Accidental Slave

Copyright © 2009 Claire Thompson
All rights reserved.
ISBN: 1-4392-2742-X
ISBN-13: 978-1439227428

Visit www.booksurge.com to order additional copies.

CLAIRE THOMPSON

ACCIDENTAL SLAVE

2009

Accidental Slave

CHAPTER ONE

The girl screamed around her gag as the whip marked her bare ass. He liked the way the flesh moved each time the strands of leather made contact. She wasn't especially pretty, but it didn't matter, not for his purposes. He wasn't looking at her face anyway. He'd bound her to a whipping post in the small, dark BDSM club that catered to the heavy scene players, the ones who understood it wasn't about pleasure or pain so much as power.

At that moment, power surged through Gary Dobbins like a drug. He released a rain of stinging leather against the girl's back and ass until she was squirming and jerking against her bonds.

"*Take it*, Elizabeth," he demanded, hitting her harder still. "You're nothing but a worthless whore. I'm going to whip you to shreds and there's not a fucking thing you can do about it."

He bit his lip and glanced around, realizing he might be observed. It wouldn't do to have the prissy club management overhear his words. They were obsessed with those tired old bywords—safe, sane, consensual.

The girl opened her eyes wide and mumbled something garbled through the pretty red ball-gag he'd wedged securely between her teeth. She tried to shake her head, but her cheek was pressed up hard against the thick post and, bound as she was, she couldn't move more than an inch or so.

She began to open and close her hands, the signal they'd agreed upon to indicate she wasn't comfortable with the scene and needed it to stop. Gary closed his eyes. He didn't want to stop. He wanted to keep whipping her, to whip away all of his own humiliation and anguish.

"You're a cunt, Elizabeth." He struck her. "Nothing but a cunt." The leather slapped at her flesh and she jerked hard in her bonds.

It should have been mine. That should be me in that corner office. That fucking bitch stole my life. She stole my career. Those bastards betrayed me. It should have been mine. It should have been mine.

He knew he was obsessing. He couldn't help it. The pain, the humiliation, the sheer unfairness of it all was eating away at him. It was like a corrosive acid that spread through every aspect of his life. Sometimes he could put it aside for hours, even days at a time, but it was always there, a secret, lurking pain—the unbearable pain of injustice. He'd been cheated—he'd been duped.

He should have quit on the spot. Yet he'd stayed on, gritting his teeth, biding his time, waiting for her to fail. Then he'd take over; then they'd see what a huge mistake they'd made.

He lifted the whip and struck the hapless girl before him as hard as he could. Her reddened ass jiggled like Jell-O. He struck it again, and again, and again, the rhythm easing the constant, gnawing jealousy and rage that were eating him alive inside.

Her hands were going like mad now, a curious bleating emanating from her drooling mouth. He wanted to smack her face, to shut her up for good, but he was, after all, in a public place. He struck her once more, hard, across the back and then dropped his whip arm.

A tall, burly man with a shaved bullet-shaped head was approaching. "Everything okay over here?" The man glowered down at Gary, crossing his arms in a threatening way. "You okay, Miss?" He bent down toward the bound woman, who gurgled something unintelligible.

"We're fine." Gary pushed himself between the man and the bound woman. "We're done, anyway. I'm just letting her down." He unbuckled the girl's gag and released her cuffs. She sagged to the ground. He steeled himself for her screeching recriminations, but for some reason they didn't come.

The bouncer seemed to be waiting, too. When she remained silent, he shrugged and walked away. It was bad form to interrupt a scene. Still, Gary knew he'd gone too far. He was lucky they hadn't thrown him out. He needed to get better control of himself.

He held out a hand to the girl, who gripped it and hoisted herself to her feet. She was a large woman, her heavy breasts dangling over a protruding belly. He grabbed the black silk robe she'd been wearing before he'd bound her to the post and tossed it at her.

"I'm sorry if I was too rough." He forced himself to apologize. "You're just so fucking hot," he lied.

"That's okay." The woman colored and smiled coquettishly. Apparently all was forgiven. "You *were* kind of rough but I got off on it." She rubbed her ass appreciatively. "I have to ask a question, though. Who the hell is Elizabeth?"

Gary went home alone. He could have brought the girl back with him—she'd made that abundantly clear—but he wasn't in the mood to entertain. He had to be at work in the morning and really needed to get to bed.

He poured himself a few fingers of whiskey, added some ice and plopped onto his sofa. Gulping nearly half the drink, he welcomed the soothing burn that spread through his body like a salve. Closing his eyes, he leaned back against the sofa and unzipped the fly of his black leather pants.

Sipping the remaining whiskey, he tried not to think about tomorrow's sales meeting. He was as ready as he would be—he'd done the analysis and crunched the numbers. Now Ms. Hot Shot Bitch would take over and run the show, taking all the credit.

Six months ago Gary Dobbins had been on top of the world. His promotion to the coveted executive vice-president spot held by his boss, Bill Moore, had been in the bag, or so he'd thought. Bill, taking early retirement, had assured Gary it was a done deal. Gary, who had given everything he had to the company for the past eight years, had naïvely believed him.

Even when he found out about the headhunter they'd hired to do a search for potential candidates for the position, his boss had reassured him. Over golf one weekend, before his hopes and dreams had been ground into dust, Bill had waved his hand dismissively at Gary's concerns.

"It's just a formality—to make it look like they're doing their due diligence. You're one of the ones being interviewed, don't forget. And I'm on the interview committee, so relax. You're the guy for the job. It's just industry practice at this level to go through the motions. You know that."

And so Gary had put his worries aside. After all, it made sense he would get the job—he knew the ins and outs of the business. Bill had taken him under his wing since day one, mentoring him and giving him every advantage. He'd been groomed for the job. It was his. He'd earned it.

Then his world had been shattered.

"I'm sorry, buddy." Bill, the betrayer, had only shrugged when he'd confronted him. "I did my best, but in the end it wasn't my decision." They'd brought in someone better, brighter, more qualified—bullshit!

Wallace had called him in, pretending to be sorry, when *he* was the one who had made the final call. He'd actually had the fucking gall to advise Gary to buck up like a good soldier—to see the bigger picture and continue to do his best for the firm, for the team, for everyone but himself.

He should have quit right then. He should have tossed his resignation letter in Wallace's face and walked out the door. But of course that was easier said than done. He had expenses and obligations. Plus, if word got out in the industry that he'd been passed over and then quit, he'd be at a disadvantage. Better to wait a while—to bide his time and make his plans on his own terms.

So he'd swallowed his pride and forced a gracious smile. He'd been there with the rest of them, welcoming their new executive vice-president, Ms. Elizabeth Anne Martin, though his guts were churning with murderous rage.

How had she won out over him? What did she have that he didn't? Her academic credentials were more impressive, he couldn't deny that, but everyone knew that didn't matter a lick once you were really out there in the trenches.

He'd done good work, no one could fault him there. Maybe her campaigns were flashier, and she'd won more industry awards, but so what? Didn't eight years of selfless dedication to the firm count for something? Apparently loyalty meant nothing. Dedication meant nothing. His life's blood and sweat meant nothing.

Somehow that bitch had blinded the top brass with her impressive portfolio and her degrees from Princeton and the Wharton School of Business. More likely, her perfect tits and a willingness to spread for what she wanted had been the real deal maker. At their first senior management meeting, Wallace had practically come on himself singing her praises. She'd probably fucked the horny old goat—that would explain a lot.

He remembered his first one-on-one meeting with his new boss with painful clarity. She knew she'd been brought in over his head. She knew she'd stolen in an instant what he'd worked eight years to achieve. She was *sensitive* to his position and the situation, the insincere bitch assured him, batting those big baby blues at him. She wanted him to be *candid* and *open*, to work together to build a strong team, to *work through* whatever difficulties they might experience as they attained a comfort level.

He'd had to bite his tongue to keep from demanding how she'd butched her way into the position that should have, by all rights, been his. He'd come dangerously close to asking who she'd fucked to get the job.

He'd toyed briefly with the idea of seducing her, and then somehow blackmailing her over it, but quickly dismissed the idea as impractical. Yes, despite his loathing of her on principal, he had to admit he wouldn't mind fucking her. He'd use plenty of rope and tie her down good. Then he'd teach her who was really in charge.

He drank the rest of his whiskey and set down the glass. Pulling his cock from his underwear, he wrapped his hand around it and pumped it to erection. He began to massage himself, imagining her at his feet, naked and bound, her mouth stretched by a spreader gag, the metal O forcing it open so he could slide in and out, fucking her face, his hands gripping her hair as he thrust hard, making her gag, making her cry....

He ejaculated, the blobs of semen spurting up and hitting his black silk T-shirt. With a heavy sigh he stood, wiping his shirt ineffectually with his fingers. He'd have it dry-cleaned. Too bad people couldn't be removed as easily as stains.

~*~

Elizabeth, briefcase in hand, unlocked her door, dreading the confrontation she knew was waiting for her on the other side. She never should have given Bryan a key to her apartment. It had seemed like a good idea at the time, but now she regretted it.

She'd promised him a cozy night. He'd rented a movie and bought a pizza, arranging to meet at her apartment at seven. She'd called to say she couldn't make it, but he'd insisted on waiting until she got home.

They had to talk, he'd insisted ominously.

Before she'd even stepped over the threshold, he was in her face, as if he'd been waiting right by the door for the past three hours. After a tirade on how inconsiderate she was in general, he moved to the particulars. "I can't believe you stood me up *again*. I don't even know why I bother. You need to get your priorities straight, Elizabeth. You need to figure out which is more important, our relationship or your damn job."

Elizabeth sighed. It was after ten, she was exhausted and she had to be at a meeting at eight the next morning. She really didn't have the energy for another argument with Bryan. A part of her was relieved he was finally forcing the issue, though. He was good in bed and someone to go the movies with, but sometimes it just wasn't worth the hassle. He was glaring at her, his arms crossed.

She shrugged. "Come on, Bryan. It's not fair to make me choose…"

"Make you choose?" Bryan laughed bitterly. "Don't make me laugh. There is no choice. Or if there is, you'll choose your work over me every time."

"I said I'm sorry. Look, if I'd walked out of the meeting at seven we would have lost the deal. Let me make it up to you. We'll spend the whole day together on Sunday. No cell phones, no email, no distractions. I promise."

"Not good enough. You either promise me you're going to reserve *all* your nights and weekends for me, one hundred percent for me, or it's over between us."

"That isn't fair. You know how important this new job is to me. I have to make my mark. Then I can ease up. I told you…"

"Spare me the bullshit. You've been there six months. You just use work as a way to keep me at a distance. I don't even think you know *how* to connect on any meaningful level to another human being. I've put up with your excuses long enough. You choose. Either back off at work, or forget it. I'll find a woman who has time for a man in her life. Someone who isn't too fucking *busy* to fall in love."

Elizabeth didn't answer. She knew on some level he was right. She didn't have time for a man, at least not a man as needy and demanding as Bryan. She looked at him, aware he wanted her to beg him to stay, to promise she'd change. Did she love him? She honestly didn't know. She knew she didn't want to hurt him.

She stood there, trying to come up with some kind of compromise, something to placate him without selling her soul. Seconds passed while he glowered at her. When she finally opened her mouth to speak he was gone, slamming the door behind him.

Elizabeth sank onto a chair and sighed. Putting her head in her hands, she let the tears spill over. She was alone—again.

~*~

Look at her. She's got the bastards eating out of her hand. Gary narrowed his eyes and pursed his lips. He scanned the faces of the men sitting at the long, oval table in the large, imposing boardroom. All eyes were riveted on Elizabeth Martin.

She was making a pitch to LTM Industries, a company the firm had been trying to woo away from the competition. A client that, if they got them, would be worth millions to Wallace & Pratt. Gary, as usual, would be relegated to being just one of the team, while she took all the credit.

He realized he was grinding his teeth. His jaw ached. He reached for his mineral water and sipped at it. He wanted a cigarette. It had been three months since his last one and it wasn't getting any easier. He was hungry. No one had touched the huge platter of pastries and donuts in the center of the table. He was dying for one, but resisted.

With his luck, the jelly would ooze from the sugary donut as he bit into it, dripping onto his silk tie. Elizabeth would wait until his mouth was full. Then she would turn her false smile, the smile that hid her steely nature from the world at large, on him and ask him for the stats to support whatever point she was making.

As if on cue, she turned to him now. "Gary, can you talk a little about the social media targets?" She turned back toward the clients, adding, "Gary is our expert on the Internet. His data will help us extend our reach beyond passive ads, integrating the message directly into the social experience and creating highly targeted ads that are both compelling and relevant. Gary?"

All eyes were now on him. She *knew* he hated to speak at these sales pitch meetings. She'd had the gall to lecture him about honing his public speaking skills. Bitch. She put him on the spot on purpose. He swallowed, relieved he had no donut sticking in his throat at least. Lifting his stack of papers, he shuffled them while he sorted out his thoughts.

He began to address the clients, gradually relaxing as they asked questions he could field. He glanced at Elizabeth, who was writing something on a pad. Probably didn't understand some of his more technical analysis. Luckily for her, he knew his stuff.

He was distracted for a moment by the curve of her breast against the silk of her blouse. Unbidden, unwelcome, an image of her in shiny, black, form-fitting latex filled his mind and hardened his cock. He'd wipe that superior smile off her face with a whip and some chain around those slender wrists.

Tearing his eyes from her, he focused on the oldest, ugliest man in the room and talked about monetizing application traffic on the Web.

~*~

Later that day Gary sat in his office; not the corner office, two walls of which were entirely glass, affording a stunning view of the skyline and the Statue of Liberty beyond. No, that was Elizabeth's office. He sat in a smaller office down the hall, the same office he'd been in since he'd arrived at Wallace & Pratt eight years before, then an eager twenty-four-year-old, still wet behind the ears.

It had been six months since the betrayal. Maybe it was time to put his name out there. Let the headhunters know he was on the market. He reached into his briefcase and extracted the résumé he'd been working on.

There was an envelope behind it, the one he had put there for safekeeping. He glanced toward his closed office door, aware it wasn't especially wise to take this particular envelope out at work, but suddenly not giving a damn. Pulling it out, he ran his fingers over the thick, fine quality paper, feeling the slight ridging caused by his name and address printed in embossed black against the creamy white background.

He extracted the card inside and read the invitation once again.

House of Usher
Slave Auction
Friday, August 8
11:00 PM

Also in the envelope were details on how to enter a slave into the auction. A portfolio, or *dossier*, as they grandly called it at the club, would be prepared so the bidders would have some idea in advance on what they were getting. It was to include a description of the slave's likes, dislikes and limits, plus the usual assortment of photos showing the slave in various submissive positions, naked, bound and exposed for the potential Master.

Gary's cock stiffened as he thought about the last auction he'd attended. Women of all shapes and sizes were put on the block, offered for a night of negotiated but erotic fun. How he'd like to put Elizabeth up for auction. He would sell her into sexual slavery—now *there* was a novel way to get rid of the competition.

He closed his eyes, imagining her on the auction block, dressed in a dark red satin corset, the waist cinched so tight she could barely breathe, six-inch heels on her feet. He'd make her wear garters and stockings, her pussy bald and exposed for the onlookers. She would be blindfolded, arms bound securely behind her, turning slowly for the bidders. Gary's cock rose in appreciation.

The intercom buzzed, jerking him from the fantasy. He jabbed at the button. "Yeah?"

"It's three o'clock." Stacy's annoying, nasal voice announced.

"Yeah, so?"

"Conference call in Elizabeth's office with Jackson & Associates. Did you forget?" Was it his imagination, or was there a certain smug satisfaction in his secretary's tone? Why hadn't she reminded him beforehand, rather than waiting until he was going to be late?

"Shit," he said aloud. Slipping the auction invitation back into his briefcase, he grabbed the files he needed and headed out of his office, casting an annoyed glance Stacy's way as he went by her desk. The smell of nail polish was ripe in the air. No time to upbraid her. Jesus, he could use a cigarette.

He couldn't quite bring himself to knock on the open door of what should have been his office. Elizabeth glanced up from her computer as he entered. Gary slid into one of the deep, comfortable leather chairs she had in front of her desk, waiting for her to look pointedly at her watch and inform him he was late for the conference call.

She ignored him for a moment, manicured nails, the polish smooth as pink glass, tapping over her keyboard. She didn't bother to look up. "One sec. Need to finish this thought." Finally she deigned to grace him with her attention.

"I think the pitch went well this morning, don't you? We had them eating out of our hands by the end."

Gary waited for her to thank him for his hard work on the project. He waited in vain. Elizabeth glanced at her watch and then at the phone. "They're a few minutes late. Just as well. Here." She held some papers out toward him. "Check this out. Do you think we should do it?" Gary took the offered papers and began to read.

"It's a service auction for charity," Elizabeth announced unnecessarily, as he scanned the information. "You know how Art's big on this type of thing. I was thinking maybe I should offer my services for the auction. I'm a pretty good cook, or I used to be, back in the day when I had time to cook more than a packaged meal in a microwave. I could offer to cook a meal for four, something like that. It would be fun."

ACCIDENTAL SLAVE

It was a brochure from the Autism Outreach Foundation, inviting "top business executives and philanthropists in the Manhattan area to participate in a silent auction of goods and services to raise money for autism research." It was a black tie affair hosted by the foundation. Art Wallace, founder and CEO of their advertising firm, loved these sorts of events and was frequently dragging one or another of the top execs with him.

Naturally he'd invited Elizabeth and not Gary. Wallace had been hitting on her since day one. If he hadn't porked her yet, it wasn't from lack of trying.

As Gary examined the brochure, he thought about the slave auction, which was, coincidentally, on the same night as this one, four weeks away. Wouldn't it be great if he could somehow trick Elizabeth into attending that one instead of this one…oh, what a delicious, diabolical situation that would be.

His mouth went suddenly dry and his heart began palpitating in a way that was almost painful. He glanced sharply at Elizabeth, who was again clacking away at her keyboard. A plan had slithered its way, fully formed, into his brilliant mind. He felt almost lightheaded as the scheme unfolded in his mind. It was ridiculous, risky, insane. But it just might work.

Elizabeth finally finished with whatever she was doing on her computer. "So what do you think? It looks like a worthy cause. Good exposure for Wallace & Pratt."

Smoothing his face into a pleasantly neutral expression, Gary smiled. "I think that's a terrific idea, Elizabeth. Is Art taking you to the dinner?" It would be tricky to maneuver around Wallace, but Gary was confident he'd find a way.

"No, actually. He gave me the two tickets the firm purchased. Evidently he bought them last year and was planning to go, but now he can't make it. I was thinking of asking you."

Gary arched an eyebrow, trying to suppress the surge of excited glee. He wasn't foolish enough to think the Ice Goddess was hitting on him—though he knew he was regarded as the best-looking guy in the office—with his boyish, blond good looks and his impeccable style. Nevertheless, the chance of a lifetime was being dropped into his lap.

Keeping his nervous excitement tightly under control, he spoke with an offhand air. "I'd love to go. Thanks for thinking of me."

"Sure. If you don't mind, have your secretary handle the RSVP, will you? And think of what you can offer for the auction. I hear you're a decent golfer. Maybe you could offer a lesson or something."

The intercom buzzed and Elizabeth's secretary's voice came over the speaker. "They're on line three."

"Thanks, Angela." She looked up at Gary. "Did you bring the analysis portfolio?"

"Got it right here." He waved a gray folder toward her. She reached out for it and he slid it across the desk, annoyed anew that he was sitting on the wrong side, though he kept his face impassive.

Elizabeth opened the folder and scanned it. "Good." She flashed a brilliant smile at him, her right cheek dimpling as she batted those impossibly blue eyes at him. She probably wore tinted contacts. "Thanks, Gary. What would I do without you?"

Let's find out, shall we?

CHAPTER TWO

"Evening, Ms. Martin."

"Oh." Elizabeth looked up, startled by the sound of the janitor's voice. "I didn't realize it was so late. How are you tonight, Mr. Jackson?"

Lord, she was tired. Elizabeth had promised herself tonight to get out before the cleaning crew came, but here she was, still working on the stupid budget for the upcoming year. Budgets were so tedious—it was all guesswork and pipedreams anyway. She much preferred the excitement of a new advertising campaign—the positive energy when her team's creative juices were flowing, the anticipation as they closed in on a deal.

At thirty, she was the youngest executive vice-president in the short but illustrious history of Wallace & Pratt, one of the most prestigious up-and-coming advertising agencies in Manhattan. She'd worked hard as hell to get here, basically putting her social life in the deep freeze, spending every moment working toward her goal.

Her job was terrific, no question about it. The money was great, the work challenging and the atmosphere at the agency one that leant itself to creativity. She had a good team. Even Gary, despite his whining and not very well hidden resentment, was smart as a whip. She had worked with guys like him before—good-looking and smart, used to getting his way with his charm and good ol' boy connections. His type had a problem with a woman being in charge. Her job was to make sure his problem didn't become hers.

At first he'd tried to charm her, complimenting her on her outfits and her hair with that sardonic smile of his, as if he were waiting for her to gush her thanks for his noticing her. That might work with his secretary and the mail girl, but it didn't fly with Elizabeth.

She'd encountered jealous men, and women for that matter, every step up the ladder of her career. She knew it wasn't about her, per se, but what she represented—what she had that they didn't. She doubted she would ever win his honest affection, but she didn't especially care. As long he remained professional and worked hard, he could nurse his little resentments on his own time.

She'd made sure he understood from the get-go she was his boss, not another simpering girl he could manipulate. She knew his type—if they were given an inch, they'd drive a truck through it. At the same time, she tried to give him as much freedom as she could. The work he'd done on this latest campaign was excellent. Asking him to the black tie affair was one way of saying thank you.

If nothing else, he would be a decent escort to take to the fundraiser. People might assume they were a couple, though she had not the slightest sexual attraction toward him. Not that he wasn't handsome. Gary was of medium height with a full head of sandy blond hair cut in a conservative but not unattractive style, with never a hair out of place. His suits were impeccably tailored, his ties of the finest silk, his cologne subtle. He had even features, a trim physique, and an All-American kind of appeal.

Not her type though. She preferred dark, swarthy men with smoldering eyes and big, strong hands. She shook her head, wondering where all the good men were. When she found time to date, which wasn't often, given the ridiculous hours she put in, the man she was with would invariably become intimidated by her self-assuredness and high-powered career.

She hadn't made it this far by batting her eyes and showing cleavage. Sometimes she wished she was more like that—able to draw on her feminine wiles to bend men to her will, but she just couldn't bring herself to use her body to get what she wanted. Nor had she needed to, not with her brains, her education and her sheer determination.

It was hardest at night, when it would have been nice to have someone to cuddle, someone to hold her and tell her she was lovely. Someone who would see past the strong, forceful image she presented to the world to the lonely woman inside.

She looked at her watch. It was after eight. She admired the filigreed gold band, thinking of Bryan, who had given it to her. She hadn't seen or heard from him since he'd walked out. The sad part was, she barely missed him.

Was there a man out there who could handle her on her terms? Who wouldn't need to be coddled and have his frail ego stroked at every turn? Was there a guy out there strong enough and confident enough to take her on, without being a bully and a prick? Maybe she was too picky. Or maybe the guy she was holding out for just didn't exist.

Sometimes she found herself longing for a man who would just take what he wanted, confident that what he offered would suit her as well. Yet she didn't want a guy who was overconfident, who thought he was God's gift to women. She knew plenty of guys like that, and she wasn't interested. She hadn't worked this hard to get ahead, only to go home to that kind of bullshit.

She was lonely, when she had time to be lonely. But at the rate she was going, she'd never have the chance to meet Mr. Right, if he was even out there. She worked six days a week and spent the seventh recuperating.

With a sigh, she shut down her computer and swept some papers and files into her briefcase, shutting it with a click. Tomorrow was another day. She would go home, take a hot shower, open a new bottle of wine and microwave something. Then in the morning, she'd get up and do it all again.

~*~

"I love your new haircut, Helen. It's a great look for you."

Helen, the human resources officer, looked up at Gary with a rarely bestowed smile. "Why, Gary," she gushed, her wrinkly cheeks turning pink. "Thank you for noticing."

In fact, Gary wouldn't have noticed, except he'd overheard two secretaries outside Helen's office discussing her new "do". It looked pretty much the same to him as her old one, not that he bothered to notice the hair or anything much else of women over fifty, as Helen certainly was.

Still, it wouldn't hurt to rack up a few points with the old broad, who coveted her personnel files as if they contained top secret documents from the FBI.

"What can I do for you today, Gary?"

"I need Stacy's personnel folder. Her annual review is coming up and I wanted to familiarize myself with last year's review and goals."

"I'll get it for you." Reaching into her desk drawer, she withdrew a small key. She unlocked the drawer marked M—Z and pulled it open. She handed the file to him. Gary took it and extracted last year's review while Helen watched him with her beady eyes.

"I'll copy it for you." She held out her hand. Gary nodded, watching with a barely concealed smile as she turned and placed the document in the copier. "That's strange," she said after a few seconds. "I thought I'd turned this on this morning." She flicked the on-off button and then flicked it again.

Gary moved to stand next to her. He crouched down and craned his neck to see behind the machine. "It's plugged in," he lied, having unplugged it himself while Helen was on her coffee break. "Maybe just leave it a few minutes and try again? Sometimes these older copiers overheat. I'll put in a word with Art to get you a new one."

"You will?" Helen beamed at him.

"In the meantime," Gary glanced meaningfully at his watch. "I am kind of pressed for time. Maybe you could use the main copier, or let me——"

"I'll do it," Helen interrupted, just as he'd expected and hoped. No one but she was to touch original documents. "You stay put. I'll be right back."

She left the office. Swiftly, he pulled the file drawer open and withdrew the folder with the words, "Martin, Elizabeth A." neatly typed on the tab. He pushed the drawer closed and slid the folder in the narrow opening between the filing cabinet and the wall.

Crouching again beside the copier, he reached behind it and pushed the plug back into place. He turned the machine on and watched it warm up.

Helen returned a moment later, his copies in hand. "Thanks. Oh, and I tried the copier again. It's working now."

As he walked down the hallway, Gary forced the thought of Elizabeth's personnel folder from his mind. He would wait until the coast was clear and fetch it after Helen, who never worked past five o'clock, had gone.

~*~

He knew he shouldn't do it. He should just skip right past the salary agreement—it was only going to piss him off. Even as he told himself this, he knew he was going to look anyway.

It was even worse than he'd expected. The bitch was getting a full $45,000 more than he was making, which was $25,000 over the $200,000 he knew Bill had been pulling down. Plus her bonus option had better terms than his.

He leaned back in his chair and closed his eyes, fighting the irrational temptation to tear the contract into shreds. Instead he carefully set it aside and continued to leaf through the papers.

Ah. There's what he was looking for—the proofs of the head shots that had been taken for the press release announcing her move to Wallace & Pratt. He removed the envelope containing the photos. It wouldn't be missed, at least not for some time. He could use shots that hadn't been chosen for the publication. They would be perfect for what he had in mind. The company's top-of-the-line photo programs would make his plan a piece of cake to execute.

He put the envelope into his briefcase and took the file back to Helen's office. All the support staff had long since called it quits for the day. Elizabeth, as usual, was still in her office, making the rest of them look bad if they tried to leave at a decent hour.

Stealthily he entered Helen's office and opened her desk drawer, poking around until he found the small key for the filing cabinet. Quickly he unlocked the drawer and replaced the file.

Unable to resist, he stuck his head in Elizabeth's office. "Working late, I see," he commented.

She was at the large drafting table, pouring over some new designs for a website campaign spread. She looked up. "I was just finishing up. Did you need something?"

"No. Just wanted to say good night."

~*~

Elizabeth examined herself critically in the three-way mirror in her walk-in closet. The saleswoman at the boutique had been so persuasive and she'd ended up spending far more than she'd intended. She had to admit, the dress fit perfectly, a sheath of pearly gray silk that hugged her curves, emphasizing her high breasts and narrow waist.

Why not? What was the point of working like a dog, if one never had anything to show for it? She deserved something nice. Anyway, it was a black-tie affair and evening gowns were expected. She turned again in the mirror, wondering if the slit along one leg was too revealing. She wore thigh-high stockings of the same pearly gray, shimmery sheer. Hopefully she wouldn't run them before she got to the dinner.

Gary was picking her up at seven. He'd really come around this past month, ever since they'd won the LTM deal, which he had been instrumental in procuring. She'd make sure his bonus reflected his dedication. Though she didn't fool herself she'd won his affection or even loyalty, at least he was behaving himself.

She slipped on the shoes she'd purchased to go with the dress, aware she would regret them by the end of the evening—at work she rarely wore anything above a one-inch heel.

Her cell phone, still on the bureau beside the small beaded handbag that held essentials for the evening, buzzed. Flipping it open, she saw the text message. Gary's taxi was downstairs waiting. Elizabeth sprayed some perfume on her neck and wrists, gave herself a final glance in the mirror, grabbed the matching silk shawl and headed out, almost feeling like she was going on a date.

The fundraiser took place in the huge ballroom of a grand old hotel. Gary and she mingled, drinks in hand, with the other guests. The auction itself was silent, with bids placed in envelopes in front of the items and services offered. There were already several envelopes in front of Elizabeth's offer to cook for four. She glanced around the crowded ballroom of the hotel, wondering who had bid.

Eventually they were seated at a table with six other people, two of whom she knew professionally. The dinner was sumptuous, with a choice of fish or beef, lavishly prepared, fresh vegetables and her favorite, Bananas Foster, for dessert. Carafes of red and white wine were placed on every table.

Gary was very solicitous; always making sure her wine glass was full. In fact, she consumed more than she wanted and realized she was feeling quite tipsy. She excused herself toward the end of the evening to use the ladies room. When she returned, Gary had added more wine to her glass.

"I don't think I need any more wine." She pushed the glass away.

"Don't be silly. It's not like you're getting behind the wheel. It's been a long week. We deserve to kick back a little. Don't be a stick in the mud."

He slid the glass back toward her and lifted his own. "To Elizabeth Martin." He raised his glass in what seemed an ironic salute. "The best damn EVP Wallace & Pratt has ever had." He smiled broadly and Elizabeth realized he must be a bit tipsy too. He had never offered her such lavish praise.

What the hell. She lifted her glass, thanked him for the kind words and drank.

~*~

Gary watched her carefully as she drained her glass. He'd only refilled it halfway, so as not to dilute the drug too much, in case she didn't finish it. He'd managed to be subtle and quick, slipping the rapidly dissolving capsule that contained the odorless, clear liquid in with the wine while she was off in the bathroom.

He'd purchased the date rape drug, GHB, online, amazed as he always was by what one could buy on the Internet. The drug promised to render its victim compliant, lowering inhibitions and inducing a kind of walking blackout. With any luck, she wouldn't even remember what happened that evening.

But he would.

It was time to move to the next phase of his carefully planned coup. He put his hand lightly over her wrist. She didn't pull away, but instead smiled at him, her expression somewhat bleary. "You ready to leave?"

"Okay." She nodded and started to rise, stumbling. The drug, coupled with the alcohol, was already doing its work, he noted happily. He hurried to his feet and steadied her with a gentle grip.

Her perfume was subtle but lingering, and her breasts seemed suspended, untouched by gravity or age in the silver-gray fabric of her clingy gown. His cock rose, despite his hatred, or perhaps partially because of it. Tonight was going to be fun. Risky, but fun.

They made their farewells to various movers and shakers as he steadily guided her toward the doors. One of the doormen procured a taxi for them in short order. Gary held her arm tight, assuring she made it safely into the cab.

He leaned forward and in an undertone gave the cabbie the address, not of Elizabeth's apartment house, but of House of Usher. He sat back next to Elizabeth, enjoying the feel of her thigh touching his.

"I feel so strange." Her voice was pitched even lower than usual, throaty and sensual. She let her head fall back against the seat, her lovely dark hair framing her face, diamond studs glinting on her earlobes.

"Say." He pretended the thought had just occurred to him. "It's not even eleven yet. I know this really cool club we could stop in, just for a few minutes. How does that sound?"

"Oh, I don't know, Gary. It's been a long week...."

"Sure. But it's the weekend. We deserve a little fun, right? All work and no play makes Elizabeth a dull girl...."

She giggled. Gary had never heard her giggle. Elizabeth Martin didn't giggle. Unless she was drunk and drugged.... He smiled grimly and patted her leg. She didn't sit up and push his hand away. She barely seemed to notice he was touching her. "I feel strange," she said again. "Woozy. Hot. Is it hot in here?"

She fanned her face with both hands, her head still back against the seat. Gary saw the cabbie in the rearview mirror flash him a knowing leer. Gary smiled back, thinking, *if you only knew what I have planned for this bitch....*

"This club we're going to, they do auctions too. It's all just in good fun, of course. They raise money for charities. I bet you'd raise a fortune if we were to put you on the block." He laughed, watching her carefully for her reaction.

"Auction?" She slurred the word, so it came out more as aw-shun. Her eyes were closed, a half-smile on her face. For a moment he worried he'd given her too much of the drug.

"Yeah. It'll be fun. Just leave it to me." She didn't answer. "You okay, Elizabeth?"

Slowly she opened her blue eyes, which looked unfocused, the pupils down to pinpoints. "I'm good." He nodded, relieved. Just to test her, he put his hand on her thigh and squeezed. Without the benefit of GHB and alcohol, she would have probably cut off his balls for daring to touch her. Now she just smiled.

He put his arm around her as they rode up to the club on the top floor of the building. "The auction is just a game. They wanted to make it fun, and it's for such a worthy cause." His voice oozed sincerity, though she barely seemed to be paying attention. She was leaning heavily against him, one lovely breast pressed against his arm, which made his cock hard.

"The theme tonight is a pretend slave auction." He glanced at her. "Like I said, it's all in fun. We might even consider it ourselves."

The elevator door slid silently open and they stepped out into a thickly carpeted hallway. There were large double-doors spaced at wide intervals along the hall. The third one down had a small brass placard to the right of the door that read, simply, "House of Usher——Private".

Gary didn't go to House of Usher often. The cover charge was very steep and there was no actual play permitted there. He'd been brought by a fellow Dom to the last auction, and had signed up for their exclusive mailing list.

Admission to this auction had cost a pretty penny, but tonight's money would be well spent if things went according to plan. He'd sent in Elizabeth's slave dossier two weeks before, complete with photos he'd meticulously created using her headshot and lurid descriptions of her qualities as a highly-trained slave girl.

He rang the doorbell beneath the placard and it was opened by a trim man in a dark suit with a black mustache and thinning black hair brushed straight back from his forehead. Speaking quietly so Elizabeth wouldn't hear him, he murmured, "Hunter. John Hunter." The man perused the clipboard in his hand, nodded and stepped back.

"Welcome to the House of Usher." His tone was subdued.

House of Usher, unlike the underground clubs Gary preferred, didn't have black walls, Techno music pumping and pornographic videos playing on screens around the room. Instead it was furnished more like an elegant sitting room in some British country house. Pretentious, he thought, but perfect for his plans. Even drugged as she was, he doubted Elizabeth would allow herself to be led into the kind of place where the real fun happened.

Here the walls were painted a muted yellow cream, with white trim and borders. What looked to be original nineteenth century oil paintings of nude women lounging on velvet chaises, silk draped alluringly over plump, pink thighs, graced the walls. The room was lit with opaque glass sconces mounted on silver art deco fixtures that cast a warm glow over everything.

Tall, wingback chairs were set in clusters around the large room, along with a number of small, round tables set with white linen, a vase with a single red rose on each. Along two walls sat plump, wine-colored velvet sofas. In the center of the room, a large wooden dais had been placed, with portable stairs beside it.

It wasn't quite eleven, but the room was already full, an underlying buzz of excitement in the air. Gary and Elizabeth were only slightly overdressed for the event. Most of the men in the room wore suits. The women, the ones who were dressed, wore dresses or skirts, though some of them revealed more than they covered.

There were several women in BDSM fetish wear—bare breasts with pierced nipples jutting over black leather bodices, stiletto heels, red lips, wrist and ankle cuffs and clanking chain. Gary steered Elizabeth through the crowd, anxiously wondering how she'd react to the scene. To his relief she didn't seem to be taking in her surroundings.

"The room is tilting. Make it stop, Bryan. Make it stop." She clung to his arm, stumbling in her high heels.

Bryan? Who was Bryan? A jolt of unease slid through Gary's gut. He'd been certain there was no one in Elizabeth's life. She spent every damn minute at the office, didn't she? What guy would put up with that?

Nevertheless, there was the possibility someone was waiting at home for her. Someone named Bryan, who would wonder what she'd been up to when she finally got home, drunk as a skunk, or worse. He smiled cruelly to himself. Let her explain her way out of this one.

Gary led her to a loveseat in a far corner of the room, settling her on it before snagging two flutes of champagne from a young woman dressed in a frilly French maid's outfit.

Gary handed a glass to Elizabeth, watching with disdainful amusement as she sloshed half its contents over her lap. Her lipstick was smeared, her eyes unfocused, her luxuriant dark hair falling into her face. Reaching for his cell phone, he flipped it open, trained it on her and snapped several pictures.

Then he sat beside her and leaned back with a satisfied sigh. So far, so good.

CHAPTER THREE

Cole Pearson sipped his martini as he glanced around the room. He still didn't see what, or rather who, he was looking for. He looked at his watch—it was only ten-fifteen. Though most of the tables and sofas were already full, with more people standing and mingling, there was time.

He sat alone at a small table near the dais. Fred Marshall, a fellow Dom and sometimes-bidder at these auctions, would join him, though he had yet to arrive. Cole picked up the three dossiers he'd selected for bidding. Slave A. was petite and very pretty, with blonde hair in a pixie cut, pierced nipples on ample breasts and a shaven pussy. Slave S. was taller, with golden-red hair and slender curves. But of the three, it was Slave E. to whom he returned again and again.

She was shown in various standard poses, bound and trussed in several so he couldn't see her face, suspended by her wrists, her body covered in a sheen of sweat, her head thrown back, dark hair streaming behind her. But it was the pose that included her face that had captivated him. She was kneeling up, her bare pussy exposed, her breasts proudly thrust out.

She was staring directly at the camera and something in her brilliant blue eyes tugged at him, drawing him back to her face again and again. There was a challenge in her expression that belied her supposedly submissive nature. It was a strong face, with a square, almost masculine chin and lush, full lips that fairly begged to be bitten. Her nose was small, which served to make her eyes look even larger. It was those eyes, so very blue, so open and compelling that he found himself falling into, even though it was just a picture.

He read some of descriptions again, trying to reconcile the slave girl in the photos with the words written beneath them. *Saucy slut girl likes it rough. Sometimes disobedient, this slave will pretend to protest, but it's just a game. Use her hard and soundly. While she's crying, "No, no, no!" she really means, "Yes, yes, yes!"*

Instruments of pleasure/pain: Flogger, whip, cane, paddle, tight bondage, ball gag, needle play, pony play.

Limits: None.

That was unusual. In staged auctions like these, while the interaction was real, there were generally pretty clear limits imposed on the Dom, because he didn't personally know the slave or what she could tolerate. Surely this girl had *some* limits?

He found himself wondering first, why a guy who had a girl like this would want to give her away, even for a night, and second, how he could say she had no limits. That could be very dangerous for her if the wrong man won the bidding. Didn't the Dom offering her for auction care about his slave girl? Didn't he cherish her above all else?

Well, if he won her, he would talk to her, get to know her a little before diving into play. Everyone had limits, and those limits should be respected. Cole took another sip of his drink and sighed, reminding himself most so-called Doms didn't share his romantic sensibilities when it came to D/s. They got off on the power of controlling another person. They were turned on by the whips and chains, the forced sex and the kinky play. Most of them didn't have a clue about the enormous potential for romance to be found in erotic submission.

Fred laughed at him when he talked like this. "Cole, buddy. That's your whole problem. It's why you go home alone night after night while an ugly guy like me has more broads than he can handle. Fuck the romance—show 'em a hard cock, some wrists cuffs and a good whip, and these girls will spread every time. They're all the same, just masochistic sluts out for a good time. Hell, that's what we're all out for. Well," he amended, "most of us, anyway. I don't know what the hell *you're* looking for. I do know you sure as hell ain't gonna find it at a BDSM club, no matter how hoity-toity it tries to be."

He knew Fred was right about that at least. But he didn't come to these auctions seeking true love. He wasn't even sure the woman of his dreams existed in real life. But he'd promised himself he wouldn't settle for less, and so far, he hadn't. The irony was, as a result, for all his wealth and supposed good looks, he was the loneliest man he knew.

He finished his martini and signaled the lovely young waitress for club soda. If he won a girl, he didn't want to be impaired when he used her. He would enjoy himself and forget about silly things like true love for the rest of the evening. This was his third auction, and while he'd enjoyed the prior two girls he'd "won", he hadn't liked either enough to keep her any longer than overnight, which was the limit for most of them anyway, on loan by their Masters.

If nothing else, it kept things neat, in terms of what came next, which was nothing. There were no expectations of a future phone call, no plans for future rendezvous. Oh, sometimes the women tried, but he had a pat story to keep his distance—his wife wouldn't approve.

In fact she wouldn't have approved, though she no longer had a say in the matter. Joanie, his college sweetheart, had been killed in a car wreck three years before. Their fourteen-year marriage had not been the best, weakened by Joanie's desperate desire to have children, and their discovery that she was infertile. They probably would have divorced by now if she'd lived, but nevertheless he'd been devastated by the loss, deeply shaken by how suddenly people can be torn from this world.

Joanie had never known of his then-secret penchant for BDSM and D/s. They'd married just out of college, and he hadn't the courage or the self-understanding at the time to admit, much less explore, his desires. For all the years of their marriage, he'd kept his true sexual nature secret, certain Joanie would reject both them and him.

For the first year or so after she died, Cole hadn't been interested in finding someone new. He was very busy then with his investment business and his real estate ventures, and still mourning her loss.

He did eventually get thrust back into the dating game via pressure from his sister and some friends, going on a few well-intentioned but disastrous blind dates. He found himself ready after a year or so to think about finding another partner. But this time around he was going to be honest with himself. This time, he would find a woman who fit his groove, who understood and craved the romance of erotic Dominance and submission as much as he did.

He would seek and hopefully find the woman of his dreams—his own personal submissive to cherish and adore. He looked again at the lovely face of Slave E., wondering what the initial stood for. Elaine? Elizabeth? Eve?

"Hey, sorry I'm late. Damn city traffic. Some cab driver almost plowed right into me." Fred sat heavily in the chair beside Cole, dropping his own pile of dossiers onto the table. The waitress appeared with Cole's fresh drink and took Fred's order.

He used the napkin in front of him to wipe his bald dome of a head and grinned at Cole. "Got a favorite picked for tonight?"

Cole slid Slave E.'s dossier toward Fred. He picked it up and whistled. "She's a babe and a half, all right. Too good looking for her own good, if you know what I mean." Cole didn't. "This is the one I want." Fred stabbed his finger on the topmost dossier he'd brought with him. The girl on the cover was plump and barely squeezed into a black leather corset, her breasts spilling provocatively over the top.

"Slave M." Fred grinned broadly. "I bought her once before. Her Master let me keep her for two days. Jesus H. Christ, that girl can suck the paint off a barn." He winked.

According to the House of Usher rules, which complied with the laws of the State of New York, no sex acts were committed at the club itself. There wasn't even BDSM play permitted at the club—once a slave was purchased, the real fun happened elsewhere.

Nor was the auction a sale of sexual favors, but rather a game designed for the amusement of the patrons, or so the story went. Fake money was used in the bidding, though it was purchased for actual cash beforehand.

More last minute stragglers were entering the club. Cole turned in time to see a man with sandy-blond hair in an expensive-looking tuxedo, his arm proprietarily around a slender woman with dark hair. She was wearing a full-length evening gown and seemed to be tottering rather unsteadily on her heels. He couldn't see her face but his heart quickened nonetheless. Was that Slave E.?

Why was she weaving like that? Was she drunk? He pursed his lips in disapproval. Alcohol and BDSM play did not mix, or shouldn't. Both partners needed all their senses intact for the heightened experience of D/s. Why would her Master have permitted her to drink before being put on the dais? Perhaps he should reconsider bidding after all. There were too many red flags with this one. Whoever the guy was, he didn't seem to have a clue.

He turned back to the table and looked over his other two choices. But I want *her*, his mind whispered insistently. Well, perhaps it would be all right, just for one night. He could be the judge for both of them. He'd been with enough submissives to sense their limits, even when they themselves did not.

The bidding was theoretically capped at fifty thousand dollars in play money, which cost ten cents on the dollar, making the actual top cost five thousand. At the previous two auctions Cole had attended, the price had never gone above two thousand. There were enough eager, willing slave girls to go around.

"Good evening, gentlemen." The maitre d' offered an unctuous smile. He glanced at his clipboard and then back at them. "Mr. Pearson, Mr. Marshall, a pleasure to have you with us this evening. The bidding will begin shortly. Since you've both participated before, I won't bore you with a recitation of the rules. Just a reminder, this is only a game. While the contracts are binding in a fictional sense, of course they're just for fun."

"Sure." Fred beamed at the maitre d', who was always keen to stress the auction was not a cover for prostitution, though technically, Cole supposed, it was, or certainly could be. He himself hadn't had actual intercourse with either of the prior girls he'd won, but he knew he could have, if he'd wanted to. Still, the BDSM play had taken place in the privacy of his own home, with a willing participant.

When the maitre d' walked away, Fred nudged Cole. "Who does he think he's fooling, anyway? If the authorities knew what really went on in this private club, they'd shut it down in a New York minute, and he knows it. Though he's right about one thing—it sure is fun."

The lights dimmed and the room quieted as a spotlight was trained on the small stage in the center of the room. The auctioneer, a tall, narrow-shouldered man in his sixties with a full head of silver hair, stepped onto the stage and hammered his gavel importantly against the podium.

"Gentlemen. Welcome to House of Usher. You all know the rules. Bidding by hand signal only. Bidding starts at five hundred." While he was talking, a man was escorting a very scantily clad young woman up the stairs beside the dais. He gave her a little shove onto the stage.

The girl looked to be about twenty-five. She was olive-skinned with sloe eyes and black curly hair that fell to her shoulders. She was wearing a gold bra and matching panties, along with high-heeled leather boots, also dyed gold. She looked like something out of a Sixties' science fiction movie.

The auctioneer turned to her with a smile and a slight bow. "Our first lovely slave girl of the evening is Slave T. She likes very tight bondage, sensual spanking and service."

"Does that mean she'll wash my car?" Fred whispered.

"Shut up."

The bidding began and was quickly up to twelve thousand dollars in play money. The gavel struck once, twice and she was sold to a large, beefy man with red hair and an even redder face. He held out his hand and she took it as she stepped carefully down the portable stairs in her boots.

A succession of six more women followed, all reasonably attractive, though none sparked much interest in Cole, who had his sights set on Slave E. Fred bid on two of the girls, but he, too, was holding out for his chosen submissive—Slave M.

"Next up, a newcomer to our fine establishment." The auctioneer glanced down at his notes on the podium and back up at the audience. "Slave E. loves all types of heavy bondage and discipline, the more intense the better. Please welcome her and let's begin the bidding at five hundred."

Slave E. did not immediately appear. Cole's heart had begun to pound the moment he heard her name. Where was she? She should have been waiting by the side of the stage for her turn. What was going on?

Heads were swiveling toward the back of the room. The blond man in the tuxedo was leading the lovely woman he'd entered with to the stage. As they passed Cole's table he heard, "Come on. It's for a worthy cause. It's all in good fun. Look, they've already called your name, so go on up and just stand there for a minute or two. Do it for the team."

The team? What team? What worthy cause? Cole didn't have time to ponder these questions for too long. Once the young woman finally made it to the stage, her designer gown shimmering over curves even more lovely than those depicted in her dossier, her dark hair wild around her face, the bidding began in earnest.

Cole had twenty thousand dollars of play money. He waited until the bidding got to a ten thousand and then raised his hand.

"Ten thousand, five hundred." the auctioneer pointed toward him with a nod.

Another hand went up and the auctioneer acknowledged him, raising the price to eleven thousand.

In short order the bidding had ratcheted to fifteen thousand. Shit! He had to have this girl, even if she was drunk and a mess and hooked up with some asshole. "Fred, lend me money if I need it, okay? I'll get you cash."

"You kidding? You'd go higher than twenty thousand? Look at her. Yeah, she's gorgeous, but she's fucking wasted, man. She looks like she doesn't even know where she is. You really want some strung-out chick?"

"Yes. I want her. You'll lend me play money if I need it?"

"Sure. What the hell. As long as I have what I need to bid on Slave M., I don't mind."

A few minutes later, the auctioneer pointed toward Cole with a smile and rapped his gavel. "Sold to the gentleman at table six for $21,500."

~*~

Gary's heart was smashing painfully in his chest. Thank God she hadn't fallen down on the stage. It had been a gamble, slipping another dose of the GHB into her Champagne. He hadn't wanted to do it, but she'd started to become more lucid, and with her lucidity, the questions became more coherent and persistent. Once she'd drunk the spiked wine, however, she became once again docile and compliant. Too bad he couldn't use it on her at work.

Though if things went according to plan, her days at work were numbered.

He breathed a sigh of relief as her auction ended, and moved quickly to escort her down the few stairs toward the man at table number six. "She's all yours, buddy." He pushed Elizabeth toward the high bidder. She sank down on the chair offered by the man, closing her eyes and leaning her head back.

The next slave girl was being brought to the dais, and Gary was eager to get out of there, now that he'd done his damage. What happened to Elizabeth from here on in was her problem. If she remembered anything about his part in it, and he had his doubts, based on what he'd read of the drug's side effects, it would be his word against hers.

The man held out his hand. "Cole Pearson." Instead of shaking it, Gary thrust Elizabeth's shawl into it. The guy looked confused. He asked, "And you are?"

"John Hunter. So congratulations and all that. I really have to be—"

The guy interrupted him. "What's wrong with her? Is she drunk? Is she sick? She looks like she's going to pass out."

Gary glanced at Elizabeth. Her head was lolling on her neck, though she was still conscious. "Uh, yeah. Sorry about that. She had a few too many. I tried to warn her, but she's a disobedient little slut. You can keep her a few days if you want, to make up for it. She should be fine by the morning."

The man scowled at him. "What's her name? Her real name?"

"Elizabeth. Listen, do me a favor. Take a whole bunch of pictures of her with her cell phone, you know, once you have her naked and tied up and whatnot. She loves to look at them at them later, okay? Her cell's in her purse." He pointed toward the small, beaded bag that hung from Elizabeth's right wrist. "Deal? You keep her an extra few days, in exchange for the pics. Oh, and if she says she has to leave, to get to work or whatever, it's just a ploy. She's unemployed. She likes to pretend, like I said in the dossier. So just ignore her and do whatever you want to her. You have my permission as her, uh, Master."

After tonight, Elizabeth's career was dead—figuratively he'd bared her breast and presented her for the sword. Now he'd leave her to fall on it herself. Then he'd assume his rightful position as Executive Vice-President in Charge of Marketing at Wallace & Pratt.

The Pearson dude started to say something else. Gary held up his hand and cut him off. "Everything you need to know's in her dossier. Sorry, gotta go. Have fun." Gary turned, forcing his way through the crowd near the stage, leaving the bitch to her fate.

CHAPTER FOUR

Cole took out his cell phone and called his driver. "Harry. Meet me downstairs in five minutes. I'm going to need some help. The young lady I'm escorting is, uh, indisposed."

"Indisposed?" Fred snorted. "She's faced, is what she is. I'm surprised you bid on her, what with your lecturing about how alcohol has no place in the scene."

"It doesn't. And on closer inspection, I'm not sure she's drunk. She seems drugged to me. I don't like this, Fred. Not one bit."

"So why are you bothering with her? Why'd you let that bastard leave without her? She's his responsibility, not yours."

Cole looked at the lovely girl. She was slumped in the seat, her head resting against her shoulder, her eyes closed. How could he possibly leave her with that asshole who clearly didn't care for her at all—abandoning her when she was in this condition, to the highest bidder.

"He obviously doesn't see it that way," Cole snapped. "I'm going to take her home and let her sleep it off. I'd like to know what she has to say about all this, once she sobers up."

The auctioneer announced, "Gentlemen, next up is the lovely Slave M. Who will start the bidding?"

"Oh, *my* girl." Fred turned excitedly toward the dais. "And look, *she's* sober." He grinned and then glanced again at Elizabeth, who hadn't moved. The grin faded to a frown.

"Maybe you better get her to an emergency room. Check her purse, why don't you? See if she has an insurance card."

Cole knelt next to Elizabeth. "Hey. Hey, wake up. Can you hear me?"

Elizabeth stirred and opened bleary, unfocused eyes. "What? Bryan? Is it time to go?"

"It's Cole. And yes, it's time to go. Let me help you stand. There's a good girl." He put her arm over his shoulders and slipped his own around her waist, hoisting her into a standing position. Fred tore his focus from the stage long enough to say, "Good luck, buddy. Hope you're happy with your prize. With any luck she won't drop dead before you get her home." He shook his head and turned back to the bidding.

Cole knew Fred was right. It was beyond stupid to take this drunk or drugged young woman home. She clearly didn't know where she was or what was going on. It was hardly a consensual arrangement. And yet the thought of abandoning her to the son of a bitch she'd come in with was more than Cole could stomach.

Not only that, he wanted her. Not drugged, of course. But her face had captivated him from the moment he'd seen her dossier the week before. He'd dreamed of kissing those lush, full lips, of draping her naked body over his knees and smoothing the soft, creamy flesh as he prepared it for her spanking....

Though his arm was firmly around her, Elizabeth stumbled and fell heavily against him. Somehow he got her out of the club and down the hall. In the elevator she revived a little, smiling up at him. "Do I know you? I think I'd like to know you. Oh my God, you're Pierce Bronson, aren't you? What happened to Bryan?"

Cole smiled, despite his concern for the girl. At least she was talking, if not exactly lucidly. Her voice was perfect, just what he'd have chosen for her if he was designing the ideal woman—low and smoky, its cadence pleasing.

"I'm Cole. Cole Pearson. I'm taking you home so you can get some rest."

"Okay." A beatific smile lit her face as she closed her eyes again and sagged in his arms. He wondered if Fred was right. Maybe he should take her to an emergency room. He envisioned the hours waiting to be seen, the hassle of explaining who she was and who he was, and all the associated mess going to a hospital emergency room late on a Friday night would invariably entail. No, better to take her home, tuck her into a warm bed and pray whatever drugs were in her system worked their way out by morning.

Harry was waiting in the front of the building, the back passenger door of the Lexus open. He moved toward them, helping Cole settle the woman in the back seat. He was far too discreet to ask questions. "Home, sir?"

"Yes." Cole climbed in beside Elizabeth. Though it was after midnight, there was still plenty of traffic to maneuver through. However, they weren't far from Cole's Fifth Avenue apartment and in twenty minutes Harry had them in the underground parking lot.

"Stop by the elevators," Cole instructed. "I'll take her up while you park the car. That's all for tonight, Harry. Thanks."

"Certainly, sir," Harry, who enjoyed formality, tipped the driver's cap he insisted on wearing toward Cole. "I hope she's feeling better."

"Me too, Harry. Me too."

~*~

It was after two but Cole was wide awake. He was sitting in the dark, staring out at the New York City skyline that lit the sky, but all he saw was her. She'd passed out completely when he laid her on the bed. He thought about just leaving her as she was after removing her high heels, but decided she'd be more comfortable out of that very expensive-looking evening gown.

Was that really the only reason he'd stripped her to her panties? Well, maybe not, but after all, he had bought and paid for her at the auction, and received nothing so far for his money. Presumably in the morning when she awoke and, hopefully, came to her senses, she be stripping for him anyway. She'd allowed herself to be auctioned off—she must know being naked was part of the deal, sex or no sex.

He hadn't been prepared for how truly lovely she was beneath the sheath of her gown. He'd told himself he wouldn't take off her bra, but she wasn't wearing one. Her perfect breasts were soft and round, tipped with enticing red nipples that rose in the cool air. He resisted the urge to flick one with his thumb—it didn't seem right while she was dead to the world.

Carefully he rolled the sexy thigh-high stockings down smooth, shapely legs, admiring her slender ankles and pretty feet. She remained limp and inert beneath his touch.

He pulled down the covers beneath her and lifted them over her. "Elizabeth?" He leaned close to her face. She didn't move. He took her pulse, which was strong, and listened to her breathe for a while as he gazed at her. He left the room, returning a moment later with one his nightshirts, which he placed at the end of the bed for her.

He filled the glass pitcher by her bed with fresh water and folded her gown, shawl and the stockings carefully over a chair, placing her shoes on the floor beside it. Finally, he smoothed a tendril of hair from her cheek and, with a last lingering look, left the room.

He stared unseeing out the huge picture window. "What would a lovely girl like that be doing with a jerk like that John Hunter person?" He shook his head, finding it hard to reconcile. Why was it submissive women so often ended up with men not worthy of them? He'd only been in the scene a few years himself, but it had been long enough to know there were more bully boys than true Doms out there.

Instead of treasuring their partner's gift of submission, they took it as their right, twisting it into something abusive and obscene. He'd seen too many public scenes where men used the guise of D/s to abuse, humiliate and torture their partners. The whip became a weapon, designed to wound, instead of an extension of lovemaking, one that, when used properly, could heighten the experience of both partners immeasurably.

Was Elizabeth a true submissive? Or just, as Fred contended they "all were", a masochistic slut out for the sensation and attention a D/s relationship might bring her.

He poured himself a brandy and sipped at it as he pondered the curious events of the night. He was hyperaware of the sleeping beauty down the hall. When he could stand it no longer, he downed the rest of his drink and stood. He would check on her once more and then force himself to go to bed.

The room was bathed in the rosy glow of a night light. She looked like an angel, her long lashes touching her cheeks, her dark hair spread over the pillow. The sheets had slid down to her waist. His cock hardened at the sight of those bare breasts and he resisted an impulse to push the sheets down farther, exposing her long, bare legs and sheer black panties. Biting his lip, he forced himself to close the door, to walk away, to wait until the morning to use the slave girl he'd won.

~*~

Elizabeth burrowed into the mound of feather pillows and tried to return to her dreams, in which James Bond was about to make love to her. It was no use. She had to pee. She opened her eyes, squinting against the bright light streaming in from the huge window to her left.

She sat up suddenly, hitting her head against the wooden headboard. She winced and became aware of a throbbing headache. She felt fuzzy and confused. Her bed didn't *have* a headboard. And her windows were along a different wall. Nor did she sleep on feather pillows.

Where the hell was she?

She opened her eyes properly and stared around the room. It was large, easily half the size of her entire apartment. The furnishings were elegant—a blond wood bureau and matching armoire, two comfortable-looking red leather chairs facing one another beneath the picture window and tasteful paintings of Impressionistic landscapes on the walls. The floor was covered with an exquisite Oriental carpet that probably cost more than everything else in the room put together and then some. This was clearly the bedroom of someone with plenty of money.

But who? Where the hell was she and how the hell had she ended up here? She leaned back against the pillows and closed her eyes, trying not to let panic overtake her. There had to be a rational explanation. She tried to recall the night before. Gary and she had attended the fundraiser. She'd had more to drink than she usually did, but surely not enough to cause a blackout of such magnitude.

She tried to remember what she'd done after leaving the dinner. Dimly she recalled Gary wanted to go somewhere else. Another function, a club, she couldn't remember. But what happened after that? Had they gone? Did she get so smashed she'd had a blackout? Would she really have done something so stupid? Had Gary had to haul her home as a result? Was she at his house?

Another horrible thought entered her head. Oh God, surely they didn't have sex....

"No way." That would be a disaster. Never get involved with people you work with—that was one of Elizabeth's cardinal rules. It was so ingrained in her, she doubted she would break it, no matter how soused. And *if*, by some bizarre chance, she did, it would *not* be with Gary Dobbins, no matter how drunk she was. The very idea repulsed her.

She looked around the room again, trying to calm her racing heart. The space reeked of "old money". She relaxed a little, seriously doubting this was Gary's place. So where then? And how did she get here?

Tentatively she sat up, waiting for the dizziness to subside. She noticed a small blue glass pitcher on the nightstand beside the bed, a matching glass fitting neatly over the top of it. Her mouth felt like it was stuffed with cotton and tasted like tin. With shaky fingers, she reached for the pitcher and poured herself a glass.

The water refreshed her, but reminded her she needed to pee. Gingerly she swung her legs over the side of the bed and realized at that moment she was naked. No, she still had her panties. Looking wildly around the room, she spied her dress folded over a chair. Then she noticed a nightshirt on the end of the bed. She reached for it and slipped it gratefully over her shoulders. It was pale blue silk with white oyster shell buttons. The silk was cool and slick against her skin. It was a man's nightshirt, the sleeves falling past her wrists, the hem stopping just above her knees.

Had she undressed herself or had someone else? She flushed at the thought of someone removing her gown, perhaps fondling her breasts, doing who knew what else. Panic gripped her again and she shook her head. This was ridiculous. Obviously someone had gone to great care to get her safely to bed. Whoever it was surely wouldn't have been so crude as to fondle her in the process. For all she knew, she was in the home of a wealthy elderly couple, who rescued her after she was hit by a cab crossing the street.

She walked toward the door she hoped led to the bathroom. It did. She examined herself in the large mirror over the sink. There were no signs of bruises and she wasn't hurt, except for the fact her entire body felt as if it had been wrung through one of those old-fashioned laundry wringers.

She used the toilet, washed her face and rinsed her mouth with the small bottle of mouthwash that had been thoughtfully placed, along with a new toothbrush and a tube of paste, a hairbrush, soap and some deodorant, beside the lovely green glass bowl with polished brass spigots that served as a sink.

She heard a faint knock at the bedroom door. She looked like a wreck, her hair a tangled mess and traces of mascara smudged beneath her eyes. Grabbing the brush, she dragged it through her hair for a few seconds, gave up and returned to the bedroom.

The knock was repeated, louder this time. A deep, masculine voice called out. "Elizabeth? Are you awake? Are you okay? I thought I heard you moving around in there."

She didn't recognize the voice, but whoever he was, he knew her name. Hurrying to the door, she took a deep breath and pulled it open. She leaned hard against it, a wave of dizziness again assailing her.

The man standing before her was tall, with broad shoulders, thick dark hair and eyes so black they looked like liquid tar. She realized with a jolt he had been the man in her dream. Despite how lousy she felt, her nipples and pussy tingled. The guy was seriously good looking. Reflexively she glanced at his ring finger, which was bare. Which didn't mean he wasn't married, lots of married men didn't wear rings. Not that it mattered——she had no time for men.

These thoughts raced through Elizabeth's head in the space of a few seconds but of course she voiced none of them, saying instead, "Uh, hi. Thanks for…" she waved her hand toward the bedroom, aware she wasn't sure what exactly to be thankful for, and what to apologize for.

"You were more than a little out of it last night. I hope you don't mind I took the liberty of bringing you home. John had left by the time I realized how, uh, impaired you were." She squinted at him in confusion. "Don't worry. Nothing happened. We can talk about the arrangements later. I thought it was better if you slept off whatever you'd done to yourself first."

"What?" Elizabeth hadn't a clue what the man was talking about. "Who's John? What arrangements? What're you talking about? Who are you? How did I get here?"

The man stared at her a moment before saying in a slow, careful voice, "Then, you don't remember? You don't remember anything about last night?"

Elizabeth wrapped her arms protectively around herself. She felt sick to her stomach and her head was pounding. "Hey." The man moved forward. "You don't look so good. Come and sit down."

She didn't protest as he palmed her elbow and led her carefully toward one of the red leather chairs. She sank gratefully down and drew her hand across her forehead. She was sweating, though the room was cool.

"Let me get you some water. You look awfully pale." The man poured water into the pretty blue glass and brought it to her. She took it and sipped. The dizziness and nausea were dissipating, though her head still ached.

"That's better." He took the glass from her and set it on the table between the two chairs. "The color is coming back into your cheeks. I thought you were going to pass out there for a minute."

"I'm okay." Elizabeth wasn't sure if this was true or not. "Except for the fact I have no idea where I am, how I got here or who you are."

The man gave a small laugh. "I'm sorry. You had me so worried I forgot to introduce myself. I'm Cole Pearson. We met last night at House of Usher when I bid on you. You were—"

"When you *what?*"

"Bid on you. You know, at the slave auction." He smiled tentatively, his expression quizzical. Despite her complete confusion, she couldn't help but notice it was a kind of lopsided grin, but thoroughly charming. Somehow it made him more appealing than a movie-star-perfect smile would have. Then she processed his words.

"Slave auction? What the...? The only auction I remember being at was the fundraiser for Autism." She closed her eyes, trying to think. A vague recollection was returning to her. Something about a club Gary wanted to take her to after they'd left the dinner. *Why* couldn't she remember? What had happened to her?

"Where's Gary?" she asked abruptly. He would know what the hell was going on, surely.

"Who's Gary?"

"Gary Dobbins. He's the guy I work with. Who I attended the fundraiser with. I dimly remember him talking me into going to a club after the dinner, but then everything's just—blank." She pressed her fingers against her eyelids, trying to fight a rising sense of panic. It was horrible not to remember. It was as if someone had reached into her head and ripped away a chunk of her brain.

"I don't remember any Gary." Cole was thoughtful. "You were with a man who introduced himself as John. John Hunter. Your Master."

She looked at him. "Master? Are you out of your mind? I don't know any John Hunter."

Cole regarded her, his black eyes penetrating her own so she suddenly found herself looking down. She forced herself to meet his gaze, daring him with her expression to explain what in the name of God was going on.

He shook his head slowly. "This whole thing is getting more bizarre by the minute. I *knew* something wasn't right. Even beyond your being drugged. Something about that guy—"

"Drugged! What—"

"At first I thought you were drunk, but now I think it was drugs. Maybe some kind of date rape drug. You were really out of it. You passed out completely on the way home in my car. He said you'd had a few too many, that you did it all the time and you'd sleep it off and be fine in the morning. Then he took off so fast I really didn't know what else to do, so I brought you home. I was pretty sure by then you were on drugs, and from your complete confusion, I'd venture to say you were drugged against your will."

"My God," Elizabeth cried, horrified. "Who would do such a thing? Who was this Hunter guy? Why was I with him? What happened to Gary?" She looked around the room for her purse and saw it on the bureau. "I'll call Gary. We'll get to the bottom of this." She stood too quickly and just as quickly sat back down as a wave of dizziness assailed her.

"This Gary." Cole knit his brows, his face creased in a frown. "What's he look like?"

"Uh, he's about five foot, nine or so, with blond hair always hair-sprayed into place. Blue eyes, smallish nose. I don't know. Handsome, in a bland kind of way."

"And he was wearing a black tuxedo last night? Black bow tie?"

The blood in Elizabeth's veins turned to ice, though she still wasn't consciously processing what Cole was getting at. "Yes. You met him then?"

"I did. Except he called himself John Hunter. According to him, you're his personal slave girl and he was quite happy to lend you out for a night of consensual BDSM play. He put you on the auction block and I won you."

Elizabeth stared at the man sitting so calmly across from her and tried desperately to make sense of his words. She failed. "I'm sorry. What? Did you say slave girl? You…*won* me?" She rubbed her hand over her eyes again, but it did nothing to clear the fog in her brain.

Why would Gary introduce himself as John Hunter? Slave girl? Auction? BDSM? Date rape drugs? None of it made any sense. It sounded the plot for a made-for-TV movie. These things didn't happen in real life.

Wait a minute. She glanced sharply at Cole. *Something* had definitely happened last night, but who said this guy, who she didn't know from Adam, was telling the truth? "How do I know *you're* telling the truth? Maybe *you* slipped some kind of drug into my drink and kidnapped me."

The man gave another lopsided grin and despite herself, her heart lurched. "Wait here a second. I'll be right back." He returned a moment later with some kind of pamphlet, which he handed to Elizabeth.

Slave E. was printed on the cover, along with *House of Usher Slave Auction.* With trembling fingers, she turned the page and gasped. Depicted there were graphic color photos of a woman bound in rope and chain, contorted in various uncomfortable-looking and sexually explicit positions. She turned the page again and there was her own face, smiling calmly back at her, inexplicably attached to a naked body, kneeling up, breasts thrust forward, a shaven mons spread wide for the camera.

"Jesus God," she murmured, as confused as she was horrified. She felt strangely lightheaded and there was a curious rushing sound in her ears. The nausea returned full force. The pamphlet slipped from her fingers, which seemed to have lost the ability to grasp.

"Elizabeth, are you all right? Elizabeth? Put your head between your knees. I think you're about to pass out." The voice sounded very far away. She could hear the words, but she couldn't make any sense of them. Bile rose in her throat and the rushing sound changed to a persistent ringing, blotting out any other sound.

"I think I'm going to…" She felt herself sliding from the chair as strong arms reached out to catch her.

CHAPTER FIVE

Elizabeth opened her eyes, confused and disoriented. She was being held in someone's arms. For a second she had no idea where she was other than that. Her head began to clear and she remembered.

Cole was carrying her toward the bed. "Hey, you okay? I caught you before you hit the floor." Carefully he laid her down and sat beside her.

Elizabeth felt weak, though the nausea, at least, seemed to have left her. "I think I'm feeling better, actually. I could use something for this pounding headache, if you had it."

"Absolutely. And something in your stomach would probably make you feel better too. Maybe some toast and a cup of coffee? No, wait." He smiled that wonderful lopsided grin again and despite herself, Elizabeth grinned back. "How about some homemade lemon pound cake? Melts in your mouth."

"I wouldn't want to put you out——"

"No trouble at all. I have a housekeeper who comes in a few times a week. She sometimes brings me treats from her daughter's bakery. They're always well worth the calories." Elizabeth couldn't help but notice Cole's trim physique and flat abs beneath his white knit shirt and blue jeans. She doubted he had to worry much about calories.

He continued. "I imagine you want to get dressed. There are some clothes that would fit you in that wardrobe there. I think they're about your size. Unless you want to wear your gown home?"

Elizabeth didn't want to wear the glamorous gown and most especially the too-high heels. But what did a guy like that keep in a wardrobe for his women friends? She had a vision of shiny black latex bodysuits and leather bustiers and corsets with garters dangling, or whatever he dressed his slave girls in for their hired play.

She knew she had to find out more about the whole peculiar, bizarre situation in which she found herself, but Cole was right. Sustenance first, then maybe she could think straight. The pound cake, and especially the coffee, sounded good. Once fortified, hopefully she would be able to organize her thoughts and collect her wits.

She looked toward the wardrobe. "What's in there? Do you keep extra corsets and bustiers for the slave girls you bring home?"

She half-expected him to take offense or act embarrassed because she'd caught him out. Instead she was the embarrassed one when a small spasm of pain washed over his handsome face. "Actually, those are some of my wife's things. My late wife. Most of it has been packed off for charity, but some of her summer things that were stored in here got passed over. I just haven't gotten around to doing anything about it, I guess."

Elizabeth felt horrible. "I'm so sorry. I didn't mean to—"

"Please, don't apologize. You didn't know. How could you? She died in a car accident. She was killed instantly, so at least she didn't suffer."

"You must miss her..." *Though not so much to stop you from hanging out at S&M sex clubs and bidding on prostitutes to take home for the night.* Silently Elizabeth admonished herself to cut it out. The man had lost his wife, for heaven's sake.

"I do. It's been three years, though, and time really does heal even the worst wounds." Cole gave a small, sad smile.

"And truth to tell, our marriage was kind of rocky. She was seeing another man and it was surely just a matter of time before..."

"She was having an affair?"

"Yeah. We'd been married fourteen years. We married too young, basically. We had drifted apart. I knew she was seeing the guy. He wasn't the first. The worst thing about it was, I really didn't care. We would have definitely split up by now."

There was an uncomfortable silence, at least for Elizabeth. Cole shook his head, shaking away the somber mood with a smile. "I'm being a terrible host, talking your ear off about stuff I'm sure you don't want to know while you're lying there starving to death. I have a pot of coffee already made. I'll be right back."

With that, he was gone. Elizabeth, who was propped against the pillows, sat up and swung her legs over the edge of the bed, waiting for another wave of dizziness. Happily, it didn't come. She scooted forward until her feet touched the ground. She didn't feel like herself, but at least the nausea remained at bay.

She moved toward a chair and sat down carefully, pulling the long nightshirt over her knees. She was about to check out the wardrobe when Cole appeared with a tray. He set it down on the small table between the red chairs. "Ah, good. You're up. You feel okay? Not going to pass out again on me, are you?"

"No, no, I'm okay." She turned her attention to the tray, reaching for the mug of steaming coffee, its aroma calling to her. She poured a little cream into the cup and lifted it to her lips, gratefully taking a sip.

Cole pulled a small bottle from his pocket and set it on the tray. "Ibuprofen," he offered. "Let me just get you some water." Striding across the room, he retrieved the water pitcher and poured a glass, which he placed on the tray as well. It had been a long time since someone had administered so kindly to her. And he, a virtual stranger.

"Thanks for doing all this. I'm still kind of out of it as to what the hell went on last night."

Cole sat across from her and raised a hand, palm toward her. "Please, don't worry about that for now. We'll figure this out. Have a bite to eat. You're still pale." Elizabeth looked down at the thick slice of yellow cake resting invitingly on a china plate and realized she was famished.

It was buttery and moist, with a tangy lemon glaze that offset the sweetness to perfection. She ate in silence, embarrassed he was watching her, but too hungry to stop.

Unable to resist, she dabbed the last couple of crumbs with her finger and put it in her mouth. She looked up to find Cole watching her with an amused expression. "Would you like some more? There's plenty left."

"No. No, thank you." She dabbed her lips with her napkin. "It was delicious." What was she doing here, in a strange man's house, wearing his nightshirt, eating his cake? She needed to get home. She needed to figure out what the hell had happened to her.

Cole smiled again, distracting her. He had a wonderful jaw line, firm and square. His face was smooth, freshly shaven though his beard was dark. His complexion was olive, his nose long and slightly beaked. It was a strong face, but a kind one. She could smell his aftershave, something light and woodsy. She resisted a crazy impulse to lean closer to smell it properly.

She took a gulp of her coffee and sat back, her brain coming more to life now that she'd eaten something. Cole Pearson didn't look like a sadistic sex pervert. He sure didn't act like one. But he *had* been at that club, bidding on girls who liked to be whipped or God knew what.

"I just can't get my head around whatever's happened. Gary Dobbins, if he and John Hunter are one and the same, works for me at Wallace & Pratt, the advertising agency. I can't believe he'd have the gall to drug me and then drag me to some sex club. I mean, the risk was enormous. It's no secret he was pissed to be passed over for a promotion for the job I landed. But Jesus, this seems like a pretty extreme response. And I was hired nearly a year ago. Why would he wait so long to get his revenge, if that's what this is?" And what I still don't get is, how did he do it? And why don't I remember anything? He's sure as hell not going to get away with it, if he's responsible. His ass is toast."

Cole shook his head. "It's hard to believe, all right. He even went to the considerable trouble of creating a false slave dossier for you. I mean, that isn't you in the pictures?" He raised his eyebrows and Elizabeth felt flames lick her cheeks.

"No! Absolutely *not*. I mean, that was my face on the last one, but that was all. The photo was obviously doctored with a photo editing program. Not hard to do, especially with the sophisticated photo programs we have at work. I don't know where he got my headshot, but that wouldn't be hard to come by, I suppose." She pondered. "How did he get me to the club? And why don't I remember any of it?"

"He probably drugged your drink. Used some kind of date rape drug. They're clear and tasteless, or at least the taste can be masked, I suppose. He must have been banking on your blacking out. I think it's one of the side effects, especially if you're given a pretty hefty dose, which it would seem you were. I imagine he got you there by simply taking you. I read up a little on the drugs that can be used, and one of the effects is they make you very compliant. They lower your inhibitions as well.

"So maybe you were even a willing participant in all of it, though I doubt you were really aware of what was going on. You did allow yourself to be led to the auction block. You were with it enough to stand up there for the few minutes it took to bid on you. You were swaying a bit, but people just assumed you were drunk. Though I personally never mix alcohol and D/s play, there are plenty that do. I took you home to get you away from him as much as anything. It was clear just from a few minutes of talking to Hunter or Dobbins or whoever he is that he wasn't a true Dom. Of course, I didn't realize at the time he was setting you up."

He tilted his head, appraising her. There was something penetrating in his gaze. Elizabeth felt suddenly naked. Both confused and aroused, she looked away.

Cole continued to speculate. "It does seem like an awfully drastic step to take just because someone got a job you thought should have been yours. I mean, usually if you're going to give someone a date rape drug, it's so you can force them into unwanted sex, right? If you don't mind my asking, is there something else between you? Were you two, uh, involved?"

"No *way*." The very idea was repugnant.

Her revulsion must have showed on her face because Cole laughed. "Sorry. So back to the revenge theory."

"Yeah. The thing is, Gary's a really bright guy and he works hard, but when the last guy in my position retired, he was passed over. He's not really a leader. He's too eager to take credit and loathe to share it. Senior management didn't feel he had what it takes to do the job. The job requires a lot of social skills and a willingness to put yourself out there with the client. Gary is more of a backroom guy. He gets flustered when he has to speak publicly. He has a hard time hiding his feelings, which are often rather negative. He tends to rub people the wrong way.

"I knew he was pissed off about not getting the job he believed he'd been groomed for. He made no bones about it, especially at first. But I had really thought, especially this past month, that he'd finally put it behind him. His whole attitude had taken a hundred-eighty degree turn for the better, or so I'd thought."

She pushed her hair away from her face and sighed. This whole situation was so strange, it hardly seemed real. The sexy guy sitting across from her was real enough though.

"You've been through a pretty rough night. Would you like to take a shower? Do you feel okay? I mean, well enough to shower on your own?"

"Why? You offering to take one with me?" She grinned and he grinned back but shook his head. Though she'd been teasing, she realized she'd been expecting him to at least flirt a little. But maybe he wasn't interested in her, not now that he'd found out she wasn't the submissive sex slave he thought he'd brought home with him.

"I'll be just down the hall in case you need me. Just press the intercom button in the bathroom and I'll hear you," was all he offered. She toyed briefly with the idea of pretending she was going to faint, to make him come into the bathroom while she was naked. Mentally she tossed the idea away, surprised at herself for even thinking it. Elizabeth Martin did not go after guys, even gorgeous ones like this. They came to her.

She kept her voice cool. "I'm sure I'll be fine. I'll be out of your hair after that. I'll just grab a taxi." Reflexively she glanced out of the high rise window, as if she could get her bearings in the city by doing so. "Where are we, anyway? I mean, this is obviously Manhattan but..."

"Fifth Avenue at Sixty third. And please, don't worry about that. Take all the time you need. I'll take you home whenever you're ready." He smiled, those dark eyes entering her soul.

She looked away, flustered despite herself. "That's okay. I can take a cab—really."

He stood, still smiling. "We can argue about it later. You should find everything you need in the bathroom. Please help yourself to anything in that wardrobe." He paused, adding, "I really think you should press charges against that lunatic."

"I'm not sure what I'm going to do, to tell you the truth. The whole thing still seems surreal to me. I don't want to accuse him outright until I speak to him. Maybe it wasn't even Gary who brought me there. Maybe whoever this John guy was only resembled Gary, and I somehow ended up with him. The whole thing is so strange and I know I'm not thinking clearly yet."

"No, you're not. Because you're forgetting about the slave dossier that was prepared and submitted to House of Usher prior to the auction. It's a private club and the auctions are by invitation only. Whoever did this, it was premeditated and planned out well in advance. You're dealing with a lunatic, Elizabeth. What he did was unconscionable. At the very least, you should fire him."

"Oh, if he did this, you can bet I will."

"Well, he needs to know what's going on, then. Or, if you want to keep it out of the office, press criminal charges. The guy's a total sleaze."

Elizabeth could no longer hold her tongue. "You know, I can't help but wonder about casting stones while in your glass house. I mean, you're the guy who *bid* on me. Who actually paid money, I presume you paid money, for a...a slave girl, no, let's be blunt here, a *prostitute*. What does that make you?"

Cole raised his eyebrows, his expression amused. "Someone who enjoys the erotic exchange of power. I make no apology for that. The club offers a service of allowing people of like mind to hook up for consensual play. It's just a game, of course, though it can be a very intense one. I'd love to have a discussion about erotic submission with you, if you're open to it, that is." He tilted his head as he peered at her. She felt he was taking her measure, gauging her interest.

Elizabeth knew something about BDSM, though not through personal experience. She had nothing against it per se—to each his own. But the idea of submitting to a man went against her grain. She was a strong, independent woman. No man would tell her what to do, that was for sure. She doubted there was a guy out there who would dare to try.

He might. And I might let him. The thought leaped into her brain and she glanced at him, glad he couldn't see inside her head.

Cole stood, looking at his watch. "If you'll excuse me, I have to make two important phone calls connected with my business. I shouldn't be long. Why don't you shower and pick something to wear? Come down to my study when you're done, okay? We'll figure out where to go from here."

He left the room, closing the door quietly behind him. Elizabeth knew she had been rather rude. It was none of her business what this man did or didn't do in his spare time, or any time for that matter. Still, she didn't get it. He seemed like such a nice guy. Yet the woman who was supposed to be her in those photos had been tightly bound in rope and chains, the shadow of a man with a long, cruel-looking whip just behind her.

Though her mind rebelled at the images, she couldn't help admit a certain perverse curiosity. What would it be like to be bound, naked and exposed for a man like Cole? A shiver of desire zinged along her nerve endings.

Her mind roiling, she moved toward the wardrobe and opened it. Inside were dresses, skirts and blouses, as well as pants and shorts neatly folded on shelves beside the hanging clothes. It was strange to think the woman who had owned them and worn them was no longer alive. She wasn't crazy about the idea of wearing a dead woman's clothing, but what choice did she have?

She selected a pale yellow brushed cotton blouse and a pair of jeans that looked like they would fit. She would have to wear her old underwear, and she had no bra, but at least she would definitely feel more comfortable going home in a cab in these clothing than in her low-cut evening gown. There were even a few pairs of shoes to choose from. She selected a pair of white leather sandals. They looked a little big, but she would only need them to get home in.

Clothes in her arms, Elizabeth went into the bathroom and set them on the counter. In the shower, she found shampoo, soap, shaving cream, face wash and even a new razor. Clearly, the man was used to entertaining overnight guests.

She turned on the water and climbed in. The hot spray felt wonderful and gratefully she turned her face up toward it. Her headache was nearly gone. She was still vastly puzzled and furious with Gary, but at the same time curiously excited by the situation in which she found herself. Cole was the first man since…well, perhaps ever, who had grabbed her attention and held it like a vise from the moment she'd set eyes on him.

Even as confused and sick as she was when she first awoke, she couldn't deny the immediate, intense attraction. It wasn't just his good looks, his deep, sexy voice or those compelling eyes. No, there was something else. Something as yet unexplored, unspoken, untapped, within herself that had responded on a gut level to something in him.

She pondered this whole BDSM thing. If a guy like Cole was into it…. Maybe her ideas of S&M, vague images of women in Cat Woman suits wielding bullwhips, and men in black leather vests, dark glasses and boots with handcuffs dangling from their belts, were the stuff of porn magazines and had little to do with whatever it was Cole was into.

The shower, on top of the coffee and cake, did wonders in clearing the last of the fog from Elizabeth's mind. First and foremost she wanted to get back to her apartment, check her phone messages and confront Gary about what the hell had gone down the night before.

Thank God no one else at the office had been witness to her allowing herself to be auctioned off to the highest bidder. How he expected to keep his job, after what he'd pulled, was beyond her.

Dressed, her wet hair brushed back, shoes in hand and purse, shawl and gown over her arm, she headed down the hall in search of her host. The study door was ajar. She tapped against it and Cole, who was sitting at a massive desk in the corner, swiveled toward her and stood.

"Perfect timing. I just finished my calls."

Elizabeth entered the room and stopped just inside.

Cole advanced toward her. "You're looking much better. Are you feeling better?"

"Yes, thanks. Almost like myself again." There was a pause. If only they'd met under less bizarre circumstances... "Listen, would you give me that pamphlet, that dossier as you called it. I don't need something like that floating around."

"Sure. Plus you'll want it for evidence, if it comes to that. Let me just get it. I won't be a second." As she waited, she scanned the room. Three of the walls were lined with books, many of them bound in fine leather and tooled with gold lettering. Another gorgeous Oriental carpet graced the middle of the hardwood floor. This place must cost a fortune, she thought.

She'd been "bought" by a millionaire. The idea almost made her giggle, if the circumstances weren't so upsetting.

He returned and held the pamphlet out to her. She took it, noticing his large hands and strong forearms. He was dressed casually in a short-sleeved white knit shirt and blue jeans. He looked good, very good. She wondered how old he was, pegged him at about thirty-five and then told her mind to shut up and say her goodbyes.

She held out her hand. "I don't know how to thank you for, uh, rescuing me."

He took her hand in his, holding it perhaps a few seconds too long. "Are you sure I can't give you a lift? My car's just down in the garage below the building. It would be my pleasure."

"No, really, that's okay. I've put you out enough as it is."

"I'll see you down, then. The doorman will get you a cab."

She nodded, since she didn't even know where his front door was. He walked her back down the hall to a small stairway that led to a very large living room, as elegantly appointed as the rest of the house. One entire wall was of glass, offering a breathtaking view of the downtown skyline. Did he own this place or rent? And had he earned the money or inherited it? None of her business, she told herself firmly.

He insisted on accompanying her all the way down to the street. "Please, keep the clothing. I've meant to donate it for ages." He pulled his wallet from his back pocket and extracted a card, which he handed to her. "This has my phone numbers and email address on it. I know we met under very strange circumstances, but I'd love to see you again."

She looked up into his handsome face. "I'd like that." She felt suddenly shy. A cab pulled over sharply to the curb, startling her. Cole opened the back passenger door for her. He grinned that infectious lopsided grin. "Let me know what happens with that Dobbins ass, okay?"

"I will, yes. And thank you again."

She climbed into the cab and he shut the door and stepped back. The cabbie pulled into the traffic. "Where to, lady?"

CHAPTER SIX

Elizabeth breathed a sigh of relief as she leaned against the door of her apartment, home at last. *My whole place could fit into his living room*, she thought. Not that she particularly wanted a penthouse on Central Park East. She was happy with her small but very comfortable SoHo apartment.

She noticed the phone light blinking and moved toward it, pressing the button. "Hi Elizabeth? It's Gary. Sorry to bother you at home. Just checking in. You were, uh, kind of out there last night." A dry laugh followed. "I mean, what you do in your private life is your own business, I guess. Uh...I just wanted to make sure you're okay and all that. Hope I'm not overstepping. I'm actually at the office right now, or you can call me on my cell. Just making sure my boss is okay." He left the number. "Bye."

"What the hell...?" Elizabeth stared the phone, stupefied. "What I do in my private life...What is that bastard talking about?" She grabbed the phone and punched in his cell number. She hung up before it connected. Whatever was going on, she would face him directly. And she'd do it now.

Quickly she dressed in her own clothing. She transferred the contents of her evening bag into her regular purse, including the slave auction pamphlet and headed back out the door.

Gary was in his office. He looked up from his desk as she leaned in. "Hi boss. Did you get my message? I was kind of worried about you. I should have insisted on seeing you home but you were adamant about going off with that guy."

"What? What the hell are you talking about? You've got some serious explaining to do." Elizabeth entered the room and sat in one of the chairs in front of his desk. "Go ahead. I'm waiting. What the hell did you pull last night and how did you think you were going to get away with it?"

"*Me?*" His tone was outraged. He raised his eyebrows and left his mouth hanging open in surprise. "What did *I* pull? You're the one who dragged me to that sex club. I have to say, I had no idea you were into leather and whips and all that kinky stuff. You never struck me as the type." He gave a brief conspiratorial grin that didn't reach his eyes. "But then, we never really know the person behind the mask, do we?"

"I dragged *you*...what? Cut the crap. You know it was the other way around. I don't remember much of the night, but I do remember you suggesting we go on to another club. You took me there. I remember that much. And when I woke up in some strange man's house—"

He interrupted. "Elizabeth, *please*. I don't need the details of who you went home with. I have to admit, I was pretty freaked out by your behavior last night, but as I say, it's your business."

Elizabeth felt her blood pressure soaring. "*My* behavior! You slipped me drugs! In my wine. Date rape drugs. Then you took me to that club and sold me at an auction."

"I did *what?* Sold you? Are you crazy? Date rape drugs? You have to be kidding. How dare you accuse me of such a thing?"

Elizabeth found herself speechless—and confused. The scenario had made perfect sense when she'd discussed it with Cole. Though it was true she didn't remember anything herself. Yet Cole had described a man who looked like Gary. And Gary had *admitted* he'd been with her at that club.

"Wait a minute. There were witnesses, you bastard. Witnesses to you *selling* me to the highest bidder in some sex slave auction. Are you denying you were there?"

Gary's voice was icy. "I would appreciate if you wouldn't swear at me, even if you are my *team leader*." He spat the last two words. "Now, as to your bizarre accusations, I'm going to give you the benefit of the doubt, and remind myself you had way too much to drink, obviously, and perhaps you didn't realize what you were doing."

Elizabeth forced herself to stay in her seat, instead of leaping over the desk to punch him in the face, which was what she wanted to do. She let him continue, her hands clenched into fists in her lap.

His voice was patronizing. "I most certainly did not drug you—the very idea is outrageous. Why would I do such a thing? I work with you, for God's sake. As to accompanying you to that club, I don't deny that. You *insisted* I go with you.

"And yes, I saw you up on that dais, but I most certainly did not *sell* you to anyone. In fact, I'd had quite enough by that time, if you want to know. I was very embarrassed to be put in that situation, frankly. I'm seriously thinking about discussing your unprofessional behavior with Wallace. I'm sure he'd be interested to know his executive VP is a drunk who drags her employees to sordid sex clubs."

"You're out of your fucking mind," Elizabeth retorted. "If you think Wallace would believe you over me—"

"And why is that? Do you have some kind of *special* relationship with him as well?"

The implication infuriated her even more, if that were possible. She stood and slipped her purse from her shoulder. Opening it, she pulled out the now-crumpled pamphlet and tossed it at him. "Do you deny this? This—this slanderous *thing* you sent in to that club, putting me on their bid list?"

Gary took the pamphlet and smoothed it flat against his desk. His eyebrows raised and he looked at her with a nasty smile. "Slave E., eh? Surely you could have come up with something more original..." He flipped through it. "Jesus, I had no idea..."

Heat seared into her face. Reaching across the desk, she grabbed the pamphlet back.

Gary leaned backed, lacing his fingers over his chest, a sneer on his face. "Christ, Elizabeth. You even made a dossier of yourself, complete with descriptions of your particular fetishes and with glossy photos. I guess I should be flattered you'd want to show me such compromising pictures of yourself but I really not into that kind of perverted—"

Deeply embarrassed, even though she knew the photos weren't of her, she cried, "Cut the crap, Dobbins. *Dossier*! You even used that same word Cole used. It proves your involvement. And damn it, you *know* that's not me in those pictures!"

Gary's voice was icy calm, cruel amusement etching his features. "Sit down. I don't know who Cole is or what you're talking about. You're making a scene. I think Jane and Hank are down in the conference room working up a presentation. Do you really want them to hear you going on about your sordid sex life?"

Elizabeth sat down heavily, dazed and stunned by what was happening. She'd been sure of his guilt. Yet he seemed to be so certain of himself now. Yes, he'd admitted he was at the club, but he claimed she took him there. Which of course was ridiculous, but it was his word against hers, wasn't it? She recalled Cole had had a conversation with him, aka John Hunter. She would call Cole. He would be her witness. Damn, if only she could remember anything about the night herself.

"That's better." Gary apparently took her silence for cooperation. "By the way, dossier is a common word. I don't see how it proves anything. As to that not being you, well, your face is shown in one of them. 'Saucy slut girl likes it rough,'" he quoted from the pamphlet, shaking his head and clucking his evident disapproval.

"I hope you don't have this stuff plastered around on the Internet," he went on implacably. "You know how easily that sort of thing is caught out. You could definitely lose your job over this, Elizabeth. I really can't believe your incredible indiscretion. Drunk or not, that was some scene you pulled last night."

"Scene? What did I..." She clamped her mouth shut. This bastard was not going to trick her into believing a word he said. He was lying through his teeth, one hundred percent. Of course he'd created that pamphlet or dossier or whatever the hell he wanted to call it. Then he'd drugged her—who else could have done it—and taken her to the club, all of it obviously planned well in advance.

"Oh my God." She suddenly remembered where that photo of her face came from. "That's one of the headshots they took for the press release when I joined Wallace & Pratt. How did you get a hold of that?"

"Me? Why would I have access to your headshots? It seems much more likely you would have that, not me."

"You got it out of my personnel file."

Gary laughed. "Sorry, but I guess you don't know Helen that well. She'd have your head before she'd let anyone get into those files. She keeps them under lock and key."

"This is ridiculous. I know you're lying. *You* know you're lying. I have witnesses to prove it. Your ass is toast, Dobbins.

I'm going to see that you're fired and I'm going to press charges too. You won't get away with this."

"Elizabeth, I suggest you take a deep breath and think this through. That dossier contains pictures of you, not me. You're the one who woke up in some strange man's house, by your own admission. You admit you don't remember what went on—sounds like a blackout, pure and simple. People who drink heavily experience them, so I've heard. It doesn't mean you were slipped a Mickey Finn by me or anyone else. Perhaps, rather than focusing your rage on me, you might think seriously about getting help for your, uh, drinking problem.

His face twisted into a sour smile. "*My* only mistake was in going along with all this. I should have realized how soused you were and made sure you got home safely, instead of letting myself be talked into going to some club where you could make a public spectacle of yourself.

"Speaking of witnesses, if it comes to that, I'm sure we could find plenty who would testify you were up there on that little stage while men bid money for your, uh, services. Sounds like prostitution to me. Are you sure you want to open this can of worms?

"I'd seriously rethink my position, if I were you. You're senior management of a high profile firm. Imagine the scandal if the news broke that the shining star they brought in from the outside was in fact a sex slave for hire by night. Now, if you're done threatening me..."

Elizabeth opened her mouth and closed it again. She'd seen her share of unscrupulous bastards as she'd fought her way to the top in a field that was highly competitive and filled with back stabbers, but she couldn't imagine anyone going to such lengths to discredit her. The whole thing was beyond belief.

He was watching her, his expression smug and confident. He was convinced, she could tell, he'd outsmarted her. Slowly she stood and walked out of his office without another word.

~*~

Cole smoothed the sheets and pulled up the covers, making the bed Elizabeth had slept in the night before. He lifted the pillow and held it to his face—he could just detect the scent of her perfume. She was so lovely. If only they'd met under different circumstances. As it was, he knew it was likely he wouldn't see her again. No doubt she would want to put the whole bizarre affair behind her, himself included.

He sighed and sat on the edge of the bed. What was it about her that made him want her so?

Because of his money, maybe partially because of his looks, he had had his share of beautiful women since Joanie had died. Yes, Elizabeth was certainly lovely, but it wasn't just her beauty that tugged at his heart. Those very blue eyes, blue as fine sapphires, seemed to sparkle when he looked into them. He sensed a spirit in her, a strength he found himself eager to explore, perhaps to tame...

His cell phone rang and he pulled it from his pocket. He was surprised but delighted to hear Elizabeth's low, throaty voice at the other end. "He denied it," she said heatedly, after identifying herself.

"What? Dobbins, you mean?"

"Yes. He twisted the whole thing." She related the conversation and her speculation as to his motives.

Cole whistled his disbelief. "What an asshole. I can't believe he thinks he's going to get away with it."

"I know. I'm just so upset and freaked out. I don't know what to do. I can't concentrate. I have work to do, but I don't even want to be in the same building as he is right now. It's like a nightmare, except I'm awake."

"Hey, calm down. It's okay. You're safe and unharmed—that's number one. Unfortunately, I doubt he's done with his elaborate smear campaign, if that's what this is, so you need to be on your guard and maybe proactive as far as your office is concerned. Where are you now?"

"I'm outside my office building. I'm—I'm sorry to bother you with this, but I didn't know who else to talk to about it."

"Are you kidding? I'm really glad you called. Say, Wallace & Pratt is on Wall Street, right? Why don't I meet you there and we'll grab a bite of lunch or something. I have nothing going on today. Maybe we could brainstorm your plan of attack together."

"Um. Okay. Thanks. Why don't we meet at Cohn's Deli? It's on the corner of Wall Street and Broadway."

"Great. See you in a few." He hung up and redialed, canceling his lunch meeting with two business associates and the massage appointment after that. Harry, his driver, was on call whenever he needed him, but he wouldn't bother him today. He laughed at himself as he stood outside his building, anxiously hailing a cab. He couldn't remember feeling this excited about a woman since…well, ever.

You know next to nothing about her, he reminded himself as the taxi began its painstakingly slow crawl through the snarled traffic. He had looked her up on the Internet after she'd gone, but the information was only about her professional life, which was in itself impressive for a woman so young. Not that he'd expected to find anything different—like maybe a secret blog in which she'd outlined her yearning to find a Dom to take her in hand and train her to be his submissive. He grinned to himself, doubting any such thoughts had ever crossed her mind. She was clearly a woman used to being in control. That realization made the thought of claiming her all the more enticing...

Cole shook his head, aware he was losing himself in a fantasy. Right now she had reached out to him as a friend, and he would respond in kind, without a hidden agenda.

He saw her sitting toward the back of the deli in one of the booths, a cup of coffee in front of her. She saw him and gave a small wave. He slipped into the seat across from her. "Hey. Sorry it took so long. Traffic."

"Sure, no problem." The waitress approached and Cole ordered a cola. They perused the menu and when she returned they placed their orders—he, a roast beef sandwich on rye, she, turkey on wheat with tomato and lettuce.

He gazed at her as he sipped his soda. Her hair was pulled back from her face. Her skin looked impossibly soft. He wanted to reach across the booth to stroke her cheek, then run his thumb over her mouth, press it between her parted lips, feel her warm, wet tongue...

She looked up suddenly and he forced his desires down, trying to ignore the rising bulge in his jeans. "Thanks for meeting me." She smiled, though her eyes were troubled. "This is all so weird."

Forcing himself to focus, Cole agreed. "Yeah. The guy's a nutcase, all right. I was thinking on the ride over here. What you need is concrete evidence. Right now it's just your word against his as to who brought whom to the club."

"But you talked to him, right? I mean, when he, uh, handed me over, or whatever he did." He smiled as her cheeks tinted a pretty pink.

"Yes. He introduced himself as John Hunter. We have him on that, at least, as proof he's lying. Though again, even that would be his word against mine. The only real crime perpetrated last night was the use of the drugs, which we would have to prove he obtained and used. Odds are he got them on the Internet, so if we could get access to his computer, maybe we could find the evidence there."

"I don't have access to his passwords. Still, I doubt he would have done it at work. If there is any evidence, it's probably on his computer at home. We'd have to get a search warrant or whatever."

"Yeah, you're probably right. The guy's been pretty slick so far, so he wouldn't do something as stupid as surf the 'Net for illegal drugs on company time. Ditto for that dossier. He created it at home. It's the House of Usher template—they send it out to all members. Say—that's another point. It proves his prior association with the club, either his own, or he has a friend who got him access to that auction. Like I think I mentioned, it's by invitation only."

The waitress returned with their sandwiches. "You go there a lot?" Elizabeth asked.

He couldn't read anything from her neutral tone and decided just to answer honestly. "From time to time. I've bid at two other auctions. It's a diversion, really. Just for fun."

"But it costs real money, right? I mean, the auction is for real cash. You actually bid on women, or on their, uh, services, for cash. Isn't that illegal?

"They issue play money. You buy it beforehand. The auction is touted as a game only. I guess the play money is the club's way around getting busted for soliciting. Nothing happens on site—not even BDSM play, which isn't illegal. If people choose to go home with each other afterwards, surely it's nobody's business but their own."

"So sometimes they don't? They refuse?"

"Not that I'm aware of. The players there are serious. Those are real Doms and subs, into the scene, into the lifestyle. Some Doms like to lend out their slave girl for an hour or a night. It's part of a game, I guess you'd call it——they 'own' the other person. She's their possession, so they can lend her out or even give her away if they choose."

"That sounds creepy. And you're into this?"

"Me? No. That is, I don't like to play in the scene——the public stuff, the underground clubs. Like I said, for me these auctions and clubs are just a diversion. If and when I find my true love, my sub girl, I would never lend her out or give her to another man. It wouldn't be like that. We would be partners. Lovers. Equals who understand and appreciate the exchange of power we both crave."

Elizabeth seemed to be absorbing this. He wondered if she understood it on any level. Would she ask him more? He wouldn't thrust his romantic vision on her. He would wait for her to ask. And if she didn't, so be it. He would, he knew, still like to get to know her better——much better.

After a moment she pursed her lips and raised her eyebrows. "So I was just a diversion, huh?" He laughed and she laughed too, with chagrin. "Sorry I passed out on you. Guess you didn't get your money's worth, huh?"

"You might like to know you were the highest bid of the night, at least to that point. I had to borrow play money to get you. I hadn't counted on the bidding going so high."

"Really?" She looked pleased. "How much did I go for?"

"$21,500. In play money, that is."

"So that's…"

"$2,500."

She frowned. "I'm sorry you lost the money. I mean, you didn't get what you paid for."

"Don't worry about it. The money doesn't matter. I hate to think you were put through this whole mess. But to tell you the truth, I'm glad *I* won you. God knows who might have taken you home if I hadn't. Someone with less scruples, someone who just wanted to have a scene and felt they had the right to it, no matter how impaired their partner was. Someone like Dobbins. To tell you the truth, I have half a mind to go over there myself and beat that little shit to a pulp."

"No, don't do that. He's probably got a fake dossier made on you too. Let's not play into his hands anymore than we already have. I'll get the bastard one way or another. He's made a huge mistake, taking me on like this." Her eyes flashed and she thrust out her chin. "You know the old saying—don't get mad, get even."

"I quite agree," Cole said, liking her very much.

CHAPTER SEVEN

They lingered after they'd finished their sandwiches. Though Elizabeth remained upset about Gary, somehow, when she was with Cole, it didn't seem to matter quite as much. He was so easy to talk to. And yes, very easy on the eyes as well.

But beneath that, beneath how kind and gracious he'd been in handling the whole hideous debacle, something was definitely sparking between them. His words played over in her head, exciting something deep inside her....*When I find my true love, my sub girl...We would be partners. Lovers. Equals who understand and appreciate the exchange of power we both crave.*

These words spoke directly to a secret place inside her. Though she was always in control and liked it that way, a part of her longed to give up, to give in, to surrender to another. She'd never permitted herself to give in to this longing, thinking it was merely a throwback to her genetic coding, the instinct of a woman submitting to man in a primal way.

There was something about Cole. Something different, something dark and exciting beneath the surface. He was so confident and self-assured. So...dominant. Yes, that was the word, though when she thought of it in terms of him, it didn't come across as chauvinistic and controlling. It was...sexy.

A little dangerous.

A lot intriguing.

She needed to understand more, though. He'd dropped various hints and casual remarks about his particular brand of D/s, but what did it really mean? What was the whole concept of erotic, romantic submission really about? Would he be the one to teach her?

"You're awfully quiet." He pulled her from her reverie. "What are you thinking?"

She avoided a direct answer. "You want to get out of here? We could, uh, take a walk or something."

"That's a great idea. If you want, we could catch a taxi over to Central Park. Walk under the trees, have a little privacy." For once traffic was on their side, and they made it quickly to the park. Neither spoke during the ride, though the silence was companionable.

They began to walk, passing a fenced-in pet area with dogs large and small leaping and cavorting about, deliriously happy to be off their leashes. They watched the animals a while and then meandered down a nearby path.

They talked about Gary and how she might go about getting some hard evidence against him. She knew she should focus on that immediate problem, but found what she really wanted to do was broach the whole BDSM, D/s thing.

She decided the time wasn't yet right. Maybe she'd just find out more about him—get a little background. "Can I ask you something? You said you'd been married fourteen years. And that she died three years ago. I have to say, you don't look old enough for that."

He shrugged. "I'm thirty-nine. We were both twenty-two when we married. And don't ask me why we married so young, because I really couldn't tell you, except that she was very eager to marry. I loved her and at the time believed she was the one for me and me for her. I spent the next decade figuring out I was wrong, but not really doing anything to fix it. I think I stayed with her so long partly because I felt guilty."

"Guilty? For what?"

"She wanted children but she had a very hard time conceiving. We spent tens of thousands of dollars on infertility treatments. She did manage to get pregnant three times, but miscarried early on each time. I was so sad and so sorry for her. But for me children weren't the be-all, end-all of our relationship. She let her infertility sort of define her life. She couldn't get past it, though she refused to even consider adoption. After a while, I have to admit, I kind of stopped trying to make things better. I think I gave up, in a way. On her, on us."

"Did she know, was she into, uh, you know...the scene, as you call it?"

"D/s? Joanie? No. No way. She had this idea of whips and chains, of brutality and abuse, of pain for its sake, of a man overpowering a woman simply because he can." He shook his head. "Though to be fair, I never really tried to explain it. It was years before I was comfortable enough with myself, and my own understanding of erotic submission. By then we'd become sort of hardened into our respective roles. Sex was vanilla, infrequent and unsatisfying."

Elizabeth laughed. "Vanilla. I like that. So what's D/s? Chocolate? Strawberry?"

Cole grinned. "It can be whatever you want. It's the intensity of experience that makes it so phenomenal. Lick the surface of the vanilla, and find layers of chocolate, of coffee, of caramel, of mango and mandarin orange. With enough trust and desire, there's no limit to what you can discover."

"That sounds kind of catchy. You ever think about writing advertising copy?" Elizabeth teased.

"You hiring?" he teased back.

They passed a bench and by mutual, silent accord they sat down side-by-side. Cole's thigh touched hers. Drawn to him, she put her hand on it, feeling the hard muscle beneath the denim. He put his hand over hers and looked into her eyes. She tried to hold his gaze, but somehow could not. She looked down instead at his hand.

She thought about his marriage, and how it had been on its way to failing. "I never married," she volunteered. "I'm not sure I'm marriage material. Sometimes I wonder if I even have the capacity to love." She bit her tongue, furious with herself for admitting such an intimate, painful truth to a man she wanted to impress. She could have bit her tongue off. Instead she rushed on. "Actually, I'm probably just too busy with my career. I don't have time to connect."

"You make the time," Cole said. "That's something I learned, but too late. I didn't make the time. When things got too difficult, we both just turned away. Instead of doing something to repair the marriage, she had affairs and I threw myself into my work."

He sighed and smiled at Elizabeth, but she could see the pain in his eyes. "Part of the problem was I was being dishonest with her. Not intentionally and not to hurt her, but because I didn't have the courage to face or understand my own desires. I've learned so much since then, and I've promised myself to be true to my own nature."

"Your nature...?"

"I'm what you'd call a Dom, which is short for Dominant. The yin to my yang is a submissive. A submissive is someone who craves the experience of yielding sensually or sexually to another person. She allows herself to be controlled, to be taken sexually to heights she might not achieve otherwise. It's a very intense experience. Very powerful for both sides, when the connection is the right one.

"Submission requires absolute trust. To me it's a sacred trust, one that must never be abused. Sadly, there are assholes in the scene, just like everywhere else. Maybe even more so, because the whole BDSM thing provides a nice cover for bullies who need to hurt women—who are clueless about the romance of erotic suffering."

"Erotic suffering? That sounds like a contradiction in terms." Despite herself, Elizabeth's nipples hardened and her mouth felt suddenly dry. She licked her lips, met his eye and looked quickly down.

"Not at all," he answered, his hand still on hers. "Not in the right context. Pleasure and pain are subjective terms. They're fluid. What you might not tolerate in one situation, can be highly erotic, even deeply pleasurable, in another."

"I don't understand," she claimed, though on some level, a level deeper than words, she did. They locked eyes again and this time she managed to hold his gaze, though she felt herself falling into those deep, dark eyes.

"I have to kiss you," he murmured, echoing her own secret longing. Oblivious to passersby, she closed her eyes and leaned toward him, answering without words.

When he finally released her, Elizabeth fell back against the back of the bench, her heart pounding, her lips tingling, her body on fire. No one had ever kissed her like that. His lips, his tongue, the passion spilling and melting between them as he held her—he hadn't simply kissed her—he had possessed her.

She tried to catch her breath, both frightened by her own strong reaction and deeply aroused. What was happening to her? It was just a kiss.

But it wasn't only the kiss. His words had ignited feelings deep and fiery inside her, something that had lain dormant and unacknowledged until now. Though she didn't yet understand his talk of pleasure and pain intermingling, or the concept of erotic suffering and romantic submission, every fiber of her being felt alive with expectation and desire.

Cole stood and held out his hand. She took it and he pulled her up and into his arms. After a moment he released her. "Come back with me to my place."

She nodded, not trusting herself to speak. Her legs were weak and she leaned against him as they walked. He wrapped a strong, comforting arm around her. She relaxed against him, as if they had always walked together like this, as if she were right where she belonged, possibly for the first time in her life.

Gary pulled out the small silver flask from the desk drawer and unscrewed the top. The confrontation with Elizabeth had gone even better than he'd expected. It was perfect, their meeting at the office, with him behind his desk at a symbolic advantage. She'd been so easy to manipulate. For all her supposed savvy, she wasn't too swift at thinking on her feet, at least not this time around.

He'd spent a mostly sleepless night, waiting for either her or the idiot who'd paid all that money to take home a zombie, to call and demand an explanation, or worse, for the police to show up with a warrant for his arrest.

What he'd done had been beyond risky—he knew that. And yet it had worked. The drugs did their job—making her compliant and docile, then conveniently wiping her mind clean by the next day. He had half a mind to send the online Mexican pharmacy from which he'd obtained the drugs a testimonial about its excellent side effects.

She was clearly confused by the night's events—what little she could remember. Not only was it his word against hers, she wasn't ever sure what hers *were*. He laughed aloud with bitter pleasure, recalling the dark red surge of color in her face as he calmly took her to task for subjecting him, her poor, beleaguered employee, to her fetishes and perversions. Oh, how good it had been to put the bitch in her place, reducing her to a stuttering, blushing mess.

She'd insisted he knew he was lying and she knew it too, but did she? He wondered just what had transpired with the guy who took her home. From the sound of things, she probably spent the night completely passed out. Not much fun to whip and fuck an unconscious slave girl. Probably the guy would be calling the club, demanding his money back.

That was another delicious irony. Though she wasn't technically his to sell, Gary had even made money on the deal. House of Usher paid the owners forty percent of their take on the auction, though it was done in the form of play money to keep it legal. Though he didn't plan to return to the club, aware he would be none too well-received after what he'd pulled, the idea of taking cash, fake or otherwise, for the hoity-toity Elizabeth Martin, vastly appealed to him.

He took a long swig of the whiskey before screwing the lid closed and storing the flask again in the bottom drawer. It was a little after six. He'd spent the entire day at the office, waiting for others on his floor who came and went to clear out.

He was reasonably sure everyone was gone, but just to be sure, he called out, "Anyone left? I've had it for today. You'll set the alarm?" He stopped, listening for a response from behind any of the closed office doors, but all was silent.

His heart picked up its pace as he approached Elizabeth's office. Reaching into his pants pocket, he removed his key ring and inserted the key in the door. His key, which all executives were given to enter the front doors of the agency during off-hours, also unlocked all the office doors, except for human resources, where employee files and payroll information were kept. Even that door used to have the same key, until fanatical Helen came on board and insisted the lock be changed.

With a glance in either direction down the silent hall, he unlocked the door and went in. He wished he had taken the flask with him, as he could definitely use another belt, but he didn't want to take the time to retrieve it. There was no knowing if some gung-ho employee might suddenly decide the best way to spend their Saturday night was at the office.

Gary turned on Elizabeth's computer, drumming his fingers impatiently on the smooth, shiny surface of her rosewood desk while it booted up.

He smiled at how easy it had been to get Sheila Murphy, one of the company's techies, to reset Elizabeth's corporate password, which worked for both her computer and email account.

Sheila wasn't unattractive but she was too thin for Gary's taste, not to mention too aggressive. Gary preferred his women with more curves and less independence.

Nevertheless, somehow they'd ended up making out in a supply closet at the office Christmas party that past winter. He'd been drunk and she'd been eager. She'd made it clear she'd like to get to know him better after that, but he'd managed to come up with enough excuses so she'd stopped asking.

Until this morning.

Earlier in the week Gary had been nosing around the tech offices while formulating his plans to slander Elizabeth. He'd learned Sheila had accepted a new job in another state. Seeking her out, he'd struck up a conversation, turning the charm on full force. She'd reacted as he'd hoped, blushing and smiling. She told him she was coming in Saturday morning to tie up a few loose ends and when he suggested breakfast with him beforehand, she'd jumped at the chance.

When he'd explained how Elizabeth's team planned to pull a fun prank on her and needed access to her password to do it, she'd been skeptical at first, spouting party line about security. But when he'd moved next to her in the booth and run his hand along her bare leg beneath her skirt while leaning over to kiss the nape of her neck, she'd begun to sing a different tune. After all, he'd assured her, it was just a joke mail to Elizabeth from her own account. Elizabeth loved practical jokes, he said with a laugh.

They'd returned to the office and he hadn't even minded the repeat of their Christmas party tussle in the supply closet. Afterwards she'd changed Elizabeth's password, admonishing him with a coquettish giggle not to tell she'd done it.

Now he waited anxiously for the computer to boot. After a few seconds the familiar blue screen appeared on the monitor with the company's logo. Gary typed in the temporary password Sheila had written down for him. He pressed enter and held his breath. The screen went black a moment, its drives whirring and clicking as it loaded Elizabeth's desktop and programs. *I did it,* Gary whispered. His heart was hammering unpleasantly but that didn't stop the broad grin from splitting his face.

After closing the reminder to change the password, he opened her Internet browser and typed in the address of a particularly brutal BDSM site he liked to frequent when home alone and in need of jerking off. He clicked through several of the pages and then typed in a new porn site address, whisking himself to an erotic bondage site that specialized in lesbian action. Then it was off to a fetish supply catalog, where he scrolled through pages of whips, cuffs, paddles, gags and restraint devices. For good measure, he downloaded several pictures of naked women in various tortured poses and saved them on Elizabeth's desktop.

He checked to make sure her browser wasn't set to delete any record of the site visits. Satisfied, he closed the browser and stared for a moment at the icons on her desktop. Looking around the large, well-appointed office—the office that would soon be his at last—he permitted himself a smile. He heard something and stiffened, his ears preternaturally pricked. Had it been an elevator door? Was someone coming in to the offices? Hurriedly he closed down Elizabeth's computer and left her office.

He returned quickly to his own, plopping himself into his chair. He strained to hear if someone had in fact come in, but heard nothing. Damn, he'd jumped the gun, his nerves getting the better of him. Well, he would finish the rest of his plan from right there at his own computer.

He logged onto the company's email server via their website. When the login screen came up, he entered Elizabeth's name and temporary password. He waited the few seconds it took to open her email, holding his breath and…he was in.

Hurriedly he scrolled through her inbox, looking for anything that pertained to him. It was all boring business correspondence. He opened her sent folder—more of the same.

Well, not for long, he thought with an evil grin.

Clicking on the compose memo tab, he typed in his own email address and the subject tag: *Sorry*.

ACCIDENTAL SLAVE

Dear Gary,

I've been doing a lot of thinking, after our little discussion this afternoon. I'm really sorry I flew off the handle like that. Of course you didn't have anything to do with what happened—the very idea is silly, once I've had time to think it through. I had obviously had way too much to drink, and I apologize for dragging you into it.

I know you were right to break off our personal relationship, even though it was pretty rough for me at the time. And though I miss you in my bed more than I can say, I would never do anything to harm you—you mean too much to me.

That said, I hadn't intended that anyone at the office find out about my secret life. I mean, it's nobody's business but my own, right? I'm a free woman and these are modern times. If I want to hang out at sex clubs and engage in a little casual S&M fun, who am I hurting?

Nevertheless, I do hope you'll maintain your discretion, especially as regards Wallace & Pratt. I really wouldn't want it to get out. You know how stuffy and prudish old man Wallace is. He just wouldn't get it.

You've done a great job on the team, Gary, and I do hope this little wrinkle in our relationship doesn't affect your ability to work with me. I wouldn't want our working relationship to become strained by any indiscretion on either of our parts. As your annual review is coming up soon, I'm sure you appreciate the delicacy of the situation.

Best regards, and, again, sorry about last night, and the baseless accusations I made today.

Elizabeth

Gary reread the email, grinning at the implication she was subtly blackmailing him into silence with the specter of his upcoming salary review. He was pleased with the personal note—enjoying the fantasy that they'd had an affair and he had been the one to break it off. He added Elizabeth's own address to the cc line since she had a habit of cc:ing herself on emails.

He held his finger poised over the button for a moment as he weighed the consequences of what he was about to do. Did he really have the balls to destroy her so utterly and completely?

He hit the send button.

CHAPTER EIGHT

Elizabeth was still struggling to recover from the effects of that breathless kiss. She stood at the large window of Cole's high-rise apartment, gazing out at the tops of the trees that filled Central Park and the ribbons of cars down below. She wanted more than just a kiss—but how much more?

Cole came up behind her, standing just close enough so she could feel his presence without his actually touching her. She stood still, aware of the press of her nipples against her bra, wondering what he expected of her. He was a Dom, used to getting what he wanted, she was sure. He wanted her—that kiss had left no doubt, but in what way?

She turned toward him, her lips parting of their own accord. She closed her eyes, eager for the press of his lips against hers. Instead he stepped back and moved to stand beside her, obviously not on the same wavelength. Embarrassed, she turned hastily back toward the view.

"This is a great place," she offered, aware her voice was over-bright to cover her chagrin.

"Yeah. It's been in the family a long time. When my parents retired, they wanted to move somewhere warmer, and I bought it from them. I like living here, but sometimes I need to get away from all the hustle and bustle of the commercial real estate business, which is what I do when I'm not bidding on beautiful slave girls at BDSM auctions."

He turned a lopsided grin on her and unable to resist, she smiled back. "Good." He nodded with approval. "I'm glad to see you can smile about it. I feel really bad about what happened to you last night. That guy should be put in jail for what he did. But at the same time, at least you weren't hurt or taken advantage of by some unscrupulous asshole."

He reached out and stroked her cheek with one finger. A shiver ran through her and her nipples ached. "And I got to meet you. To take you home. To…kiss you."

Elizabeth's heart skipped a beat and again her lips tingled in anticipation. Her legs felt rubbery. Was it still the after-effect of the drugs? Why did she feel like a trembling teenager around this guy? She should say something—something clever and sassy, something to show she was in control of both the situation and herself. She opened her mouth but no words formed.

He took her shoulders and gently but firmly pushed her against the thick glass. His dark eyes seemed to be searching hers, looking for something she wasn't sure she was ready for him to see. She held his gaze as long as she could, then buried her head against his chest. Her heart was pounding as she rested against him, waiting, knowing he was going to kiss her again, wanting it.

He put his arms around her, tightening them as he pulled her close. All at once his mouth was on hers, his kisses urgent. His tongue teased and darted between her lips while his hands roamed over her body. She felt as if she would melt into the floor, her muscles liquid, held up only by his strong embrace.

He let her go, holding her by the shoulders, his eyes again searching her, as if trying to penetrate secrets she barely knew she was keeping. He led her to the sofa, gently pushing her down. Caught in a web of her own desire, she didn't resist him. She desperately wanted him to kiss her again.

"Just lie back and relax." He lifted her legs onto the sofa, maneuvering himself so he was sitting beside her. There was easily room for them both on the deep sofa, which was upholstered in rich, soft leather.

He stroked her cheek with the back of two fingers. She resisted an impulse to turn her head and take them into her mouth. She willed her heart to stop its wild flutter. Cole was like no man she had ever met. She knew she was out of her ken, out of her depth, but she didn't care.

"Trust me," he whispered.

She nodded and closed her eyes.

He leaned over her until his lips touched her forehead. His kiss was light as the touch of a petal on her eyelids, the bridge of her nose, her mouth. He traced the line of her lips with the tip of his tongue. He kissed her, the velvet press of his lips soft against hers as his tongue danced in her mouth. When he pulled back, she leaned up, not ready for him to stop, never wanting him to stop.

"Un unh," he admonished, pressing her shoulder back against the couch. "Stay still. Let me take you to a new place—a new way of experiencing your desire." His lips were smiling but his eyes were burning into hers. She wasn't entirely sure where he was going but she knew she wanted to come along for the ride.

Gently he laid one hand over her eyes, forcing them closed. "Yes. Stay like that, relaxed, eyes closed." Elizabeth felt very vulnerable, but also deeply aroused. He removed his hand from her face. She remained with eyes closed, her heart fluttering wildly. Cole's fingers closed around her wrists, pulling them up and pressing them onto the sofa above her head. Her eyes flew open. Her natural instinct was to resist, and she did, struggling against his firm grip.

"What...?"

"Shh, it's okay. Just flow with how it feels, give in to it." Elizabeth's heart was smashing against her ribs and she couldn't seem to catch her breath.

"Don't struggle. Relax. Close your eyes again." He leaned down, his mouth brushing against her ear. "Slow your breathing. You're safe here. Give in to your own desires."

He kept her wrists pinned over her head. Her blouse had ridden up, exposing the skin of her midriff. Cole stroked the flesh, his touch electrifying her. She pulled against his grip and he tightened it just a little.

His free hand roamed, moving down her thighs and passing over her bare skin again. She shuddered and pressed her legs together, keenly aware of her pulsing clit. She felt his hand at her throat, the thumb lightly pressing beneath one ear, the fingers curling easily around her neck. She gasped, her heart bucking, and jerked her wrists, which he held steady.

One hand on her throat, the other pinning her arms high over her head, he murmured, "Do you want me to stop?" His voice was low and sultry, a ripple of challenge beneath the surface of the words.

She looked at him, opening her mouth to say yes. Her mind told her to *demand* he let her go that second. Her body, yielding, wet and aching with lust, overruled, and she closed her mouth without answering.

He narrowed his eyes and smiled a predatory smile. "No, I didn't think so." He moved his hand from her throat, twisting it so his fingers dipped into the cup of her bra beneath her blouse. He found and rolled an already stiff nipple, making her gasp. He kissed her throat, his tongue gliding down to the hollow between her collarbones.

"You're so beautiful," he whispered throatily, sliding to lie down beside her, her wrists still caught in his firm grip. She trembled, feeling his passion and heat mingling with her own. His cock was hard against her thigh. His free hand moved down between her legs, sliding against the thin cotton of her slacks. Her clit throbbed beneath the press of his fingers and it was all she could do to keep from grinding against them.

All at once he released her wrists and pulled her into his arms. She wanted those fingers back at her sex. She wanted, she realized with astonishment, to feel his grip on her wrists, rendering her helpless, taking the decision from her. She wanted to pull off her clothing and rip off his shirt and let him take her——caveman style. What was happening to her? Who was this guy who could draw such reactions from her?

Her mind whirling, her body on fire, she tried to collect herself. He held her close and she could feel the beat of his heart against hers. He murmured in a low voice, his lips near her ear. "That is just a taste, Elizabeth. The tiniest whisper of the passion we could share."

He let her go, sitting up and twisting to face her. He was watching her with dark, solemn eyes. She too sat up, pushing her hair from her face and straightening her blouse, two buttons of which had popped open.

She was flustered and curiously let down. Why had he stopped? She rubbed her wrists, conscious she wanted to feel his grip on them again. She bit her lip, aware her panties were wet, wondering if the stain of her desire showed at her crotch. She pressed her legs together and looked away from his mesmerizing stare. "I don't know..."

"You don't know..." he prompted her to continue. Slowly, almost against her will, she looked back at him. His dark hair was tousled, the bangs, which had been brushed smoothly to the side, falling over his forehead, into his eyes. He shook back the hair and waited for her to continue, a small smile on his lips.

Why was she behaving like a tongue-tied schoolgirl? Elizabeth was used to making high-powered deals with the movers and shakers of the business elite. She never hesitated to let a man know how she felt and she was always honest, even brutally honest. Surely she could express herself now. Admit to him her confusion, if not her desires.

She blew out a breath and turned resolutely toward him. She wanted him to explain to her what it was she was feeling. Yet she lacked the words or the courage to ask. "I don't know what you mean. About—about this being a taste of…of what we could share. The passion…" She trailed off.

"Don't you?" His voice was soft, coaxing. "I may be wrong, but I have a strong feeling about you, Elizabeth. About us. My instincts are rarely wrong. Yes, I realize I was mistaken last night. I brought you home under false pretenses, through no fault of my own, but nevertheless, I spent the night fantasizing about when you woke up. I believed, as you know, that I'd purchased the charms of a willing submissive for a night's, or in this case, a morning's casual BDSM play.

"Yet, as you know, that's not what I found. I found you—not only the most beautiful woman I've ever seen, but a captivating, intelligent, strong woman who, I sense, has a great untapped well of passion lurking inside her.

"What I want with you is most definitely *not* an evening of casual BDSM play. And, just so you know, when I bring a woman home from an auction or that sort of casual thing, the play doesn't go beyond the scene. That is, I don't make love to those women. It's just an outlet—a release, I suppose you'd say."

"What do you do?" Elizabeth couldn't resist asking. "This causal BDSM play you keep referring to. What does it involve?"

Cole raised his eyebrows, an amused expression on his face. "Since you ask so directly, I'll answer directly as well. I have a playroom. I converted the attic into a BDSM playroom. All the usual accoutrements—a restraint cross, a spanking horse, suspension equipment and a nice assortment of floggers, whips, paddles, cuffs, chains, gags and blindfolds, among other things."

"My God." Elizabeth was thoroughly shocked.

"Don't worry. I have no intention of introducing you to any of that unless or until you expressly ask for it."

"Unless I ask..." Elizabeth shook her head, stunned to think he actually thought she would *ask* to be tied to a cross and flogged. The very idea was beyond her comprehension. And yet...and yet despite her shock, the image of herself, naked and bound, Cole standing behind her, a whip in his hand, flashed into her mind with such vivid clarity she blushed, as if he too were privy to her thoughts.

"Listen to me, Elizabeth. I want you. I think you know that. But I have no intention of dragging you into something you're not ready for, or not interested in. As I told you last night, I don't regard the pleasure I take in using a woman, a woman who wishes to be used in that fashion, as a perversion. But by the same token, I would never thrust my feelings or desires on someone else. On someone who didn't ask for it willingly and with complete understanding of what it entailed."

He moved closer, his hand sliding along her thigh, sending shivers through her she couldn't hide. Her breath caught in her throat as he moved closer still. His wonderful woodsy scent was intoxicating, blending now as it did with something else, the musky rise of his lust, and her own answering pheromones.

"When I take you, it will be because you offer yourself to me—completely and without reservation. I know you're not ready—yet. Still, you can't deny something happened between us just now. Something beyond the simple thrill of being with someone new. I know what you were experiencing," he asserted. "I know it in my bones. I was born knowing it, as you were, though until this moment you may not have realized it. I felt what you felt when your wrists were pulled taut over your head, your body stretched and exposed for my touch, my caress, for whatever I chose to do to you.

"I could sense your feelings of helplessness, the loss of control, coupled with the fierce, almost overpowering heat of your own lust. You wanted it, Elizabeth. You may deny it, but I'll know you're lying."

She had in fact been about to do just that, but he stopped her by pressing two fingers against her lips. "I saw the spark in your eyes, Elizabeth. I felt the pounding of your heart, the heat between your legs."

Elizabeth's cheeks burned. She crossed her legs and turned her body away from his. In a soft, gentle voice, he continued. "Please don't misunderstand me. I don't say this to embarrass you, or to accuse you of something you aren't comfortable with. I only want you to understand I know what you're feeling. I know it because I know you. On a basic, primal level, you and I are already lovers. I am the other half of what you don't yet realize you can become. I can sense the submissive potential in you, Elizabeth. I would love to explore it with you."

Elizabeth sat up straighter, wrapping her arms protectively around her torso. She felt hot and wondered suddenly if she were going to faint again. She waited for the unwelcome rise of nausea and the ringing in her ears, but it didn't come. His words were burning her as if they'd been branded into her psyche. Unable to cope with the full import of what he was saying, she grabbed onto his last words, ready to combat them.

"Submissive? Me?" She gave a laugh, aware it sounded forced. "I'm an executive vice president at a prominent Manhattan ad agency, one of the youngest in the business. You really think I got there by being submissive? I'm not one of those women who need a man to complete her or define her. I sure didn't get where I am by submitting to a *man*."

She knew she sounded defensive. She knew she was talking around what he really meant, but she couldn't seem to stop herself. She was running scared, not of him, but of her own feelings.

"No, of course you didn't." Cole smiled. "Though I think semantics are getting in the way of what I'm trying to say. You're telling me you're not *passive*. That you've achieved what you have in your profession because you're strong, intelligent, forthright and confident." Elizabeth nodded, somewhat mollified.

"I would suggest being sexually submissive is not at odds with strength, confidence and intelligence. In fact, it takes a good deal of courage to submit with grace. To relinquish control to another, with the understanding he would never take you further than you need to go."

"I don't know what you're talking about." A small voice whispered deep inside her—*yes, you do*.

He moved back and shifted on the couch so he was facing her. She looked down at her lap, trying to avoid those dark, captivating eyes. With thumb and forefinger, he lifted her chin, forcing her to look at him.

He moved his finger, tracing the line of her lips. Slowly, carefully, he pressed it between them until they parted. He pressed harder, forcing her mouth open, pushing his finger down on her tongue. Elizabeth caught her breath. The gesture was somehow both a violation and a supremely erotic act.

He withdrew his finger, tracing a wet line down her throat. Elizabeth was aware of her ragged breathing. She had never been so excited, so scared and so thrilled all at once. Things were moving too fast, but she didn't want them to stop. She didn't know what she wanted.

"I wasn't expecting you, Elizabeth." He smiled, shaking his head. "But now that I've found you, I don't want to let you go. Not without at least introducing you to the potential of romantic submission."

He stood, which surprised her, as she had expected him to take her again into his arms. That was precisely what she wanted him to do, she now realized. Instead, he walked back a few paces and turned toward her.

"I want you." His voice was calm but she could sense the urgency beneath it. "But only on your terms. I'll wait as long as you need. We'll go at your pace. I ask only that you don't shut me out. Let your mind open. Let your heart open. Trust me. Trust yourself with these new feelings."

Elizabeth nodded, unsure what was expected. She too stood, moving uncertainly toward him. He opened his arms and she moved into them, again hiding her face against his strongly-muscled chest, wishing it were bare so she could feel his skin with her cheek.

He lifted her head with a finger beneath her chin, but instead of kissing her lips, he planted a chaste kiss on her forehead and dropped his arms, stepping back. "You must be exhausted after your ordeal. I'm taking complete advantage of you and I apologize. Take some time. Think over what I've said."

She stared at him, not sure she was hearing him correctly. He continued. "I can come down with you to get a cab, want me to? Or would you rather have Harry drive you home? I can have him downstairs within fifteen minutes."

"What?" She couldn't have heard him right. He was dismissing her? Sending her away like some kid after the lecture was over? What the hell? She started to say something, to protest, but the words died on her lips. What, after all, would she say? *Don't send me away, let's go into your bedroom and explore this submissive thing right now.* Or, *How dare you get me so hot and bothered, and then turn around and say see ya' later?*

In fact she *was* exhausted, bone-weary and worn out. Then there was the whole creepy, bizarre mess with Gary to straighten out. The irony was, since he was now sending her away, she wanted to stay. She was even willing, she realized with some astonishment, to go to bed with him then and there. More than willing.

Maybe he was just using reverse psychology on her—telling her to go so she'd want to stay. Well, it wouldn't work. Nobody manipulated Elizabeth Martin. She forced a bright smile to her lips. "A cab is fine. I can see myself down——"

He caught her in his arms, pulling her close as his lips crushed hers. She was falling, falling into the kiss, falling into his strong arms, falling beneath his spell the instant his lips touched hers. When he finally let her go, she stumbled and he caught her, drawing her into his warm, safe embrace.

"I'm not sending you away. Please don't think that. Or if I am, it's because I want you so much. I don't want to take advantage of your vulnerability right now. When you come to me, I want it to be from a position of strength. I know what I'm thrusting on you is new. I think your body understands, and your heart, but your mind needs time to catch up."

He clutched her shoulders, his expression at once commanding and pleading. "After you've had a good night's rest, and a chance to think over what we've talked about, come back to me. You don't even have to call first. I'll put the doorman on notice to expect you. I'll be here—waiting."

"And if I don't come back?" Elizabeth couldn't resist asking.

"You will. Now that you've had a peek into the Pandora's box of D/s, you won't be able to resist."

"Yeah, right." Elizabeth tossed her head with a defiant laugh. But she knew he was right—she would definitely be back.

CHAPTER NINE

"Pearson, you're an idiot."

It was nearly dawn. Cole had given up lying in his bed, tossing in the twisted sheets, his eyelids flipping open like broken shades on a window. Instead he sat in his study, staring out at the slowly lightening sky.

Why had he sent her away? Everything in her demeanor said she wanted to stay. He'd seen the startled, hurt look when he'd said she was tired and needed time to herself. Had he miscalculated? Should he have kept her there until he'd broken down all her defenses?

Naked beneath his robe, his hand fell to his cock, which was rising at the memory of Elizabeth, stretched so beautifully and vulnerably on the sofa, her eyes closed, her lips parted, her breath ragged with a mixture of fear and desire that had very nearly cost him the tight control he maintained on his lust.

He stroked himself absently, wishing she was there with him now, naked and sleeping in his bed, already his lover, his possession.

Yet, despite his physical longing, he knew he'd done the right thing in sending her away. D/s was powerful, and it had the power not only to draw one in, but to frighten one away, if offered too quickly. His own natural impulse was to claim her at once. He knew if he hadn't sent her packing, he would have pushed her too far, too fast.

Was she the one?

He shook away the thought, but it slipped persistently back into his brain. In the three years since Joanie's death, he had been exploring D/s, slowly evolving his own take on the whole thing.

At first he'd just played around, checking out the scene online, engaging in erotic chats with so-called slave girls on BDSM sites, getting comfortable with the lingo, the mindset, the players. He'd moved on to the clubs, even briefly joining a group that met once a month to discuss various esoteric aspects of BDSM, hold demonstrations on whipping techniques and the latest toys, and generally pat each other on the back for being such serious, high-minded players in the scene. He'd quickly tired of the group, which was comprised mostly of insecure, needy men posturing as Doms, and insecure, needy women posturing as subs.

He'd made his own share of mistakes, he couldn't deny it. At first, heady with the newfound freedom of being single and, for the first time, honest about his dominant orientation, he'd been indiscriminate. He'd been too quick to connect with any reasonably attractive woman who showed the promise of submissive desire. Most of them were not, in fact, submissive, but just horny, lonely women eager for something different. Sure, they got off on an ass-reddening spanking and some aggressive lovemaking, but ultimately failed to appreciate the nuance of a D/s relationship.

He knew he was too romantic—too poetic. Joanie used to tell him he was born in the wrong century—too gallant and old-world for his own good. He understood what she was saying, but disagreed. Since when was seeking true love an old-fashioned idea? He refused to believe it, but that refusal had left him very lonely.

In the first year or so of his explorations, he brought a number of potential sub girls home, only to be disenchanted in fairly short order. Though the sex and D/s play were fun, the underlying spark of passion was never there. Sadly, all too often it turned out what they were really seeking was someone to take care of them—someone to support them financially and emotionally. While he wasn't averse to taking care of someone, he contrived to hold onto his romantic dream of finding his soul mate.

Had he found her in Elizabeth?

He'd sensed her profound reaction to the light bondage of his holding her wrists down. He'd felt the thump of her heart and the seen the quickening of her breath. Her nipples were hard as pebbles when his fingers grazed them. She was definitely intrigued and turned-on, but that didn't mean she was submissive. It didn't mean she wanted what he wanted.

Cole watched the sunrise by observing a certain high strip of windows, noting their glass changing from black to gray to white to the blurred yellow dazzle of reflected sun. Would she come back today? Or, after a night's sleep to provide some distance, would she lump him into the same category as that asshole who worked for her?

A very patient man in most things, he found himself fidgeting, his fingers tickling to call her cell, wake her up and insist she come to him at once. He sighed and turned toward his desk, reaching for his favorite fountain pen.

More proof, he supposed, to support Joanie's assertion he was in the wrong century, Cole vastly preferred the smooth, fine line of real ink moving wetly over the page, to the scratchy scrawl of a modern disposable pen.

He held the pen, enjoying its well-balanced heft in the palm of his hand as he admired it. It was onyx black, with dark cream and burgundy marbling at either end, and a gold art deco band at the base of the cap. He unscrewed the cap, which protected the flaring gold nib that narrowed down to a fine point. He reached for a piece of paper and pressed the nib to it, writing the single word over and over...*Elizabeth.*

~*~

Elizabeth bent unseeing over some work she'd pulled from her briefcase in a vain effort to distract herself. The coffee beside her was cold and she felt restless. It was eight o'clock, too early to call him.

You don't have to call before you come, he'd said. Well, she certainly wasn't just going to show up. It had rankled, his amused certainty that she'd be back. Did he think just because he was rich and handsome, he could have his pick of women?

Well, she had to admit begrudgingly, he probably could at that. Not that she was interested in him for his money. She had enough of her own, earned by the sweat of her brow. Easy for Cole, obviously old money, to invest in Manhattan real estate like other people bought groceries. She had earned her money, every penny.

She looked around her small, bright kitchen with its Italian-tiled walls, marble counter tops and shiny brass pans hanging from the ceiling over the island in its center and smiled with satisfaction. True, she still owed a hefty mortgage, but she knew she could sell her condo for plenty more than she paid for it, if and when she chose to do so.

No, it wasn't his money. Or even, if she were honest, his looks, though they were pretty terrific. No. It was the way he had kissed her while he held her down, and the strange, almost fierce look in his eyes when he'd asked her if she wanted him to stop.

She hadn't wanted him to stop. She had wanted him to continue. To take control—complete control. She'd been nonplussed and confused when he'd so abruptly stopped. Had he purposely been teasing her, testing her?

Never in her life had she been so electrified, so completely aroused by a man, and all with her clothing still on and nothing exchanged between them but a kiss! She'd barely made it home in the cab, her fingers itching to slip down into her panties and rub away some of the aching need.

She'd made herself come once she got home, but it had only taken the edge off the lust. Smoldering coals of desire still burned deep in her belly, disturbing her sleep and coloring her dreams.

Then there was Gary. Not only what he'd done—which defied belief in itself—but how he'd denied it when she'd confronted him, acting like she was the one who had manipulated and compromised *him*. He'd been so persuasive, so insistent, she'd very nearly found herself doubting her sanity.

How the hell was she supposed to deal with him now? How could she work with a man like that? The answer was obvious—she could not. He would have to go. Unfortunately, she couldn't fire him herself. But Art could. Yes, she would go to Art first thing Monday morning. No, she would go to him today.

She looked at the clock on the wall. Eight-fifteen. Definitely too early on a Sunday morning to be calling her boss. What about Cole? Was he awake? He'd certainly been in a hurry to get rid of her. Did he have a date or something? Was he even now lying in the arms of another woman, all thoughts of her pushed aside?

The thought bothered her more than she was willing to admit. Which was silly. They hardly knew each other.

Yet even now her nipples tingled and stiffened at the memory of the way he'd held her stretched and helpless before him, his kiss and his touch making her tremble with a strange combination of fear and animal desire. She touched her lips, recalling the press of his finger, the way he had gently forced them apart, entering her mouth in a way that was deeply sexual. It was evocative, she suddenly realized, of a man's cock entering a woman. She shivered, though the warm sunshine shone through the window in a pool of light.

This was crazy. She was obsessing about a man who had a BDSM sex dungeon right in his home. He was a pervert, pure and simple. No, she knew even as she tried to force that thought into her mind that it was a lie. He'd explained and she'd understood on a gut level, that what he offered wasn't about sadism. It was something that spoke to her deepest, most secret longings.

For the first time in her life, a man was reaching past what she claimed to want, what she professed to need. He had gone for her essence, scaring her silly in the process. She was Elizabeth Anne Martin, a savvy, strong-minded career woman making it in one of the most competitive cities in the world. How did she reconcile the trembling girl she'd been on his couch with the strong, confident image she projected to the world?

Maybe she didn't have to reconcile them?

She was making her head hurt with all this introspection. She took a sip of her cold coffee and made a face. She looked at her laptop, which was open on the other side of the small kitchen table. She hadn't even glanced at her work email since Friday afternoon. She made a deal with herself. She would handle whatever was in there, and then, as a reward, she would go out for bagels. "I wonder," she said aloud in the habit of people who live alone, "if Cole likes bagels."

~*~

"You've reached the voice mail of Art Wallace. Sorry I missed your call. Leave a message and I'll get back to you." The phone beeped in Elizabeth's ear and she sighed with frustration. This wasn't something she wanted to leave in a voicemail.

She took a breath, willing herself into her professional persona. Her voice was crisp. "Good morning, Art. It's Elizabeth. I need to speak to you about an urgent matter. It's regarding Gary Dobbins and it's very, uh, sensitive. I'd appreciate a call back at your earliest convenience."

She flicked the phone shut and looked out the window of the taxicab, barely noticing the throng of people pressing forward in front of it as the light changed. The bagels, from her favorite neighborhood deli, were still warm in the bag on the seat beside her.

She hadn't called Cole. She'd started to, but hadn't been sure of what to say. She would, she decided, give him a casual ring when she got to his building.

She paid the driver and stepped out onto the curb. Usually quite confident about her wardrobe, Elizabeth was suddenly self-conscious in the pale blue sundress she had spent way too much on, but which showed off her bust and narrow waist. It had spaghetti straps, which precluded the wearing of a bra, but its pleated bodice held her breasts nicely in place. It was her sexiest sundress. Would Cole think she'd overdressed for a Sunday morning casual drop-by?

Stop, she admonished herself. *I'm thirty-years-old. I don't need a man's approval. I dress how I want.* She reached in her purse and fished out her cell phone, scrolling to find Cole's number from when she last dialed it. Staring up at the imposing pink granite building with its large glass doors flanked by uniformed doormen, she pressed the button and held the phone to her ear.

"Cole Pearson."

"Hi. It's Elizabeth. Elizabeth Martin."

"Hey." His voice was warm and animated. "It's great to hear from you. Where are you?"

"Actually," she gave a self-conscious laugh, "I'm outside your building. I, uh, I have bagels."

"Well then. If you have bagels." Cole laughed. "Just give one of the doormen your name. You're on the list."

Keeping her voice bright, hoping it didn't betray the sudden butterflies in her stomach, she quipped back, "Oh, the *list*. Well, I guess I *have* arrived, to be on your list."

"You have, no question about it," Cole joked back. "And guess what, you're the only one on it."

She wasn't sure how to respond so she didn't, not directly. "Should I just go up? Tenth floor, right?"

"Wait in the lobby. I'll be down in a second."

She closed the phone and slipped it into her purse. She pulled out her compact and inspected her face. She was wearing very little makeup—just some bronzer beneath her cheek bones and a little mascara. Luckily, having avoided sun all her life, her skin was still fresh and unlined, despite her thirty years. She pulled out her favorite lipstick and applied just enough to give her lips some shine. Satisfied she looked as good as she was going to, she put away the makeup and headed toward the doors.

An impassive but polite doorman greeted her, consulted a small palm pilot when she gave her name and then held the door wide for her. She stood in the large lobby, admiring the marble floors and high ceilings while she waited for Cole.

In a moment the elevator doors opened silently and there he stood, if possible even better looking than she remembered. He was wearing a white button-down shirt, open at the throat, revealing a swirl of black chest hair. It was tucked into black jeans that fit neatly over soft, black square-toed boots. Her eyes traveled appreciatively down and then back up again to his dark, smiling eyes and wide, funny smile.

"Elizabeth. Welcome back." He held out his hand and she took it, charmed when he raised it to his lips and brushed it with a kiss.

She held out the bag, suddenly shy. "Bagels," she offered.

He took the bag and drew her gently into the elevator. As they rode up, he put his hand on the small of her back. The gesture at once excited and comforted her. It was a possessive gesture, of that there was no doubt.

Once in his place, he pulled her into his arms. "I'm so glad you came back, Elizabeth. I've been waiting for you."

"I couldn't stay away," she answered truthfully.

He pulled her closer, dipping his head to kiss her lips. The kiss was light at first, even tentative. She was the first to open her mouth, pressing the tip of her tongue against his lips until they parted. He bent her back, pressing his hard body against hers as he kissed her harder.

After several breathless moments he released her, though he kept his arms loosely around her while she collected herself. She was annoyed with herself, aware by the heat in her face she was flushed. She couldn't quite get her breath. She wanted him to kiss her again. Would it always be like this—him offering and then withdrawing so quickly?

Impulsively she reached for him. "Kiss me again." She was aware it sounded like a command, but she didn't care.

He obeyed with a small delighted laugh, pulling her back into his arms. Her nipples perked against his hard chest, her body pressed tight against his from groin to shoulder. She felt herself melting again, yielding to the inexplicable power of his touch.

Something began to buzz and vibrate against her side. It took her a few moments to realize it was her cell phone. Cole must have felt it too, because he let her go. "Coming from your purse. Not a bomb, is it?" He grinned.

Elizabeth struggled to open her purse, her fingers not working properly as she tried to shift from being ravaged to professional mode. By the time she got it open, however, she had missed the call.

"Damn it," she swore under her breath.

"Important call?" Cole's tone was sympathetic.

"My boss. I left a message. I figured I'd better fill him in on this whole mess with Gary. I should have called him yesterday. I wasn't thinking clearly."

"You'd been drugged, for God's sake. I think it's good you're contacting him now. Being proactive before that slime bucket does any more damage."

She nodded and pressed the button to retrieve voice mail. Instead of Art's gravelly voice, the chirpy, high-pitched sound of Art's secretary, Mary Beth, reached her ears. "Hi, Elizabeth. Mary Beth here. I'm calling back for Art. He left me in charge of retrieving his messages while he's away on the fishing trip. You said something about Gary Dobbins? He's not ill, is he? Is everything okay? I can't reach Art right now, but he should be back late tonight. If it can wait, he'll be in the office in the morning. Okay, well, take care."

That's right—she'd forgotten. That was why he'd given her the tickets to the Autism fundraiser in the first place— he'd had a conflict with the fishing trip on the yacht of one of their high-powered clients for a three-day weekend. Well, she consoled herself, at least it hadn't mattered that she hadn't called the day before.

"Everything okay?"

"Yeah. I forgot my boss is out of pocket for the weekend. On a yacht off the coast of Newport, Rhode Island. He left his cell phone with his secretary, who just retrieved my message about Gary."

Cole pondered a moment. "What exactly did you say in the message?"

"I was fairly vague, thank God. Mary Beth is pretty tight-lipped, but I doubt even she would be able to keep quiet about one employee selling the other at a BDSM slave auction."

They looked at each other. A tendril of a smile curled up Cole's lips and Elizabeth found hers twitching in response. They both began to laugh, and, catching each other's eye, laughed harder still until Elizabeth doubled over, holding her sides, tears spilling down her cheeks. Even while a part of her knew this was just an emotional release valve, it felt good to let it out and she let herself go. They collapsed together on the sofa, the laughter finally sputtering into hiccups and sighs.

Cole was sprawled against the sofa, his long, strong legs out straight in front of him, his hands clasped easily over his flat stomach. "I can't remember when I laughed that hard," he remarked after a moment of comfortable, easy silence.

"Me neither," Elizabeth answered, wiping her eyes with her fingers. Cole at once pulled out a starched white handkerchief from his back pocket. Who carried a handkerchief in this day and age? Nevertheless, she took it, smiling at him as she dabbed at her eyes.

"Coffee," Cole announced, sitting up straight. "I need a cup. How about you?"

"That would be great. And if you're hungry, those bagels had just come out of the oven when I picked them up. They're from my favorite neighborhood bakery."

"Sounds delicious. Come on into the kitchen and we'll have ourselves a feast."

Elizabeth wasn't surprised the see the kitchen, which was easily three times the size of hers, had been equipped with all the latest stainless steel appliances. The countertops were granite, the flooring thick planks of dark hardwood, the cabinets with glass doors, revealing fine china and stemware inside.

While Cole busied himself at the coffeemaker, he turned toward her. "There's cream cheese and butter in the 'fridge. Help yourself. Oh, and if you wouldn't mind, you can pull out the cream too."

Elizabeth set the items on the table, feeling more relaxed and at ease than she had in ages. The shared laughter had brought them closer, somehow, than hours of talking could have. Despite the persistent niggling worry about Gary and that whole sordid business, she was happy.

Soon Cole brought a hot pot of coffee to the table, along with two ceramic mugs. He poured them each a cup, returned the pot to the warmer and sat down across from her. They each helped themselves to a bagel and ate quietly for a while. The coffee was hot and delicious and she sipped it, thinking how much better it tasted than the store brand she bought and used in her ancient coffeemaker. Or was it just because she was with him?

She glanced up at him, sensing a subtle shift in the mood between them. He was watching her with those dark eyes, the heavy lids giving him a sleepy, sensual look. "You came back, Elizabeth and I'm so glad. But I want you to understand, I need you to understand that I'm not looking for a vanilla relationship. At least, not ultimately. I want something deeper, something more fulfilling. I want to teach you to submit—to surrender not only to me, but your deepest, most secret desires."

"I'm—I'm not sure what you mean," Elizabeth faltered, her heart skipping a beat.

"Let me ask you this. Have you ever found a man who made you feel the way I did yesterday? Who made your heart pound, who made your breath catch, who made you wet and aching after just one kiss?"

Elizabeth, startled by these blunt questions, hid her embarrassment with a retort. "You're pretty sure of yourself, huh? God's gift and all that? What makes you think you were that good?"

"Oh, I don't. Please don't misunderstand me. I'm not that good. I'm nothing special, not on my own. No—it was *us*, Elizabeth. You and me. Together we can find what each of us has been looking for. Give it a chance—take a risk. Give *us* a chance."

"I haven't been looking for anything." Even as she said the words, she knew she was lying. The few men she'd cared about or tried to care about over the years went parading past in her head, each one coming up woefully short when compared to this dynamic, compelling, sexy man.

"I want you," he whispered fervently. She could feel his power like a live thing descend over her. She realized with sudden clarity she wasn't attracted to him in spite of his talk of D/s and the erotic submission, but because of it.

She met his burning gaze head on. "I want you," she replied, barely hearing her own words over the beating of her heart.

CHAPTER TEN

"Never, huh? Not even a playful swatting?"

"They wouldn't have dared." Elizabeth jutted her chin forward. Cole laughed and she found herself laughing with him. They'd spent a pleasant morning chatting over bagels and coffee, moving to sit outside on Cole's terrace and enjoy the warm morning sun.

For a while it was "first date" talk, getting to know about each other's lives and backgrounds, and discussing the current events of the day. In addition to being sexually attracted, Elizabeth found herself genuinely liking this kind, engaging man who, despite his obvious wealth and good looks, didn't seem to take himself too seriously.

They'd moved back inside as the sun rose higher, glinting through the haze of the Manhattan skyline on what was shaping up to be a muggy August day. The mood had subtly shifted as they settled side-by-side on the sofa where, the evening before, he'd pinned her wrists over her head and kissed her as if he'd owned her.

At Cole's question if she'd ever had a proper spanking, she immediately and vehemently denied it, but couldn't deny the sudden sharp increase in the tempo of her heartbeat.

Cole regarded her appraisingly. "I imagine you're a bit more than most men can handle. Beautiful, successful, smart, sexually defended."

"What? Sexually what?"

"Defended. Protected. Forgive me for presuming, but something tells me you've yet to be with a man who could get past that defense. Break down the armor that keeps you safe, but also keeps you shielded from the intensity of experience a passionate, mature woman deserves."

"I've had serious relationships." Elizabeth knew she sounded defensive.

"And you're not with them now, are you? I doubt it was they who left you, am I right? They lost you, because they didn't understand what you need or how to reach past your natural reserve to meet those needs."

"And you're going to tell me you're the man to meet those needs, huh?" Her tone was flippant as she tried to compensate for the blush she knew was rising to her cheeks.

"I'd like to be." His tone was gentle, unassuming, and yet there was no doubting the power behind it. Everything about him seemed to radiate power, albeit understated and restrained. She could easily imagine his persevering in the business world, getting what he wanted not with bluster and arrogance, but with a certain understood authority. He was the kind of man one instinctively wanted to obey.

He moved closer, dropping his hand to her bare thigh, slipping his fingers just beneath the silky fabric of her dress. His touch instantly alerted all her nerve endings. Gently he stroked her skin.

"Sensation," he offered, "occurs along a spectrum. From the lightest touch—" his fingers moved feather-soft along her flesh, "—to more intense contact. You'd be surprised how you can be taught to experience what you might have one time defined as pain, as simply a more intense sensation. A spanking is an excellent way to begin."

"Why would I want to begin? Why should I *want* to redefine sensations, as you call them?"

"Because," his voice was low, and as he spoke he slid his hand farther up her thigh until his fingers touched the silky panties that covered her mons. She jumped at his touch. She was wet, she knew she was, and her pussy tingled and ached. "...you need this. You're longing to give up control on some level in your life. You need someone strong to share your secrets and let you experience your deepest longings in a safe, sensual environment."

"No..." she tried to protest, though something inside her yielded at his words. Elizabeth Martin never gave up control. Never...oh, his fingers were slipping beneath the panties. She knew she should stop him, deny whatever it was he was saying about her. She wasn't a sub girl just because he wanted her to be...no, oh God, she was slippery wet. Strong fingers slid upward, finding and catching her clit, making her gasp. Her head fell back and he leaned over her, his hand buried at her sex, his lips meeting hers.

"Yes," he murmured, before kissing her. "Yes."

It felt good, so good, to have someone touching her, stroking her. He did it just right, too, not too hard and too fast like some guys, who thought their enthusiasm should make up for their lack of finesse. She moaned, pushing back against his hand, desperate for his touch.

Quickly, too quickly, he brought her to the brink of orgasm, his mouth still against hers, his tongue in her mouth flickering in tandem with his fingers at her sex. Literally seconds before she came, he pulled away.

Flustered and frustrated, she urged, "No, don't stop. I was so close. Please..."

"You have to earn it, sweet Elizabeth."

She opened her eyes, not entirely processing his words, her focus still on her pussy and the not-quite-achieved orgasm. "What?"

"That's right. I'll let you come, but first you will earn it with a small spanking. An introduction to the redefining of pleasure and pain."

"I don't know what you're talking about."

"Yes, you do." He leaned forward and kissed her forehead. Then he gathered her in his arms and pulled her up and over onto his lap.

"Hey," she protested weakly, but she didn't fight him. He was going to *spank* her. The strangest thing was, instead of being furious or indignant, her pussy throbbed at the thought, though the idea frightened her.

"You're not going to hurt me?" Her voice trembled.

"I will never harm you. You will learn that pleasure and pain are subjective terms that have no specific meaning in a D/s relationship. I'll teach you. You'll see. You'll know. Trust me."

He pressed her down against his lap. Still hovering on the edge of climax, she rubbed her pussy against his thigh, aware she was acting like a slut, too hot to care. He flipped up the back of her dress. "You're perfect," he murmured. He stroked her ass, his touch light but firm.

His erection poked hard against her pubic bone. What was she doing—a grown woman, permitting herself to be placed over a man's knee for a spanking? It was crazy.

But her pussy didn't seem to agree. It was wet and throbbing, and she felt so needy she almost began to hump his thigh. She was distracted by a sudden, light swat to her behind. She jerked against him. He placed a hand firmly on the small of her back and swatted her again.

"Relax against me. Experience the sensations. Turn off your mind, if you can." She tried to obey him. Her ass was tingling and she realized she was holding her breath, waiting for the next swat. He was smoothing the flesh and then he struck her, harder this time. The sound of his palm against her ass resounded in the air.

It stung a little. It was the sound more than anything that made her yelp. He stroked her again, but kept one hand firmly on the small of her back, holding her in place. Again the palm came down, this time harder, catching both cheeks with the blow.

Elizabeth jerked and squirmed against him. "You're doing great," he insisted, still holding her down. "Just a little more. Let me take you a short way down the path you need to be on."

He sounded like some Buddhist philosopher, but she was distracted from his words by a series of hard, stinging blows landing with force on each cheek, making tears spring to her eyes. "Hey! You're hurting me."

He ignored her, continuing to smack her several more times. She jerked beneath him, finally twisting over onto her back. Her dress had ridden up her thighs, exposing her panties. Without missing a beat, Cole pressed her thighs apart.

With deft fingers, he slipped past the silk. "You're soaked," he informed her, his eyes glinting. It felt too good to stop him, too good to protest, resist, pretend she wasn't more turned on than she'd ever been in her life.

"Oh," she whispered, elongating the vowel with a breathy sigh.

It took only seconds to send her careening into a scorching, trembling, dizzying climax. She bucked and shuddered beneath his fingers, all trace of modesty gone as she took her pleasure.

Afterwards she lay inert, her head lolling to the side, her heart thumping wildly. He smoothed the hair away from her face. Slowly she opened her eyes. He was watching her with those dark, dangerous eyes, as if he knew the secrets of her soul.

She felt, she realized, amazing. Better than amazing. Terrific. Incredible. She sat up and reached out to him, wrapping her arms around his neck. He pulled her up into his lap and buried his face against her neck. "You see?" he whispered. "I knew it. You were born for this."

She didn't respond, except by holding him tightly. She wanted to feel him inside her. She wanted him to make love to her. She wasn't entirely sure what it was he was so certain she was born for, but she knew if it involved him, she was ready to find out.

He stood, holding her in his arms as if she weighed no more than a child. With a long, confident stride, he carried her from the room and down the long hallway to the master bedroom.

~*~

Cole couldn't remember wanting another woman as much as he wanted Elizabeth. He laid her on the bed, forcing his lust under control for the moment, resisting a nearly overwhelming impulse to rip her clothing from her body and plunge himself into her.

He was relieved in a way that she'd squirmed away from his spanking, because each time she'd jerked against his lap, rubbing his erection in the process, he'd nearly come. He couldn't wait to properly restrain her and introduce her to the fierce, delicious passion of erotic suffering. Mentally he shook his head.

Slow down, Pearson, slow way the fuck down. Give her all the time she needs.

Thus reminded, he kicked off his boots and lay beside her, still fully clothed. He took her into his arms and they kissed a while. She pulled back from him and reached toward his chest, where she began to unbutton his shirt. He let her, his cock straining in his jeans.

She pushed his shirt from his shoulders and nestled her cheek against his chest. He was nearly shaking with repressed desire. He wanted to fuck her. Instead he stroked her hair and back, trying not to imagine how a black leather flogger would look, its tresses raining against her white, soft flesh…

"Make love to me," she whispered, lifting her face toward him.

He pushed himself from the bed, only long enough to shuck his jeans and underwear. He saw her eyes fall to his groin and he grinned, hoping she liked what she saw. She sat up and slipped her sandals from her pretty feet, letting them fall to the ground. While he watched, she reached behind her, unzipping the dress and pulling it over her head.

As with her evening gown, she wore no bra. This time he had the right to gaze at those perfect orbs and he greedily devoured them with his eyes, his mouth actually watering in anticipation of biting and sucking the stiffening nipples at their centers. How glad he was she hadn't turned out to be just a casual play toy purchased for a few hours of meaningless fun. How lucky he was the twisted fates had somehow brought her into his life.

She lay back against the bed, her dark hair in a swirl on the pillows, her very blue eyes shining toward him. Hurriedly he opened the drawer in the chest beside his bed and grabbed a condom.

He rolled it into place and lay down beside her, cupping her crotch. The little panties were soaking wet, which pleased him. On an impulse he slipped his fingers beneath the fabric, gripped the other side with his thumb and pulled.

Elizabeth gasped as the flimsy fabric tore away. He reached instinctively for her throat, recalling her strong, visceral reaction the day before to the primeval gesture of dominance.

A series of shudders racked her body, almost orgasmic in nature, as he gently tightened his grip around her long, slender neck. With his other hand he pressed her open, exploring the hot, velvet clasp of her tunnel.

She lifted her arms of her own accord above her head, the gesture submissive and, to Cole, deeply erotic. "Jesus, I want you," he murmured, still holding himself in check, though barely.

He rose over her, loving the feel of her soft breasts crushing beneath his chest, the nipples rising to meet him. He moved between her thighs, positioning himself, the head of his cock nudging at the entrance, gauging her readiness.

Carefully he pushed forward and she took him in, tight muscles clenching along his shaft, the pressure nearly unbearably sweet. She was trembling beneath him, her eyes closed, her breathing rapid, her cheeks flushed. He groaned, reaching for her wrists, pulling her arms taut and pinning them to the bed, his body pinning hers beneath his. He could feel her heart pattering too fast against him.

Tenderness for a moment overtook his lust and he leaned down, kissing her face—her eyelids, her cheeks, her lips. "Shh, it's okay. I'm going to make love you, beautiful girl. You belong to me."

She opened her eyes, nodding. "Yes," she said breathlessly. She tested his grip on her wrists and he knew she didn't want to be released. He tightened his grip and she moaned, arching her hips up to take him deeper.

He began to move inside her, reveling in her tight, wet embrace. He wanted her so much—too much. "God," he groaned.

"I'm sorry. I can't…it's just too good. Oh." Shit, he couldn't help it. All the pent-up longing he'd held so tightly within himself since the moment he'd seen her swaying on the dais, and then laid bare and sleeping in his guest bed, spilled over in an orgasm more worthy of a teenager than a grown man.

He lay still on top of her for a few seconds trying to recover himself. His fingers, he realized, were still tight around her slender wrists, pulled high over her head. He let them go and she wrapped her arms around him.

He grunted an embarrassed laugh. "I'm really sorry. That just came over me so fast."

She put a finger to his lips. He looked down into her face, aware of her complete power over him, aware of the illusion of Dom and sub, of Master and slave. At that moment, it was she who owned him. "It's okay." Her grin was saucy. "I take it as a compliment. Anyway, first one's always free."

He laughed, his embarrassment evaporating. "Well, I'm thirty-nine, not seventeen, though you wouldn't know it from that little performance." He grinned, glad she grinned back. "But give me a little while and I'll make proper love to you."

He sat up, drawing a circle around one perfect nipple. "I have an idea. I have a hot tub in the bathroom. It's very relaxing. Would you like a soak?"

"That sounds great." Elizabeth reached for her dress, slipping it on over her head. Cole found her modesty touching, though he would soon cure her of that. For now he said nothing, though he himself remained naked.

He led her into the master bath, mildly pleased as she ooh'd and aah'd over the bath fixtures and the marble floor and most especially over the oversize Jacuzzi set into one corner, surrounded by varnished wood.

Removing the lid, he flipped the switch to start the water jets. "How about a little atmosphere?" he suggested. He moved around the room, lighting the myriad candles he had set up all along the walls in crystal glasses that reflected and refracted the light. Once they were lit, he turned off the overhead light.

Standing close, Cole reached around Elizabeth and unzipped her dress, pushing it from her shoulders and watching it puddle at her feet. She didn't protest, which pleased him. He helped her to step into the hot water, watching her seat herself before climbing in himself.

"This is incredible." Elizabeth sighed with pleasure, leaning her head back.

He settled across from her, for the moment content just to look. The jet streams felt good pummeling his back and shoulders and frothing against his thighs. He leaned his own head back, letting the hot water work its magic.

When he opened his eyes, he saw a thick, moist steam had risen against the candlelight. It was as if they were sitting beneath a cloud of liquefying light. Elizabeth's eyes were closed. Beads of moisture lay like pearls on her cheeks and sparkled on her lashes. Her wet hair clung in tendrils to her slender neck. He could just make out the curve of her breasts above the water.

His cock rose and he touched it beneath the water, surprised to find it fully erect. He moved along the seat until he was beside her. Elizabeth sighed deeply and leaned her head against his shoulder. Beneath the water he took her hand, placing it on his erect shaft.

Her eyes opened. "That was fast." She grinned mischievously. He laughed and kissed her, aware he wasn't falling in love—he was already there.

CHAPTER ELEVEN

Art Wallace was pursing his lips, his pale eyes narrowed above the tent of his fingers, against which he was leaning his nose. He sat back, his grizzled eyebrows furrowing. "These are some very bizarre, and frankly, very unsettling accusations, Elizabeth."

Elizabeth frowned. She's expected him to be shocked, certainly, but also at least a little sympathetic. She touched her earring in a nervous gesture and dropped her hand back into her lap. She'd dressed carefully that morning in one of her more conservative suits, the cut severe but feminine, the narrow skirt stopping just below the knee. Her hair was pulled back in a twist, her pearl earrings as conservative as her suit.

She'd barely slept the night before. She'd stayed at Cole's place until nearly midnight. What an amazing night it had been. They'd made love several more times, taking breaks to doze, to eat Chinese takeout, to slip into that wonderful hot tub again. Each time he'd made love to her, he'd been a little more dominant, a little more forceful. She'd thrilled to it—she couldn't deny it.

Yet she had to work the next morning, and she'd finally found the will to leave. Cole had insisted on driving her home himself, and waiting at her curb until she was safely inside her building.

Once alone, worries about Gary reared their heads again, crowding out the happiness and excitement thinking about

Cole engendered. She should have tried calling Art again, but Cole had distracted her so completely, she'd forgotten. When she got back to her place she checked her phone, frustrated to see she'd missed Art's call, no doubt oblivious in the arms of her new lover when he'd called. He hadn't left a message. She didn't dare bother him after midnight, and so tried to read herself to sleep, with the aid of a glass of wine.

That morning she only took the time to throw her briefcase in her office before marching down to have a word with Art. Trying to remain calm, she walked down to his office, knocking at the ajar door.

He'd looked up at her, not with his usually broad smile, but with a frown. "What can I do for you, Ms. Martin?"

Ms. Martin? If anything, Art tended to err on the side of informality, often calling her Liz, or even worse, Lizzie. She closed the door and sat in front of his desk, putting her hands, palm down, on the glass surface.

As succinctly as she could, she outlined what had happened after the Autism fundraiser, including her suspicions of date rape drugs, how Gary had left her at the slave auction, and his later wild denials and repudiations. She left out any reference to Cole—it wasn't relevant at any rate. Art glowered as she went on, not responding at all in the manner she had expected—that of paternal outrage.

Instead came his dry comment about unsettling accusations. She sat back, trying to compose herself, wondering what the hell was going on. In the pressing silence, she added, "There's definitely something wrong with the man, Art. I can't work with someone like that. I'm seriously thinking of pressing criminal charges."

"Hell hath no fury..." Art murmured.

"What?"

Art reached across the desk, patting her hand in a patronizing way. "He told me, Elizabeth." He shook his head. "He even said you'd probably be in here first thing, making up some cock and bull story to cover your a—er, your tracks."

"My what? Who? Gary? You talked to Gary?"

"Yes. Last night. I called you back, but I got your voice mail. Mary Beth said you'd left a message about Gary. He left one about you as well. He actually stopped in at my place out in Scarsdale."

"Gary stopped in?" Elizabeth was still trying to take in what Art was saying.

"He did. And I must say, Ms. Martin, I was shocked by that little flyer you put together. I mean, what you do on your own time is certainly none of my concern, but—"

"Art! *He* did that. He created that piece of filth to *frame* me. He cooked this whole sick thing up from start to finish. It's all an elaborate plan to discredit me. He's been after my job since day one. You know that." Elizabeth paused to draw a breath. She was dizzy with outrage and confusion. This couldn't be happening. Art couldn't possibly believe that piece of shit Gary over her.

He stared at her impassively. "Look." The distaste was evident on his face. "You know I don't approve of getting involved with one's co-workers and this is exactly why. It appears the two of you are having a particularly nasty little spat. I know you're getting up in age and want to marry but really—"

Elizabeth rose to her feet. "What the *hell* are you talking about? Are you implying Gary and I were *involved?* What has he been saying to you? You have to know that's beyond ridiculous."

"Sit down, Elizabeth. You're hysterical. And lower your voice." He glared at her until she sat. "I'm nearly eighty-years-old," he informed her. "I've been around the block a time or two, and I know lovers' quarrels can turn very ugly. I'd like to put this whole matter aside. You and Dobbins are two of Wallace & Pratt's most valuable assets. I'd hate to see you lose your jobs over something so ridiculous and, frankly, so sordid."

Elizabeth was nearly shaking with rage. She took a deep breath, swallowed and closed her eyes, willing her blood pressure to lower itself to something less than stroke level.

"Mr. Wallace." She kept her voice reasonably calm, consciously using his surname as he had used hers. "I appreciate your *confusion* in this matter, as obviously Gary has filled your head with a lot of twisted lies and slander. For the record, Gary Dobbins and I have never had any relationship other than our professional relationship at work. Period. I would never date someone from the workplace, and even if I knew Gary purely socially, I would never choose a man like him.

"Be that as it may, what he did was unconscionable, and I won't stand for it. Nor will I stand for his slander on top of it all." She put her fingers to her temples, trying to think her way out of this. She needed to stay calm, and appeal to Art's innate sense of logic.

"Okay. You say you've seen that—that slave pamphlet?"

"Yes." Art fairly spat the word, though his tongue darted over his lips in a way that made her uncomfortable.

"Think about the one photo that showed my face. Isn't that picture familiar?"

"Oh, I—I barely glanced at it." His eyes shifted. "My wife was in the next room, for God's sake."

Elizabeth pressed on, determined to make her point. "I'll tell you what it's from. It's my headshot for the news release when I joined the firm. It was pasted onto that body! That's *not* my body. I would never pose for those pictures——not in a million years."

Art still didn't answer, but he seemed to relax a little, his expression slightly less glowering. "Next point." She continued. "Let's say for the sake of argument those were actually me in that pamphlet, and I was involved in some kind of underground S&M sex thing. Do you really think I'd risk my career to get back at some supposed boyfriend by making up that he drugged my drink and forced me into a slave auction?"

Her laugh was brittle. "I mean, come on. How ridiculous does that sound? It's absurd on its face."

Grudgingly Art nodded. "It does sound awfully silly, the way you present it. But Gary was very convincing. And the ways of the heart, especially the heart of a woman scorned——"

"Oh, *stop* it, Art," Elizabeth snapped. He bristled and she at once regretted the outburst. Speaking in a calmer tone, she added, "Art, women of today, women like me with high-powered careers don't worry about things like the scorn of a man. I'm sorry, but that's just laughable, especially when the man in question is Gary Dobbins."

I'd rather eat dirt than be involved with that little prick. Of course, this thought remained unspoken. She needed to keep her emotions out of this. Despite other good qualities, Art was a chauvinist. No point in giving him fodder to confirm his belief all women were hysterical.

To her relieved surprise, Art said, "Well, my gut instinct is to believe you, though the whole distasteful thing has me very puzzled. Especially because he says he has proof. Evidence."

Elizabeth's eyes narrowed. "What sort of evidence?"

"I didn't press. Frankly he had me so disturbed last night, I just wanted him out of my house." He pushed the intercom on his phone.

In a moment a bright voice responded, "Yes, Art?"

"'Morning, Mary Beth. Listen, is Gary Dobbins in? Find out, will you? And send him down to my office, pronto."

Elizabeth half-rose from her chair. Art waved her back down. "Let's get this out in the open, shall we? No more he said, she said. Let's deal with whatever the hell is going on face to face."

Elizabeth nodded, though adrenaline was spurting through her blood at the thought of facing that bastard head-on again. A moment later the door opened, and Gary, impeccably dressed as always in a finely-tailored suit, entered the room.

"Good morning, Art." His voice was warm. Upon seeing Elizabeth, it became decidedly colder. He nodded stiffly in her direction. "Elizabeth."

Elizabeth didn't return his greeting. She stared at Art, clenching the arms of her chair to keep from jumping up and strangling Gary with her bare hands.

"Sit down, Gary. Elizabeth and I have been talking this morning and it seems, uh, there's some discrepancy in your stories. She denies most of what you've said."

"Aw, baby." He put his hand on Elizabeth's arm. She jerked it away as if burned. "This isn't the way to handle things. Really. Come on, we can take care of this after hours." He turned to Art, his hands raised in a gesture of surrender. "She's still hysterical. I'm sorry we're—"

"Stop it!" Elizabeth's voice rose nearly to a scream. She felt like she was in the middle of some horrible nightmare. *Baby?* Had the prick just called her *baby?* She was aware of Art watching her steadily with his cold, pale eyes. Why had she never noticed how cold they were?

Her voice was controlled steel when she spoke again. "Gary. Whatever crap you're pulling, you won't get away with it. Art says you have proof that you're telling the truth in whatever your latest slander is. So out with it. What's your *proof?*"

Gary smiled benignly at her, though she noticed beads of perspiration on his upper lip, the only hint of nervousness he betrayed. He reached to pat her again but her glare must have deterred him because he dropped his hand back into his lap.

"I don't have the proof. You do." He turned to Art with an ingratiating smile. "Oh, and Art, you do too. I take it you haven't checked your email yet. This regrettable situation is just getting worse, it seems." Again he turned back to Elizabeth, the smile plastered on his face not reaching his cold, dead eyes. "I'm sorry, Elizabeth. But you willfully violated the company's Internet policy. I honestly don't know how you expected to get away with it."

Elizabeth felt her blood freeze, certain whatever he was referring to had been of his making. Between clenched teeth, she spit, "What're you talking about?"

Ignoring her, he turned back to Art. "It's come to my attention Elizabeth has been surfing the Internet for porn. Not only that, she had the bad judgment to download some of the filth to her computer." His face twisted into a sneer. "If our security worked like it should have, she'll have been shut out of her account and the details would have been emailed to you, per company protocol." Gary shook his head in mock disappointment.

"And you know this how?" Elizabeth snapped.

Gary didn't answer, his face still on Art, who was typing on his computer. "My god. He's right. The report is right here." Art stared with bulging eyes. "You've violated company guidelines and your access to the network was revoked, based on last night's scan. What the hell were you thinking?"

"I wasn't thinking anything because I didn't do it. This whole thing was concocted by this—this man." She bit off the word she'd been about to say and took a deep breath. She had to keep her cool and think her way out of whatever the hell Gary had cooked up to destroy her. She stood. "Come on. Now. Let's go. I'll prove there's nothing on my computer. Then we'll check *your* computer, Dobbins."

"Fair enough." Both men stood and the three of them trooped down the hall. Elizabeth felt as if she were moving in some kind of dark, murky haze. She was scared now—scared at how confident Gary had seemed about "proof" on her computer.

They entered her office and Gary shut the door. Elizabeth booted up her computer and typed in her access code. It was denied. She turned helplessly toward the men. "I can't get in."

"You'll need to call tech, Sir," Gary said to Art with a small, sour smile. "They'll give us a temporary password for Elizabeth's account. Then you can decide if you want to give it to her."

"Get 'em on the line," Art said gruffly, refusing to meet Elizabeth's eye. He sat at Elizabeth's desk, typing in the information he was fed over the phone.

Once they were logged in, Gary, who along with Elizabeth had been hovering behind Art, said, "The most obvious first step is to check the history."

"Her what?"

"Here, I'll show you. It's a log of where she's been on the Internet." Gary leaned over Art, opened the browser and clicked on the history tab. Then he stepped back. "See that tab there? *Show all history?* Click on that and then we'll see."

He seemed awfully sure of himself. She was surer than ever now he'd somehow broken into her computer and planted incriminating evidence of some kind. Art was peering down the list. He clicked on one marked **XXXBDSM** and the screen opened to a pornographic site featuring scantily clad girls bound in rope, with promises of hot XXX videos for $19.95.

He whipped his head back toward Elizabeth. "*Well*. I guess Gary knows you better than you thought, hmm? I must say, this is troubling. Not that I particularly care if you visit these sites, Elizabeth, on your own time. But at these offices. *Really*. I'm afraid your credibility has been severely damaged by your foolish actions."

"There were more, did you see? A whole bunch of them," Gary interjected eagerly.

Elizabeth staggered over to her sofa. She felt as if she'd been sucker-punched. Why didn't Gary just get out the knife and stab her in the guts and be done with it? "Art. I am completely innocent in all this. Whatever he's done, I have to hand it Gary for sneakiness. He gets the underhanded nasty awards of the century. If you choose to believe him over me, that's your prerogative. I had a job before I got this one. I'm sure I can get another. I've brought several very lucrative clients to this firm. I'm sure you'll understand if their loyalties lie with me, not with Wallace & Pratt."

She knew her threat was thinly veiled. She didn't give a damn. At this point she was ready to quit on principle. The only thing that held her back was the knowledge then Gary would win.

"There's, uh...there's one more thing, Art." Gary's expression was one of pure malice when he glanced toward her. "The email. The email she sent me after she had the bad taste to drag me to that sex club."

"I never——!" Elizabeth roared. Both Gary and Art glanced toward her closed door.

"You're distraught," Art's voice was nearly kind. "Why don't you take the rest of the day off?"

"No." Anger had restored her somewhat. She spoke carefully through clenched teeth. "Show us the email, Gary. Now."

He bowed toward her in a mocking manner. "As you wish."

~*~

Elizabeth drifted in and out of a dream, trying to wake up. She was standing on a raised platform. She was naked except for rope wrapped around her legs, hobbling her. Wallace and Dobbins were in the audience, along with all the rest of her team at work, plus a whole pack of leering dirty old men. Though she couldn't see him, Cole's deep voice intoned, "Who will bid fifty? Do I hear fifty for this slave?"

She jerked awake, her body covered in sweat, the sheets twisted around her legs. There was a bitter taste in her mouth. Sunlight shone through the cracks in her blinds and she squinted at it, at first not recalling how she came to be home in bed, the blinds drawn, sleeping in the middle of the day.

The memories flooded in and she groaned, falling back against the pillows. As a final nail in her professional coffin, Gary had opened his email, showing them both that message crammed with lies, obviously written by him, sent from *her* email address.

Gary printed the email and handed them each a copy. Elizabeth scanned hers, astonishment and outrage again rendering her temporarily speechless. She read more quickly than Art. When she glanced up at him, he was still reading. His eyes were wide, his skin reddening.

She had to hand it to Gary. He'd packed it all in to the email—her supposed culpability regarding the slave auction, her secret life as a sex pervert, their now-defunct love affair, the veiled threat of rigging his annual review if he dared betray her and even a dig at "old man Wallace"—a term she never would have used.

It had been too much. Hot tears sprang to her eyes, infuriating her, as she made it a staunch policy *never* to cry in a professional setting—no matter what. But she'd never been faced with something like this. The magnitude of Gary's deceit and willingness to destroy her had completely disarmed her. The email was the last straw. Somehow he'd hacked into both her computer and her email, using them to falsely incriminate her in so many ways.

If Art believed him over her, he'd have no choice but to fire her. If she'd really done what she'd been accused of, dragging an employee to a sex club while seriously intoxicated, and surfing the Web for pornography on company time, not to mention having sex with a guy who worked for her, and then subtly threatening to withhold his raise if he didn't keep his mouth shut—how could she expect Art, or "old man Wallace" as he now believed she thought of him, to keep her on?

To his credit, he hadn't fired her then and there. Instead he said again, "Go home, Elizabeth. You don't look well. Take as much time as you need. We'll talk when you're feeling more yourself."

She nodded, deeply embarrassed at the tears now spilling shamelessly down her cheeks, cursing her inability to hide her feelings the way most men could. They'd left her alone, shutting her door with a soft click. She knew the buzz would be all over the office by the end of the day that something was wrong with her. Probably Gary would let "slip" all sorts of slanderous lies about her, lies that would further cripple her ability to be an effective manager going forward.

Now hiding out in her apartment and feeling hugely sorry for herself, Elizabeth reached for the bottle of Jack Daniels that had sent her into the midday mini-coma in the first place and poured herself several ounces. She threw it back, glad for its warming, if false, sense of temporary peace.

Her cell phone rang and she reached for it, peering at the caller ID. It was Cole. Despite her misery, her heart took a little leap of delight at seeing his number. She clutched the phone, not answering. It has hard to believe she'd been so happy the night before—spending an amazing evening with the most exciting, charismatic man she had ever met, and now her world was literally crashing down around her. How could she admit to him what a mess she'd made trying to handle the Gary debacle on her own? How humiliating to confess she'd let that little twerp somehow get the better of her.

The phone rang several more times and then went to voicemail. Elizabeth poured herself another drink, gulped it and buried her head beneath her pillows.

CHAPTER TWELVE

The persistent buzzing finally penetrated a deep sleep. Elizabeth struggled to come awake, reaching for her alarm clock. With eyes still shut, she found and depressed the off button, but the buzzing continued.

Full consciousness returned and she sat up in bed, trying to identify the sound. It was her intercom—someone was downstairs in the lobby of her building, someone to see her. She looked at the clock, shocked to see it was after six in the evening. She'd spent the entire day in a drunken sleep, hiding from her problems, hiding from the world. Now, it seemed, the world was trying to find her.

She stumbled out of bed, hurrying into the living room toward her front door. She depressed the button on the intercom box, her voice breathless. "Yes?"

"Elizabeth. Are you all right?"

"Cole? Is that you?"

"Yes, I'm sorry, yes. It's me. I hope I haven't overstepped by just coming over, but when you didn't answer your cell and they told me you'd left the office quite a few hours earlier—gone home sick, your secretary said—well, I was worried, based on what you had to face this morning. So, you're okay?"

"Yes, I'm fine." Her response was automatic and not entirely honest. She took a breath and tried to clear her head. She wasn't used to drinking so much, and certainly not in the middle of the day. What had she been thinking? "Come on up. I'll buzz you in. I'm on the third floor, second apartment on the left."

She pressed the lock release button, holding it down for a good five seconds to give him time to get in. She hurried to the bathroom and splashed her face with cold water, gargled with some mouthwash and ran her fingers through her disheveled hair. She looked awful, her eyes puffy and red, the mark of a wrinkled sheet down one cheek like a scar.

She was still wearing the blouse from her suit and a half-slip. She rushed into the bedroom, took off the slip and pulled on some jeans. The doorbell sounded and she went to open it, figuring she looked as good as she was going to at that point.

Cole stood at the door with a large box of chocolates with red ribbon around it. "For you." He held it out to her.

She took it, laughing. "How did you know I'm on a special chocolate diet?"

"Never met a woman who wasn't," he teased. She led him in, feeling better than she had all day. Somehow when Cole appeared, things didn't seem quite so bleak.

"Nice place." He looked around. "Cozy."

Elizabeth set the chocolates down on the coffee table in front of the loveseat. "You mean tiny. But yeah, I like it. Thanks." They stood smiling at one another. Then Cole held out his arms and she stepped into them, grateful for his firm, masculine embrace. He didn't try to kiss her, perhaps sensing she only wanted to be held at that moment.

She leaned against him, feeling at least for the moment protected and safe. The whole hideous situation leapt into her mind and tears sprang into her eyes. What a mess everything was. She pulled back with a sigh.

Cole peered at her, his expression concerned. "So tell me what happened. How come you left in the middle of the day? Did you get my calls?"

She sat on the sofa and leaned forward, putting her head in her hands. He sat beside her, putting his arm around her shoulders. She willed herself not to cry. She was not going to cry. She was not going to act like a pathetic, helpless little girl in front of Cole.

Instead she lifted her head and turned to him, trying to smile. "I didn't get your calls, sorry. I was, uh, sleeping. The buzz of the intercom is what woke me up, actually."

"Sleeping? Are you sick? Can I get you something?"

"A gun to kill Gary Dobbins with. Have you got one lying around?"

She outlined the events of the morning, feeling her blood pressure ratchet up as she repeated each horrible detail. Cole didn't interrupt, though he shook his head throughout most of her story.

When she was done, still he said nothing. Cole sat back, pondering. "There's always that one detail," he said slowly. "That one thing the criminal does that is his undoing. At least that's the case in the murder mysteries, right? Gary's been awfully smug throughout this whole thing, but he's bound to have made at least one mistake. All we have to do is figure out his mistake and we can nail his ass."

"That's all, huh," Elizabeth retorted dryly. "Why didn't I think of that?"

"Hey, Miss Smartass, I'm serious. Let's go over the events carefully and think things through. First of all, there's your domain password. How did he get it? You didn't have it written down somewhere, did you?"

"No, I didn't. There's no way he could have gotten it. Not even our tech guys know the passwords. If you forget yours, they have to reset it for you—give you a temporary password until you go in and change it yourself."

"Maybe he did that. Convinced a tech to reset your password and give him the information."

Elizabeth shook her head dubiously. Cole continued, "Well, he obviously got them somehow, and he managed to hack into your computer, setting the scene of the crime by visiting various sex sites and leaving a trail in your history folder. We can't prove he did that—it's his word against yours, and his word carries more weight at the moment, since the stuff was found on your supposedly password-protected computer."

Elizabeth stared glumly at Cole without responding. He went on. "It's more of the same with the accusations about the club. He claims one thing, you claim the other, and he got to Wallace first and apparently was very convincing. He provides you with a motive—woman scorned—" Elizabeth winced. "and backs it up with proof in the form of an email from you to him."

"Yeah. Which really doesn't prove anything, because if he hacked into my computer, why not my email too?"

Is the company's email located on a server?"

"Yeah. But it's also accessible via the Internet, from our website."

"Can you log on now? Show me the email? It's probably still in your sent folder."

Elizabeth groaned. "I don't even have access anymore. I got shut out for supposedly downloading porn. I left this morning in such a tizzy I didn't even ask Art to give me the password he was given." She pressed her fingers to her eyes, refusing to let the tears building behind them come out. "The whole thing just makes me sick. The thought of that little prick, nosing around in my email, invading my personal files, violating my personal space…"

She dropped her head into her hands and this time the tears won out. "I can't believe this is happening to me. That monster has ruined my career and I never saw it coming."

"No he hasn't. He's just staked out the battle lines and now it's our turn to fight back. Don't forget—there are many battles in a war. And this, my dear girl, is war."

~*~

Though it was after seven, there was a chance there were still people at work and Elizabeth steeled herself for that possibility. She reminded herself she had a right to be there. She hadn't been fired—yet. Cole palmed her elbow solicitously as they entered the wide doors of the offices of Wallace and Pratt. A few office doors were open but all the support staff was long gone.

Cole had convinced her to call Art and ask him to allow her access to the network. "I need to prove my innocence, Art. I'm asking you as a friend—please trust me for a few more days. If it turns out I can't prove it, I'll resign without protest."

To her immense relief, Art had cleared it for her with the tech department, though it was obvious he was still in Gary's camp. If she hadn't had Cole by her side, Elizabeth knew she might well have given up altogether just to avoid the humiliation.

She took Cole to her office, moved toward her desk and booted up the computer. To her relief the system accepted the temporary password, which she promptly changed. She opened her email and clicked on the sent folder. The offending email had been sent at six-seventeen p.m. on Saturday, August ninth with a cc back to her own email address.

"Open a few other emails, if you don't mind. I want to check the IP addresses against this one." Cole frowned as he stared at the computer screen. "It was sent from the same IP address as your legitimate emails, but computers in the same office can share an IP address." He looked at her. "What you need is for someone to check the web service logs and trace the transmission path back to the actual PC used. If we could prove it was sent from his computer, that would be pretty damning."

"I could check with Nick," Elizabeth offered. "He's one of our IT guys." She didn't mention that Nick had a huge crush on her, though she'd never encouraged him. She paused as she realized the implication of asking for Nick's help. "He'll read it then, won't he? He'll read that horrible, disgusting email supposedly sent from Gary's jilted lover." She put her head in her hands.

"Desperate times call for desperate measures." Cole continued his war theme from earlier. "Yeah, it'll be embarrassing, but if it helps clear your name, it's worth it. Dobbins is fighting really dirty. We have to fight back."

She smiled at him, pleased despite the whole mess at his use of the word *we*. She reached for her phone and dialed Nick's extension. When she got his voice mail, she left a message. "Hi Nick, it's Elizabeth Martin. Listen, I have a very important favor. Could you check the email log files and track down an email sent from my email address this past Saturday at six-seventeen p.m. with the subject line of 'Sorry'? I need to find out what PC it was sent from. If you could let me know, I'd really appreciate it. I didn't write that thing and if I don't find a way to prove it, I could be out of a job. Thanks for your help."

She hung up and groaned. "If it *was* sent from my computer, we're back at square one."

Cole came behind her and put his hands on her shoulders. Gently he kneaded the muscles, which were knotted and aching with tension. "We've done what we can for now. Let's see what your IT guy comes up with."

"Okay. And Cole, thanks. Thanks for putting up with all this crap. Not exactly the best foot forward in a new relationship." She felt herself blushing and was glad he couldn't see her face. Had she just said that loaded word—*relationship?* They'd spent one night together. Why had she said that?

He continued to massage her shoulders, apparently unfazed by her use of the R word. "What that creep has done to you is unconscionable. It will be my distinct pleasure to help in any way I can to nail the bastard."

The elevator touched down in the lobby and they stepped out. Cole was looking up at the ceiling. He turned back to Elizabeth, his face lit up. "What? What is it?" she asked.

"We've been over-thinking this thing. Forget computers and Internet Protocol and transmission logs. Focus on cameras. Good, old-fashioned security cameras." He pointed toward the small cameras mounted on either side of the entrance, and a third pointing toward the elevators. "Building security should be able to review the film and see who entered and left the building on Saturday."

"But I was there Saturday too."

"Yeah, but not at the time the email was sent. You'd already left and this film could prove it. Whereas, assuming he sent the email at the same time as he hacked into your computer, *he* would have still been here at six-seventeen, sending slanderous emails to himself in your name. We prove he left sometime after that, while you left before it and I'd say that's pretty definitive, wouldn't you? Your IT guy's corroboration would just be icing on the cake."

Real hope began to surge through Elizabeth for the first time since the beginning of the whole ordeal. Impulsively, she reached up and wrapped her arms around Cole's neck. She hadn't planned it, but his lips soon found hers. Her body relaxed and she let him hold her, his strong arms pulling her close as he kissed her. For a whole minute Elizabeth forgot everything except how good it felt to be in his arms. Then, recalling the cameras, their red eyes no doubt recording the embrace, she pulled away.

He drove her back to her place. "Want to come up?" Despite everything going on, Elizabeth wanted him. She wanted to feel his skin against hers, to press her cheek against his manly chest, aswirl with dark hair that tapered down his flat belly toward his groin.

"I would." He found a parking space not too far down the street, a small miracle in itself.

Once inside, Cole asked, "Have you had dinner? We could order something." She was glad he hadn't suggested they stop and get a bite while he was driving her home. She was still physically out of sorts from drinking whiskey and sleeping most of the day away. Her head ached and her shoulder muscles were still knotted. Yet she was hungry, having eaten nothing since a small breakfast.

"I'm starving, now that you mention it. What would you think of my whipping up an omelet? It would be fast and easy." *So then you could make love to me all the sooner.* He seemed to read the subtext in her eyes because he smiled a slow, sultry smile, his dark eyes glinting.

He stepped behind her, lightly massaging her shoulders. She sighed and leaned against him. "That feels so good. I hate when I do this—hold tension in my body."

"You need to let it go." His fingers pressed into the twisted muscle and she closed her eyes in pleasure. "I have an idea. Why don't you take a nice hot shower before we eat? Let the tension drain out of you. Just show me where things are and I'll make the omelet."

The thought of hot water spraying against her knotted shoulders sounded wonderful. And she loved the idea of someone else doing the cooking. "You talked me into it."

Elizabeth's theory that food always tasted better when someone else made it held true that evening. Cole had found and sautéed fresh mushrooms, which, along with grated cheddar cheese, he had added to the eggs. Elizabeth emerged from her shower to find hot buttered toast and a perfectly cooked omelet, along with a glass of chilled white wine.

She smiled gratefully at Cole. "You're quite the chef, huh?"

"I've lived alone the last few years. Had to learn to fend for myself." He smiled back and raised his glass. "You look beautiful, Elizabeth."

She ducked her head, pleased. She had debated whether to dress again or not. After all, they both knew they were going to make love. Why pretend otherwise? She had opted for a pale blue satin nightgown with a low, square-cut neckline and its matching robe. She hadn't washed her hair in the shower, not wanting to hassle with wet hair. Instead she'd pulled it back and pinned it loosely in a French braid, letting several errant tendrils frame her cheeks.

They ate in silence, soon finishing the delicious food. Cole poured them each a second glass of wine, both tacitly agreeing to leave the dishes until later.

Once in Elizabeth's bedroom, which was about one-fifth the size of Cole's, most of the space filled with her four-poster bed, Cole took Elizabeth into his arms and kissed her. "I want you," he whispered. "I want to claim you."

Elizabeth shivered, understanding from their earlier lovemaking that this meant more than a symbolic claiming. Was she ready for what he offered? Her body was aching with need for him, every nerve ending jumping with anticipation.

Impulsively, she pulled out of his embrace, dropping her robe to the ground, aware of his eyes on her breasts, the nipples clearly visible beneath the thin satin. She sank to her knees in front of him, any trace of lingering shyness burned away by her lust.

With greedy fingers, she pulled open his fly and dragged his pants down his strongly-muscled thighs. She noted with self-satisfied pleasure that his cock was fully erect. She glanced up at his face. He was staring down at her, his lips parted, his expression almost fierce. With her eyes locked on his, she pulled down his underwear, allowing his large, hard cock to spring free from its confines.

For a moment she leaned her face against it, capturing it between her cheek and his stomach, savoring its hot pulse as she inhaled his heady, sensual musk. She turned her face until her lips met the throbbing vein along the satin hardness of taut skin. Again looking up at him, aware of her seductive pose, she licked along the shaft until she arrived at the spongy crown.

She slipped her mouth over it and flicked her tongue along the slit and then in a circle as she lowered her head. Cole groaned and closed his eyes, his hands coming to rest on her shoulders. She suckled her way down, finally taking him deep into her throat. Aware of her skill in pleasing a man in this way, she knew it wouldn't be long before she drove him over the edge. The awareness gave her a sense of power that was most decidedly not submissive. She was in control. Despite his whispered words, she was, in fact, the one claiming him at that moment.

When she reached to cup his balls and the base of his shaft, Cole's voice startled her. "No. No hands. Put your hands behind your back." She knew he was close to coming. Why was he stopping her? She decided to ignore him and again reached for his cock with sure fingers.

He pulled back, his cock falling from her mouth. "I said no, Elizabeth. Put your hands behind your back and don't move. Keep your mouth open for me." He hadn't raised his voice at all, but there was something in his tone that brooked no disobedience.

Elizabeth's heart had begun to thump and her legs suddenly felt weak. How quickly he had turned the tables. While a portion of her mind resisted, thinking she should reassert her control, her body ignored this completely. Her clit was swollen, throbbing persistently, and her nipples were so stiff they ached.

He waited until she had obeyed, moving her hands behind her back, before permitting her to touch his cock once more. "Good girl." His voice was gentle and he actually patted her head. The lingering bit of her mind that could still think tried to bristle at the condescension of his action, but failed utterly.

With a few deft movements, he pulled the pins that held her hair in place, and it fell in waves to her shoulders. He gripped either side her head, wrapping his fingers in her hair. "I want you to look at me. Look in my eyes, Elizabeth, while I use your mouth. While you're on your knees, with my cock in your pretty mouth, I want you to think about how you feel. Be honest with yourself and with me. Keep your hands behind your back, no matter what I do. Understand?"

"Yes," she whispered above the thundering of her heart. He smiled, the smile almost cruel. The slightest frisson of fear moved through her, weaving itself into the tapestry of her lust, yet she stayed still as he had commanded, her eyes locked on his.

With slow deliberation, he eased his shaft into her mouth, nearly choking her as he slid past her soft palate. When she started to suckle him again, he shook his head. "No. Stay still. Just receive me. Accept me." He pulled back just as slowly until the shaft was nearly out of her mouth and then pressed it back again.

His cock slid into her mouth, pressing her tongue down. This time when the head touched her soft palate, she pulled back, her gag reflex activated.

"Relax. Open yourself to me." She closed her eyes and tried to do as he said, aware she was trembling and so aroused it was all she could do to keep from reaching beneath her nightgown to rub her swollen, wet pussy.

His grip tightening in her hair, he began to move faster and deeper while she struggled to remain in position, hands clasped behind her back and mouth open to his onslaught.

All at once he released her and pulled her up onto the bed. Kicking out of his clothing, he flipped up her gown, pressed her legs apart with his thigh and touched the entrance of her drenched sex with the head of his cock, slick with her kisses.

She could feel his heart tapping against her chest. "Do you want me?" he murmured.

"God, yes." *Fuck me, fuck me, fuck me.* She wanted to scream it, but a certain natural decorum kept her from doing so. Instead she arched her hips up toward him in invitation. He pulled at the hem of her gown and lifted it over her head. She lay naked before him.

"Do you have something?" It took her a moment to realize he was asking for a condom.

"No, no, I don't care. Just fuck me. *Please.*" She was aware of how she must sound, but too desperate for his cock to care.

"I want you, Elizabeth." He let his weight ease over her, pinning her to the bed with it. She was unable to control the deep shudder that shook her body as his unsheathed cock entered her. She wasn't on birth control and she knew they should be practicing safe sex, but she was too far gone to care.

He thrust himself into her, his cock sending spirals of melting ecstasy swirling through her body. For several delicious minutes he moved inside her, the pleasure mounting like an impending storm. When he kissed her mouth, her body exploded in an unexpected and particularly intense orgasm. She bucked beneath him, its power ripping through her like a bolt of lightning.

With a groan of passion, Cole pulled himself from her, his semen landing in hot spurts against her stomach and breasts. She wanted to open her eyes and look at him, to see his face in the throes of his passion, but she was too spent even to lift her eyelids.

She heard him moving beside her but still she couldn't find the strength to move. She heard him in the bathroom, heard the water running and the toilet flush. In a moment he was back, his weight causing the bed to shift as he lay beside her. She opened her eyes when she felt the warm, wet washcloth sliding against her, wiping away his ejaculate. This was followed by a dry washcloth, and then by his lips brushing her skin.

She was moved by his thoughtful, sweet gesture. How could he be at once so dominant and so tender? He pulled her into his arms. "May I stay?"

She turned toward him and smiled, the endorphins from the orgasm leaving her suddenly giddy with emotion. She wanted to shout, *Yes! Don't ever go. Ever, ever, ever.* Instead she just nodded and nestled against his broad chest, closing her eyes, safe in his warm embrace.

CHAPTER THIRTEEN

She came into the office early, hoping to avoid the curious stares and questions of her staff, at least for a while. She knew Art probably didn't expect her in, but hiding wasn't going to get her anywhere. Resolving this quickly was the only way to move forward and begin to repair whatever damage Gary had done during her absence the day before.

There were seven messages on her voicemail, but none of them were from Nick. She called Art's office. Mary Beth answered. "Hi Elizabeth. We weren't expecting you in today." Elizabeth held her breath, wondering what Art had told her and what gossip was burning through the office like a brushfire, courtesy of Gary Fuckwad Dobbins. Mary Beth continued. "Art said you might not be coming in for a while…" She let it hang. Elizabeth couldn't tell if the secretary knew anything or not yet about her impending fall from grace.

Giving nothing away, Elizabeth responded. "I'm much better, thanks. Listen, is Art in by any chance?"

"He just called to say he's running a little late. I expect him by eight-thirty. Is there anything I can do for you?"

"Just let me know the minute he gets in, if you would. I have a matter of some urgency to discuss with him."

"You got it."

Elizabeth hung up and stared at her inbox, which was piled with letters to sign, projects to review and the minutia of everyday office life. She grabbed a stack of paper, forcing herself to concentrate on her work.

At eight-ten her phone rang, the double ring indicating it was an interoffice call. Nick Davis showed on the caller ID. She grabbed the receiver. "Hey, Nick."

"Good morning, Elizabeth. I, uh, got your message. I did what you asked." She could tell from the marked discomfort in his tone he'd read the offending email, but that couldn't be helped.

"Yes. And what did you find out?" She reminded herself it didn't really matter where Gary had written the email from—this would just be, as Cole had called it, icing on the cake.

"I had to check the web-based mail logs but that email was sent from Gary Dobbins' computer." Elizabeth let it sink in for a few seconds. "Okay. Thanks, Nick. I really appreciate it."

At eight-thirty-two her phone rang again. Mary Beth. "He's here."

"Thanks, Mary Beth."

Elizabeth walked down the hall, passing Gary's office along the way. He was in there and looked up as she passed, but she ignored him. At Art's office, she knocked lightly on the door.

"Come in," came the gravelly voice.

Elizabeth entered and walked resolutely toward his desk.

"Elizabeth." Art looked surprised. "I had thought you'd be—"

"Home, licking my wounds while Gary prepares to take over my job?" She sat down, crossing her legs with confidence, desperately relieved to be operating from a position of power for the first time since Gary had pulled this crap.

Art coughed, clearly uncomfortable. Elizabeth looked him in the eye, keeping her voice professional and as devoid of emotion as she could. "I have proof, Art, that Gary set this whole sordid thing up. Yesterday I was so blindsided by the depths of his deception and slander I wasn't thinking clearly. Today, I am."

Without giving him a chance to respond, she continued in a firm voice. "I have three things to say. One——call building security and ask them to review the security camera records for Saturday. Tell them it's urgent and must be done this morning. You will find that Gary and I were both at the office, but that I left by noon and didn't return. I am certain you will find that Gary was still in the building when the email was supposedly composed and sent by me at six-seventeen p.m.

"Two——I had Nick Davis check the email transmission logs, something we should have done yesterday, but I guess none of us was thinking on our feet." She tried to control her glare toward her boss, but failed.

Art still didn't seem to be getting it. He held out his hands with a placating gesture that made her want to smack him. "Look, Elizabeth. You should know this whole thing has made me very uncomfortable. I never liked the idea of employees getting involved with one another and this mess is really getting out of hand. Whatever happened between you two, I'm willing to forget——"

"No, you listen to me, Art." Elizabeth's voice was steely, though miraculously she managed not to raise it. "I'll repeat myself. Nothing, absolutely *nothing* is going on, ever went on, or ever will go on between Gary Dobbins and myself, except possibly a lawsuit to clear my name, if it comes to that."

Art opened his mouth to speak but Elizabeth barreled on, determined to make him listen. "Nick has confirmed that the email was sent from Gary Dobbin's computer. *Not* my computer. *Gary's* computer. His password-protected computer. The email logs and the fact Gary was here when the email was sent and I was not are sufficient to prove, beyond any doubt, that Gary is lying. Not only that, he somehow hacked into my computer in his effort to further incriminate me in this web of lies." Art gaped at her.

She wanted to reach over his desk and shake him. Instead she said in a low, controlled voice that made tougher men than Art Wallace quail, "If additional proof is needed, there are witnesses at that club Gary dragged me to, who will swear, under oath if necessary, that Gary Dobbins presented himself as one John Hunter and offered me, while drugged against my will, for sale at a pretend slave auction. Hopefully we won't have to go to those lengths, but I'm fully prepared to do so to protect my reputation."

She stood. "Finally, once you ascertain that he was in the building at the time of the email while I was not and confirm for yourself that the email was sent from his computer, I demand that you fire Gary Dobbins immediately."

Art's mouth was hanging open. She stared him down until he managed to close it. Either he would dismiss her out of hand, or he would check out her claims. She waited on tenterhooks, prepared to walk out and not look back if he declined to take action.

To her immense relief, he pressed a button on his phone and barked, "Mary Beth, get building security on the phone. Pronto."

While Art made his calls to confirm Elizabeth's assertions, she returned to her office, determined to catch up on some of her work and stop letting Gary dominate her thoughts.

"Didn't expect to see you here today." Elizabeth looked up sharply at the sound of Gary's nasal tenor. He dared to poke his perfectly coiffed blond head around her door, his smile bland and cruel, still unaware what awaited him.

"I imagine you didn't," she answered coldly. He stood lingering in the doorway and she forced herself to resist the impulse to wipe off that smirk with her fist. She didn't want to waste any more time on Gary Dobbins. "I'm busy. Please close the door on your way out."

"As you wish," he intoned, making a ridiculous bow like some courtier in a bad movie.

Once he had gone, she stuck her head out of her office. "Angela, cancel our team meeting. We'll reschedule for tomorrow." She knew Gary would think she'd canceled because she was hiding with her tail between her legs. She didn't give a damn what he thought at this point, but she wanted to wait until after his termination to talk to the rest of her team. She didn't plan to give them too much detail, except to say Gary had been caught behaving illegally and had been terminated. If Art wanted to tell them more, that would be up to him.

Two hours passed, dragging and limping along as she tried to focus on a campaign. Mercifully she was distracted by phone calls and emails. Finally her phone rang, Art's name showing on the screen. "Yes?"

"Get down here, will you?" She waited, but he said no more, clicking off.

Elizabeth's heart began an uncomfortable thump as she hurried down the hall. She entered Art's office without knocking and stood in front of his desk, too agitated to sit.

He gazed up at her with pale, apologetic eyes, slowly shaking his head. "It's unbelievable. You were one-hundred percent correct. I can't apologize enough. I hope you understand, given the evidence, er, the *apparent* evidence Gary presented yesterday. I was completely taken in. I just can't believe he would do something like this. The magnitude of it—the sheer nerve. It defies belief."

Relief washed over Elizabeth like a flood. She sagged down onto a chair and closed her eyes. The horrible nightmare was coming to an end. Rallying herself, she sat up and looked at her boss. "So security was able to prove he was here during the time the email went out, and that I wasn't?"

"Yep. And I checked with the tech boys too. The email definitely originated from his computer, not yours. Not only that, someone in the tech department reset your password on Saturday. None of the guys there take responsibility, but they say Sheila Murphy, who was in the building Saturday morning, might have done it. She doesn't work here anymore but I'll have someone in HR follow up. I'm not exactly sure what the implications of that are, but I imagine Gary had something to do with that too. Meanwhile, you're in the clear. He's in the mud. Speaking of which, let's get the little shit in here and read him the riot act."

He buzzed Mary Beth, telling her to get Dobbins into his office ASAP. "Oh, and call security while you're at it. I want two guards up here right away."

Elizabeth sat on the edge of the chair, her body held rigid as she waited to confront the smug bastard with the cold, hard evidence of his failed scheme. Gary entered a few minutes later with a confident swagger. He stopped short when he saw Elizabeth, but quickly composed himself and moved toward the vacant chair beside hers.

Art glared at him. "Well," he barked. "What do you have to say for yourself?"

"Excuse me?" Gary's confident smile faded, confusion registering in his face. His eyes slid nervously toward Elizabeth, who gazed back at him impassively. He looked back to Art and took a deep breath. Slowly he smiled and Elizabeth had to hand it to him, the bastard had balls. His voice was smooth and confident when he spoke.

"Look. I'm willing to put this whole thing behind us." He bestowed a condescending smile on Elizabeth, who kept her face stony, though he didn't seem to notice or care. "I've been giving it a lot of thought, and if Elizabeth is willing to agree to a change in the hierarchy of the team dynamic...." Elizabeth could scarcely believe her ears. He still thought he had the upper hand. He still thought he could finagle her job for his own.

Art cut him off. "Save it, Dobbins. The jig is up. I don't usually have other employees in the office when I fire someone, but I think Elizabeth has earned the right to witness this firsthand."

It took Gary a moment to react. Things clearly weren't going the way he thought he'd so carefully orchestrated. He opened his mouth, stuttering. "What? She? Me? But she's the one...."

Art held up his hand. "Save it for the courts. That is, if she chooses to press charges for the drugging of her drink and the slander of her good name." He turned to Elizabeth. "I would if I were you, Elizabeth. This bastard is dangerous." He returned his glare to Gary and went on.

"You're fired. As of this instant. You're a bright guy and I have no doubt you'll land on your feet, though I'll do everything in my power to make sure it isn't in this town. I've got a lot of connections, and I'll make sure every one of them knows the depths of your filthy character. Now get out of my office. You have fifteen minutes to collect your things."

As if they'd timed it, two uniformed security guards appeared at Art's door, with Mary Beth hovering nervously just behind them. Art waved toward them and then looked back to Gary. "Leave your laptop in your office—it's company property. Leave your keys with your secretary. These gentlemen will oversee your packing and escort you from the building."

He turned toward the guards. "He is not to take one single file or scrap of paper that he can't prove belongs to him personally. I'll send in someone from human resources to make sure."

Throughout all this Gary sat as if frozen, his face pale, a small muscle at his jaw jumping. Elizabeth imagined she could almost see the wheels turning furiously inside his head as he tried desperately to think of a way to wriggle out of the incredible mess he'd created for himself. He opened his mouth as if to speak, appeared to think better of it and snapped it shut again.

As the guards approached him, he swayed and Elizabeth thought for a second he was going faint. He recovered himself, however, when one of the guards reached for his arm. He jerking it away. "I can walk by myself. Don't touch me." He stalked from the office without looking at either Art or Elizabeth.

Elizabeth sank back into the chair. She didn't feel elated or even happy at what had occurred. She'd come too close to losing everything she'd worked so hard for. She shook her head. "What a waste. He's destroyed his career and his reputation. I still can't believe he stooped so low just to get what he thought had been stolen from him."

"Well, good riddance to bad rubbish," Art said. "I followed my gut in not promoting him in the first place and it's a damn good thing. He's a sneak, a liar and a sore loser. I hope you press criminal charges."

Elizabeth said nothing. She knew it would be next to impossible to definitively prove he'd drugged her drink, or that he'd been the one to take her to the club rather than vice versa. And the thought of presenting the explicit slave pamphlet and the nauseating email to the scrutiny of a court of law gave her chills. No, he'd been punished more than enough by losing what he'd obviously coveted to a ridiculously dangerous degree. She believed Art's threat and that he could make good on it. Gary's career in advertising, at least on the east coast, was definitely over.

She stood, relieved her voice sounded reasonable steady, though inside she still felt shaky and little sick. "Thanks for believing me."

Art looked embarrassed, no doubt because he *hadn't* believed her, at least not at first. His voice was gruff. "How's the Baker proposal coming along?"

Glad for a chance to at least pretend at normalcy for the first time that week, Elizabeth sat back down and discussed the project, answering Art's questions and brainstorming about various key aspects of their pitch.

When she walked back to her office, she was relieved to see Gary was gone. Word was already circulating like wildfire through the office, with clusters of staff huddled, talking in low voices. She'd have to tell her team what had happened—not the details, but the fact he'd been involved in some unsavory business and had been let go. But that could wait until tomorrow, when the dust had settled.

When her cell phone rang, Elizabeth was at her drafting table, reviewing the layout of a series of magazine ads. She retrieved the phone, surprised to see it was already six o'clock. She recognized Cole's cell number. She'd left a message for him several hours earlier, with only the single word, "Victory!"

She flicked open the phone, smiling broadly. "Hi there."

"Hey there, it's Cole." As if she wouldn't recognize that deep, sexy voice, even if she didn't have caller ID.

"Did you get my message?"

"I sure did. I'm sorry it took me so long to call back. I was stuck in a series of endless meetings with my financial advisors." He chuckled, adding, "Victory, huh? I want to hear the entire story, not one word omitted. Are you still at work?"

"Yeah. I didn't realize it was so late. I'd promised myself I'd leave early today, just on principle after all this insanity, but time, as usual, got away from me."

"We'll have to work on that."

"Oh, we will, huh," Elizabeth retorted. The few serious men in her life had always chafed under her intense work schedule, but that's just the way it was. She hadn't made it to where she was by working nine to five. If Cole was going to be in her life, he'd simply need to adjust to her schedule.

There was a smile in his voice, but something else too. It was an air of quiet confidence, of control, that set her heart fluttering. "Yes, we will. It's important to manage your life to leave time for your personal growth. I'll teach you. So far you've proven an excellent student."

Elizabeth swallowed, feeling the sudden shift in mood between them. How was it, with just a word or a gesture, he could switch the balance of power between them, rendering her at once defenseless and yet yearning to please him?

She didn't respond, and was relieved when he changed the subject. "May I take you to dinner? I'm actually in the car right now. We could be there in fifteen minutes. I can't wait to hear every detail of that bastard's crash and burn."

She looked at the project spread out before her and again at her watch. "I've wasted so much time and psychic energy on that creep. I'm way behind on two proposals I'd hoped to have done by the end of the week. And, as much as I'm thrilled he's gone, I've lost my right-hand man. I'll need to fill that position as fast as I can."

"You will. I'm sure of it. But for tonight, if you can, let it all go. I'll take you to this excellent French restaurant

I've recently discovered. We'll get a bottle of champagne to celebrate your success and then I'll take you home. I promise while you're with me, you'll forget all about Gary Dobbins and Wallace & Pratt and deadlines and due dates."

Recalling the subtle yet powerful way he'd taken sensual control from her each time they'd been together, Elizabeth believed his promise. She shivered with delicious anticipation, almost blurting out she'd rather skip the restaurant and go straight to his place for some serious play. Jesus, she was turning into a slut. It must just be because she hadn't had sex for several months, and he'd reawakened dormant passions. Maybe she wouldn't even let him take her home. She'd play harder to get and insist he drop her at her own place, claiming exhaustion.

Who was she kidding? If he told her to strip in the car and spread her legs, she knew she'd do it. What the hell was happening to her? She tried to ignore her perking nipples and moistening panties. "Dinner sounds great. I'll be outside waiting."

CHAPTER FOURTEEN

Cole leaned over and blew out the candles on the dining room table. He'd forgotten he'd lit them over an hour ago when she'd texted him she would soon be on her way. The salad looked limp in its wooden bowl. At least he hadn't cooked the steaks yet.

He glanced again at his watch, irritated she was late. Not just a little late. Two hours late. And this wasn't the first time. In the three weeks they'd been dating, she'd arrived twice at least thirty minutes late at restaurants, and missed one dinner altogether, calling him belatedly to say she'd been caught up in a team meeting or some project or other and hadn't realized the time.

He'd excused her each time, aware she was a busy executive, and not only that, but was still shorthanded, as they'd yet to hire Gary's replacement. He poured himself a second glass of red wine and carried it with him out to the terrace. It was nine o'clock on a Wednesday.

They'd seen a lot of each other since they'd met, the romance going at full tilt. The sex remained fantastic. She was easily the loveliest, most sensual and passionate woman he had ever been with. It was hard sometimes, very hard, to restrain himself from moving too far too fast when it came to D/s.

They had talked about it at some length, one night staying up until four in the morning. She was fascinated, she told him, with the D/s lifestyle, one she admitted she hadn't properly understood before they'd met. He'd given her several links to websites that were informative and honest. She'd done her homework, and more, telling him with wide eyes about the blogs she'd found.

"There was one, she calls herself Slave Anna. She writes this kind of live journal, tracking her submissive experience with a man she just refers to as 'Sir.' She writes beautifully, and while I have to admit some of the stuff they do kind of freaks me out, I find myself getting really turned on and intrigued by the whole experience. I mean, I never thought of myself as a masochist or whatever, but the way she writes makes me want to experience it too—the kiss of the whip, the searing pleasure of the cane...." Elizabeth had trailed off, shivering, her eyes shining, thrilling Cole with possibility for their own fledgling D/s connection.

She was open to each advance, but he knew sometimes she was scared too. The last thing he wanted was to scare her away. In such a short time, she'd come to mean too much to him to risk that. He closed his eyes, remembering the first time he'd tied her slender wrists to the wrought-iron frame of his bed, turned-on by the wide-eyed look of fear and lust at war on her face.

She'd asked him to tie her down—"Just to see," she had said. He'd only secured her wrists, not sure she was ready to be properly bound and spread for him, but she'd responded ardently, bucking and moaning against him when he'd entered her, her pussy gripping him like a velvet vise.

"I want more," she had whispered late one night as they were drifting off to sleep. I want you to take me to that amazing place Slave Anna seems to have found."

Did she really understand what she was asking? He wanted nothing more than to take her to that place—the submissive headspace she was referring to, where pleasure and pain truly lost their meaning as separate sensations, where to serve was to be served and to submit was to exalt. It had long been his dream to find a woman he could take to such heights, but it didn't happen overnight. Was she really ready for that kind of commitment?

He hadn't seen her last night. She'd been working late, as usual, and he hadn't pressed the issue. He didn't want to suffocate her and he appreciated it was wise to slow things down. Infatuation had a way of burning fast and furious, and then fizzling to a disappointing end. He'd much rather stoke the slow embers of love.

Love.

He hadn't told her he loved her, though he'd wanted to. Nor had she said it to him. He sipped his wine, wondering, not for the first time, what exactly he was doing and where he thought he was going with this relationship, if that's even what it was. She was nearly ten years his junior, and she'd never been married. She seemed wedded to her work—a classic workaholic, using that work as a way to keep herself distanced and safe from too much intimacy.

He understood that well. He'd done the same thing in his marriage to Joanie. He'd promised himself going forward that wouldn't happen again. So far he'd never let his work get in the way of seeing Elizabeth, but she had, and quite often.

If only she belonged to me, he thought wistfully. *Truly belonged to me as my submissive.* Would that make a difference, he wondered. Would it allow her the space to slow down? He understood her better now after these few weeks.

She literally could not stop. He wouldn't go so far as to call her manic, but she was driven. She couldn't sit still. She always arrived at his place with her briefcase, stuffed to the gills with folders and work. He took secret pride in making sure she never opened it. He knew very well how to distract her.

The only time she slowed and stilled was when they were making love. He knew if he could teach her to truly submit, she would find even greater peace, peace she could take with her beyond the bedroom. It was something he'd witnessed and read about, and as a Dom had experienced firsthand.

Interestingly, most true subs he had known were very in control in their day-to-day lives, women like Elizabeth, powerful and driven, confident and sure of themselves. They weren't the passive little rabbits he'd met all too often at the BDSM clubs, girls looking for a man to take over their lives and make all their decisions.

No, the most sensual and satisfying subs to train were women like Elizabeth, strong and smart, and sexy as hell. To claim someone like her, to own someone like her…he sighed heavily and pulled out his phone, in case she'd sent him a message he'd missed.

It rang at just that moment, startling him. He saw her name and, because he was annoyed with her at standing him up, answered formally. "Cole Pearson."

"Cole," she said breathlessly in that low, sexy voice that never failed to give him an erection. "I'm so, so sorry. I hope you didn't hold dinner for me. I kept trying to get away to call you but the negotiations weren't going well and I've wanted this account forever. And guess what, I think we *got* it. I was able to meet every one of their demands and objections with a solution and I think we sold them. This could mean millions for the agency and a big fat bonus for me."

She paused, no doubt expecting his praise and admiration. He was too pissed off to give it. "That's good," he said curtly.

There was a pause, then she rushed on. "Oh, Cole. You're mad at me. I know, I know, I said I'd be there two hours ago. I don't know what to say. You know how busy I am."

"Yes. It's all right." He cut her off. "Don't worry about dinner. It's not a big deal. You've obviously got a lot on your plate at work right now. I'm afraid I'm rather busy the rest of the week myself, but maybe we can get together this weekend." He knew he sounded stiff, even cold.

There was a brief silence at the other end of the line. She sensed, correctly, his rebuke. "All right. Well, have a good night—what's left of it." He could hear the hurt in her voice. She clicked off.

Cole shook his head. *That was childish of me,* he chided himself. *I'm punishing her for standing me up.* He thought about calling her back and apologizing—telling her she could come over any time, no strings.

But he didn't pick up the phone. Maybe a few days apart would be a good thing. They had been moving very fast. Maybe she welcomed the break and he'd only thought she'd sounded hurt, because he had been. He snorted and shook his head. He was definitely over-thinking this thing. He never experienced this sort of confusion and indecision in his professional life. How was it that a woman could reduce him to feeling like he was back in high school?

He thought about making one of the steaks, but didn't really feel like eating a full meal without her. Instead he poured himself some very fine Scotch, grabbed a handful of smoked almonds and went into his study.

He did a little work at his computer and then checked his email. While clicking through mostly junk, he thought about Gary Dobbins, who had hacked his way into Elizabeth's private email account as part of his elaborate attempt to bring her down. Elizabeth said they hadn't heard a peep from him at the office, for which she was relieved.

The magnitude of what Dobbins had done was incredible, and it was only through sheer luck and determination Elizabeth had been able to bring him down. On the one hand, Cole was oddly grateful to Dobbins, not for what he did to Elizabeth, but for the fact Cole never would have met her otherwise. As exasperating as it was to share her with her first love—her career—he was happier now than he could ever remember being.

Still, Dobbins had been a real prick on so many levels. He should be punished for what he did. Cole could understand why Elizabeth didn't want to press criminal charges and have her named dragged through the muck of it all, but it irked him the creep got off so easily. Yes, he lost his job, but a guy like him would find another, of that Cole was certain. Maybe not in Manhattan, but he'd land on his feet.

It infuriated Cole to think the smug bastard was still at large, hanging out at clubs like House of Usher, a bully posing as a Dom, doing who knew what further damage in the world. Cole sat back in his chair and stared down into his drink, recalling what Elizabeth had said that first day—don't get mad, get even.

~*~

He didn't hear from her the rest of the week, nor did he call her. *Give her space*, he told himself during his more mature moments. *We'll connect this weekend*. He started to call her a hundred times, but pride kept him from doing so. In his decidedly less mature moments, he told himself if she was too busy to connect, he was damned if he'd chase her. He knew he was acting like a fool, but still he didn't call her.

Saturday morning he was awakened by a text message on his cell phone. "Hey, stranger," it read. "Just happened to be in the neighborhood. I've got bagels!"

Joy rushed through him. Grinning broadly, he texted back. "Well, since you have bagels…come on up!"

He jumped out of bed and went into the bathroom to wash up. Quickly he pulled on some jeans and a shirt, combed his hair and rushed into the living room to wait for Elizabeth. He realized he was grinning like an idiot and told himself to get a grip.

He opened the door just as she was about to ring the bell. She was carrying a white sack from the bakery and, to his delight, no briefcase. She stood just at the threshold, her expression uncertain, even shy. He felt a rush of tenderness and remorse.

Forgetting his resolve to go slow and careful, he blurted, "It's *insane* how much I've missed you." He held out his arms and she stepped into them, pressing her cheek against his shoulder. It was so good to hold her.

"I'm sorry," he whispered.

"Me too," she replied.

Letting her go, he stepped back to look at her. Her hair was down and the turquoise of her silky sleeveless blouse caught and mirrored the color of her brilliant blue eyes. "I had forgotten how incredibly lovely you are. I'm sorry I was such a jackass. I know you're busy at work and I need to make allowances for that."

"And I know I tend to use work to keep from getting too involved. I don't want to do that this time. Not with you. And it was rude of me to stand you up for dinner again." She gave a coquettish grin, adding, "I probably should be punished."

He raised his eyebrows. "Let's discuss it over bagels. You *have* been a very naughty little girl." He laughed, enjoying the flush rising in her cheeks.

In the kitchen, he prepared coffee while Elizabeth put the bagels on a plate and set the table. He liked having her there, the two of them moving about it like a real couple, doing the mundane, domestic things necessary to prepare a meal. He wanted that with her. He wanted more than that—much more.

Elizabeth was quiet at first and it was obvious she was nervous but, at the same time, excited. Who would have dreamed this lovely girl would be asking for a punishment, even if she was half-kidding? Cole's cock was swelling at the thought, but he forced himself to tread lightly. Hoping to help her relax, he asked about her work week and how it was going with the search for Gary's replacement.

It was she who brought the conversation back around to the topic of punishment. "You know, when Slave Anna misbehaves, she gets punished. Sir calls it a correction. He says he's teaching her to behave correctly in order to please him at all times."

She'd brought it up again. It was time to pay attention "Just what exactly are you saying, Elizabeth? What are you asking?" He kept his tone light, but watched carefully for her reaction.

Elizabeth's eyes widened and she caught her breath, her tongue sliding nervously over her lower lip. "Well, I, um. You know…"

"Say it. I want you to say it."

"I, um…" She looked down, her voice low, "need to be corrected." He studied her lovely face and dropped his eyes to her breasts, pleased to see erect nipples poking toward him.

He tried to keep the exaltation out of his tone. "I agree. I think we'll start with a spanking. Not the little tap I gave you the other day, but something you'll remember. You ready for that?"

"Yes." It was no more than a whisper. Their bagels forgotten, they both stood from the table. She looked up at him, her eyes shining, the color high in her cheeks. Yes, she was definitely ready to move to the next level in their D/s adventure and he was more than ready to take her there.

He gestured for her to precede him, enjoying the sight of her shapely ass in her tight jeans as she moved gracefully along the hallway toward his bedroom.

Once there, she turned toward him, wrapping her arms around herself, her lower lip again caught in her teeth. Taking pity on the nervous girl, he moved toward her and pulled her close. "Relax, sweetheart. Yes, the spanking will be real this time, but I've said this to you before and I'll say it again, as often as you need to hear it, I will never take you further than you feel safe going. You've said you want to explore this lifestyle with me, and we will continue to do so, but you have to trust me. Okay?"

He held her shoulders and peered into her eyes, needing her to trust him before he would go further. "Yes," she whispered, dropping her arms at her sides and managing a small smile.

"Take off your jeans and panties and lie down on your stomach." He watched her, his cock straining in his jeans as her lovely, long legs were bared. She was wearing lacy pink panties, which she pulled down her slender thighs, her eyes on his face as she did so.

She started to lift the hem of her blouse. "No. I didn't say to take off your top. I'm going to punish you, not fuck you. You don't deserve to be fucked right now. First you must be…corrected."

Her eyes flashed and he waited for her retort but none came. Instead she nodded and lay across his bed, her gorgeous ass offered up for him, her face turned away.

He reached into his jeans and stroked his cock, which ached to thrust into her. He sat down beside her and rested his hand lightly on one rounded cheek. Elizabeth jumped at his touch. Gently he smoothed her skin, stroking her ass cheeks and lower back to calm the skittish girl.

When he decided she was relaxed enough to begin, he gave her bottom a light pat. She wriggled against his palm and he smiled. She was ready. He smacked her across the right cheek, admiring the way the flesh moved. Elizabeth gasped lightly but stayed still. He smacked the other cheek, a little harder. He wanted to take her over his lap so he could feel her body against his, but he knew that would make the experience too sexual for her.

It would be sexual eventually, but he would control the pace. First he'd put her to the test and see just how sincere she was about experiencing the lifestyle, as she had put it. He began to spank her in earnest—hard, steady swats, alternating cheeks.

"Ouch. It *hurts*." She covered her bottom with her hands.

"It's supposed to hurt. This is a punishment. Keep your hands at your sides or I'll have to tie you down." He waited to see if she would obey. Slowly, she removed her hands and put her arms at her sides. Her hands were balled into fists.

"Unclench your hands," he ordered. Again she obeyed. Her ass was already a nice shade of pink. "Thirty swats. You can count out loud or in your head or not at all, but that's what you're going to get." He struck her three more times, much harder than before, the sound of his palm against her flesh reverberating in the air.

She gasped and immediately clenched her hands into fists again. He tapped at one fist. "Unclench your hands. It shows resistance. You are not to resist me." Again she uncurled her fingers. She was breathing hard, her head turned away from him.

"Turn your face to me. I want to see you." She turned her head. He smoothed away the hair that had fallen over her face, tucking it behind her ear. He stroked her cheek for a moment, resisting the urge to bend down and kiss her. This was, after all, supposed to be a punishment.

"You're okay," he assured her. If she couldn't handle a simple spanking, there was no way he was going to introduce her to the whip or the cane, no matter what she said she wanted.

She nodded. "Twenty-two left."

It took him a moment to realize she had been counting. He grinned at her, pleased. "That's right. You earned every swat, too." He watched her face as he began to spank her again, just as hard as before. She squeezed her eyes tight and began to breathe in a rapid staccato but she didn't clench her hands and she didn't protest.

Her ass was turning a lovely shade of red, his handprint landing white and darkening rapidly as the blood moved below the surface of her smooth, perfect skin. She began to whimper, her hands again clenched. He tapped a fist and she opened her fingers.

He continued to spank her, aware she was nearing the limit of what she could tolerate, or rather what she thought she could tolerate. *"Twenty-three,"* she cried suddenly. "Oh, Jesus. I can't do it."

She rolled away from him, covering her ass with her hands. He rolled her back to her stomach and gripped her wrists, pulling her arms up over her head. She jerked against his grip, but he held her fast.

"Of course you can, silly girl. Only seven left. You do know, if you stop a spanking before it's done, we have to start over. Do you want to start over?"

"No," came her small voice.

"No, I didn't think so. So just relax and take what's due you. You earned this. You deserve it. You need it. Don't you?"

There was a long pause. He let her wrists go. If she still protested, he would stop. She didn't move her hands from over her head, but left them lying against the pillows. "Yes." Her voice was now a whisper.

"Yes, what?"

"Yes, I need this."

He grinned broadly, hugely pleased at this unexpected capitulation. He had expected her to say she deserved it. To say she needed it implied more, so much more. He cupped his palm and smacked her ass seven more times in rapid, stinging succession. Elizabeth whimpered and tensed, but didn't otherwise resist him.

He bent over her and gently kissed the tender flesh, turning his cheek to feel its heat. She moaned. "I'm so proud of you." He meant it. He kissed her again, his lips trailing down toward the back of her thigh.

He brought a hand between her legs, pressing them apart. He touched her pussy with the tip of one finger. Despite the sting of the spanking, or, dare he hope, because of it, she was wet and swollen. This time her moan was more ardent, and she spread her legs farther of her own accord.

He pushed her onto her back. Crouching between her legs, he licked along her outer labia, savoring the spicy-sweet taste of her. She gasped with pleasure as his tongue sought and found her clit, hard as a pebble beneath its hood. Lightly he teased her with his tongue, while sliding a finger into the tight wetness he would soon claim with his cock.

Later he would talk to her and help her process her reaction to the spanking but for now he would just adore her, licking and teasing her until he drove her to the edge of ecstasy. In short order he did just that. She was panting and moaning, writhing against him. "Oh, oh, oh," she cried, her orgasm seconds away.

He pulled away and rolled from the bed. Her eyes flew open. "Don't stop. Don't, *please*, let me come." She was imploring.

He pulled off his clothing and hurled them away, reaching to the night table for a condom, which he quickly rolled onto his straining cock. He stared down at her, loving the sight of her, the smell of her, the sound of her pleading for him. "Take off your blouse and bra." She obeyed quickly, lying back down, her breasts tipped with dark red, distended nipples. He fell heavily onto her, grabbing her wrists and pulling them taut over her head.

Maneuvering himself between her thighs, he plunged into her impossibly hot, tight cunt and groaned with pleasure. She at once began to buck beneath him, writhing and gasping. "Yes, *yes*," she cried. He could feel the heat from her spanked ass against his balls as he moved inside her.

It wasn't long before her body began to shudder in a long, convulsive climax. He released her wrists and wrapped his arms around her, savoring the clasp of her wet, satin pussy milking his cock. A moment later he, too, climaxed, the sound of her breathy cries pushing him over the precipice.

Once his heart slowed a little, he rolled onto his side, his cock still inside her, pulling her along with him into his arms. She nuzzled against his chest in that disarmingly sweet way she had. He stroked her hair.

"That was amazing." There was wonder in her voice.

"You took that spanking pretty well. I wasn't easy on you."

"It was amazing," she repeated. "I mean, yeah, it hurt." She pulled back to look up at him with a rueful grin. "But I don't know how to explain it. It was just so...hot. Sensual. I felt, I don't know, so *alive*."

"That was just a taste of what we can share, if you're really serious about exploring D/s together."

"I am. I want to. I want more." She gave a small laugh. "I can't even believe I'm talking like this. If you'd asked me a month ago, I'd have laughed in your face. I mean, I was clueless. I thought the scene was the crap Gary is apparently into—violence for its own sake, subjugating a woman just because you can—you know, abusive stuff. I totally didn't get it before. And then, reading about it online and stuff, that's been really interesting and eye-opening. And I love when you hold me down when we make love—the masterful aspect of it, the sense of sensual helplessness." She paused, thoughtfully rubbing her ass.

"But today. I mean, I know it was supposed to be a *punishment*." She wrinkled her nose at him. "But it was so much more than that. I really felt like I was letting go. For the first time in my life, I was relinquishing something, but in a good way. I was..."

"Submitting," he offered.

CHAPTER FIFTEEN

"I want to see the dungeon."

"The what?"

Elizabeth, lying naked and sexually sated in Cole's huge bed, lifted herself on an elbow. "Your dungeon. You know, the room you told me about, filled with whips and chains and all that stuff." In the six weeks she'd known him, he'd never offered to show her the room, and up until that moment, she hadn't asked.

"Ah, you mean the playroom. I think of it as a place for erotic play, though I suppose dungeon is apt enough." He caught her with his dark, piercing gaze and her heart skipped a beat.

"Well, I want to see it," she persisted.

"Why?" He stroked her breast, tweaking a nipple to punctuate his question.

"Just to see." His fingers sent a shiver of desire directly from her nipple to her pussy. "Just curious."

"All right." Cole swung his legs over the side of the bed. She watched him, admiring his broad, strong back. Though they'd just made love, her body stirred. He pulled on a pair of jeans, not bothering with underwear or a shirt.

Elizabeth climbed out of the bed and moved toward her pile of clothing but Cole stopped her. "No. I want you naked. Subs aren't permitted to wear clothing in my playroom."

She opened her mouth, barely managing to stifle a small gasp. Subs, in the plural. Of course she knew he'd had women there. He'd told her himself. Was she just another in a series of pretend slaves?

He was watching her in that way he had, as if her thoughts and feelings were scrolling across her face. "I'm not sure you're ready, Elizabeth. Not for the playroom. Remember, if I take you there, it won't be for casual play. I don't want that with you."

"I didn't say I want to *do* anything. I just want to look. Can't a girl look?" An image she'd seen online, of Slave Anna bound at a wooden cross, her body bathed in sweat and covered in welts from a cane, flashed into her mind's eye. She swallowed, a finger of fear drawing down her spine. No, she didn't want that. She just wanted to look.

"Okay. I'll show you. But the rule stands—you'll stay naked." She licked her lips and nodded, aware his words and his authoritative tone, not to mention his gorgeous body, had all conspired to make her pussy wet and tingly.

He walked to his bureau and slipped a key ring into his pocket. "Let's go." He led her past the guest bedroom to a door at the end of the hall. Her heart was pattering as she watched him unlock it. Beyond the door was a short, narrow staircase.

She followed him up the stairs, which opened onto a large, windowless room. When Cole flicked on the lights, she gasped as she tried to take it all in. Having spent a number of hours on various BDSM sites online, she knew what she was looking at, but seeing it for real, knowing it belonged to Cole, knowing he had used it, was something else again.

Set along one wall was a padded bondage table complete with stirrups, a black cross shaped like an X and what looked like a vaulting horse, also padded with black leather. In one corner, huge eye bolts had been affixed into a concrete beam in the ceiling. A suspension swing hung from two of them. Leather restraints dangled from two more. One wall was entirely covered in mirrors. The rest were hung with a vast array of cuffs and shackles, ropes of varying lengths and textures, floggers, paddles, crops, straps, slappers, canes and whips.

"Wow." She was barely aware she had spoken aloud.

"You like it?" Cole grinned wickedly. "No one goes in here without my express permission. My housekeeper has never seen the inside. She thinks I have a safe and keep important documents for my business in here and I let her think it."

His voice lowered, its cadence seductive. "The walls are soundproofed." He touched her bare shoulder, sliding his fingers toward her throat.

Elizabeth's breath quickened and she stepped away from him, swallowing hard. He let his hand fall. "Seen enough?"

"What's that?" She pointed toward a large box-shaped item on the floor by the mirror. It was covered with a black sheet.

"Ah, that." Cole advanced into the room. Elizabeth remained by the door. He plucked off the sheet, revealing a large steel dog cage, its door padlocked shut. "I call it the puppy cage. I only use that for serious infractions. A willful breaking of the rules. In my experience, it's a sub's greatest punishment—to be isolated and left alone. Far worse than a whipping."

She stared at the cage, unable to stop the vision of herself locked inside, a prisoner in a soundproofed room. "You—" Her mouth was dry, her voice hoarse when she tried to speak. She cleared her throat and tried again. "You actually use that? I mean, for real?"

"Only on very naughty girls." He laughed and moved toward her, taking her in his arms. He kissed the top of her head. "I think you've seen enough. Let's go back to bed. Or would you like to soak in the hot tub?"

She allowed him to lead her away, though she couldn't resist a last look at the room. The setup was incredible. What would it be like to be bound to that cross, to feel leather tresses striking her ass, her breasts....

She had told Cole about Slave Anna and her testimonials. She hadn't admitted her own strong reaction to a site she'd recently found where women were being trained as submissive sex slaves. Of course it wasn't real, she knew that, but she'd been riveted to the video clips, at once fascinated and horrified as she watched them bound and whipped for their Masters' pleasure.

She had tried to tell herself she wasn't interested in that sort of thing. Cole's brand of gentle dominance was much more to her taste. But what did she really know of Cole and his tastes? This dungeon wasn't the place of a casual player. He'd put a lot of time and money into building and stocking it, that was clear.

How many women had he used there, cuffed and spread, eager for the whip, the cane, his kiss? She followed him wordlessly back to the bedroom, distracted by her thoughts. They returned to the bed, Cole slipping out of his jeans to lie naked beside her.

"You're awfully quiet," he observed.

"I might want...to try it." She couldn't bring herself to say what she really wanted.

"Try what?" Damn it, why wouldn't he read her mind?

She tried again, embarrassed to be so tongue-tied and decidedly unused to it. "Um...You know. The stuff. In the playroom. Maybe try...something."

To her annoyed surprise, he shook his head. "No. Sorry. You're not ready."

"How do you know?" she retorted hotly.

He grinned sardonically at her, though his eyes were kind. "Well, for one thing, you can't even say what it is you want. Being chained to a cross and flogged is a far cry from a sensual spanking. Don't get me wrong, I love the exploration we're doing and I'm very willing to go as far as you're ready to go—when the time comes. It's not here yet, that's all. Trust me. If I took you in there now and gave you what you think you want, you'd freak out. Don't forget, just a month ago, you were horrified by the whole scene. Whips and chains, sadistic abuse of women, perversion...."

"That's because I didn't know any better," she snapped. "And who are you to tell me what I'm ready for? You don't own me."

As soon as the words were out of her mouth, she realized their import. His smile fell away, his eyes hooding. "No. Not yet."

~*~

Elizabeth glanced anxiously at her watch. It was already seven-fifteen and Cole had asked her to meet him for celebratory drinks at seven-thirty. He'd called her earlier that afternoon, excited to have just closed an important real estate deal he'd been working on for several months. It made her feel warm and happy that she was who he called with his good news. She'd assured him she would be there—no problem.

Tonight she'd promised herself she'd be gone by six, home in time to shower and change into something sexy before she met Cole at the Plaza. Now she'd just have to shoot over there in her work clothes and sensible pumps.

Inwardly she sighed—there was no helping it. When Gene Mueller, their prime candidate to replace Gary, had called back, agreeing to a second interview, she'd had to seize the moment. He was going to be out of town the next week, and she wanted to strike while the iron was hot, since he was up and away the best candidate they'd seen so far for the job. She hadn't bargained on his getting stuck behind an accident in the Holland Tunnel and being two hours late for the interview.

Art was holding forth about what the company had to offer the guy, should he come onboard. They all three knew it was a done deal at this point. They wanted him and he wanted them. Still, there was a certain rhythm and ritual to the interview process, and Art was making the most of it. Elizabeth tried to control her impatience, reminding herself the clients Mueller would bring with him were worth plenty, even if he never produced another campaign.

Not only that, once he was onboard, it would free up some of her time. She had promised both Cole and herself to pull back some. There was no real reason she had to put in the kind of hours she did—not anymore. Her one weakness, one she was quick to admit but loathe to address, was a difficulty delegating. She knew she needed to make the effort, not only to prevent burnout before she reached thirty-five, but because it was nearly impossible to sustain a personal relationship when one was always either at the office or passed out from sheer exhaustion.

She had been doing better this past week, leaving earlier than usual and, more often than not, going to Cole's place to spend the night. He still continued what she thought of as his gentle dominance. The thing was, as each day passed, she found herself wanting more. He'd laughed off her request to try a little experimenting in the playroom, which had pissed her off. He kept telling her she wasn't serious. What did he know about it?

He wasn't the one who woke up in a sweat, rope and leather weaving through her dreams, leaving her breathless. She loved when he used scarves to tie her wrists and ankles to his bedstead—somehow the feeling of helplessness heightened her sexual experience. And when he spanked her, which he had begun to do on a regular basis, sometimes so hard she was left with faint bruises, yes, it hurt, but it hurt so good.

Did that make her a masochist? Because she got off on the pain? It wasn't so simple, and she was beginning to appreciate that on a personal level now. Somehow during the course of the spanking the stinging pain of his palm seemed to shift, to metamorphose into a stinging pleasure. It wasn't that it no longer hurt—it was that she was beginning to experience the pain, or more accurately, the sensation, differently.

Whatever was happening, she knew the sex that followed the spanking sessions gave her the most intense, incredible orgasms she'd ever experienced in her life. She couldn't help but wonder how much more intense they might be after a sensual flogging, while bound to the X of the St. Andrew's Cross, or bent over the padded spanking bench in Cole's playroom.

"Don't you agree, Elizabeth?"

Elizabeth looked up, realizing she hadn't heard a word either man had said for the last five minutes. Hoping she wasn't agreeing to something she'd regret later, she smiled brightly and nodded. "Absolutely."

"Well then." Art stood and brushed at his pant legs. "Let's seal it with a drink, shall we? Maybe get some dinner. There's a Japanese place I've been wanting to try."

"Not me, thanks," Elizabeth said quickly. "I'm sorry." She smiled toward Gene, who smiled back. He was short and dumpy, his brown suit wrinkled and ill-fitting. Quite a far cry from the perfectly dressed and stylish Gary Dobbins.

Nevertheless, he had a brilliant reputation in the ad business, and from what she'd observed at their two interviews, would be a pleasure to work with.

She extended her hand and shook his warmly. "I'm very pleased you'll be coming onboard. I wish I could go out with the two of you tonight, but I've got a prior obligation."

"Not a problem," he assured her.

She finally made it to the Plaza and spied Cole sitting at the bar, talking to, or rather listening to, a very attractive if somewhat over-made-up lady who was leaning toward him, ample cleavage offered for his inspection. The woman put her hand on Cole's sleeve, tossed back her very expensively-dyed blonde hair and laughed a trilling little scale Elizabeth could hear from across the room.

Elizabeth experienced a twinge of jealousy, but she wasn't really threatened. Cole was just being polite, she was sure. She stood back a moment, admiring him from a distance. He looked so elegant in his suit—she was used to seeing him in jeans. She knew he dealt in million dollar real estate deals as a matter of course, and his apartment was located in one of the most expensive parts of Manhattan, but so far it hadn't made much of an impact.

Probably because of her busy schedule and limited time, so far they'd spent most of their time in bed, in the Jacuzzi or eating takeout at his kitchen table. This evening, seeing him in his suit, the elegant sapphire cufflinks on the fine white sleeves showing beneath a pearl gray silk suit that looked as if it had been tailor-made for him and probably had been, she was reminded this guy had some serious bucks.

She wondered how many women pursued him, not because they particularly cared about him as a man, but saw him as a meal ticket, a sugar daddy, a way out. She was glad she didn't even have to think about those kinds of things. She had her own money—she had her own life.

But she was very happy to have him in hers, however strange the events leading up to their meeting had been. Idly she wondered what had happened to Gary, though she was heartily glad to have seen the back of him. What was he doing now? Had he found a new job? Had he left the city? As far as she knew, he hadn't been hired at any of the Manhattan firms.

Elizabeth approached the bar. The woman pursed her lips, flashing daggers toward Elizabeth when she touched Cole's shoulder, as if to say, *he's mine. I got here first.*

At her touch, Cole turned to her and his face lit up, making her smile in return as warmth flooded her veins. "There you are." He stood and took Elizabeth's hand. She couldn't resist a triumphant glance at the blonde.

Ever the gentleman, Cole turned back toward the woman. "It was a pleasure meeting you. I hope you enjoy the rest of your evening." She gave him a tight smile that didn't reach her eyes, and turned toward the much older and less attractive man on her right.

A hostess appeared from nowhere to escort the two of them to a small, choice table near the window. Moments later two waiters appeared, one carrying a champagne bucket filled with ice, the other a bottle of fine champagne and two crystal flutes. The cork was popped and the glasses filled, then the waiters melted discreetly away.

Cole raised his glass. "To us." He smiled.

She raised her glass and then sipped at the champagne, which was dry and delicious.

"Got held up again, hmm?" Cole's voice was low, with no trace of reproach. Still, she glanced up sharply to see if he was upset.

"I'm really sorry," she began. "The guy we were interviewing was late and—"

Cole held up his hand to stop her. "It's okay, Elizabeth. I'm coming to understand this is just how it's going to be between us. I accept that. You've got your career and that comes first—"

"*No!*" Several people at nearby tables looked curiously at Elizabeth. Embarrassed, she lowered her voice, but went on. "No, it doesn't come first. I've been doing a lot of thinking, Cole. I want more. I want of the D/s lifestyle you keep dangling in front of me and then pulling away. I want to find out for myself. I want to experience the heightened sensations I've read about and heard about. Please. I'm sorry I was late tonight. You have to admit, I was doing much better all week."

Cole put his hand over hers. "It was never my intention to dangle the lifestyle at you and snatch it away. It's not like that. It's just…" he paused, as if gathering his thoughts. "…you can't do this piecemeal. Believe me, I know. Not and make it something meaningful. If you're serious about exploring the lifestyle, as you say, you have to be willing to make the commitment to it, and to me. It's not just something you sample on the weekends. At least, that's not what I want. Not with you."

"What are you saying—that you want me to quit my job?"

"Not at all. I don't want you to do anything you don't want to do, ever. It's just I honestly don't think it would be fair to you to expect you to learn to submit while trying to juggle the rest of your life. In order to do this right, to really give of yourself the one hundred percent I would require, you need concentrated, committed time to focus. For a few weeks at least, I would need your full attention, 24/7, to properly train you. Time you just don't have."

Elizabeth toyed with her glass, watching the bubbles. Did she really want what she claimed to want? To find out what it was like to submit completely to another person? To willingly give up power, or, as he put it, to agree to an exchange of power?

Because she liked the sexy spankings, did it really follow that she'd thrill to the whip or flogger, to being bound and at his mercy? If she didn't obey him, would she find herself in the cage?

Since she'd met Cole, she'd never felt more alive. And it wasn't just because he was fun and sexy and handsome. It was what he offered—what she'd barely tasted, but had whetted her appetite and left her ravenous for more. She did want it, she realized with a sudden, blinding clarity.

Slowly she looked up. He was watching her. She felt at once hot and cold, her bones melting as she lost herself in his mesmerizing gaze.

She took a resolute breath, set down her glass and put her hands, palms down on the table, looking him straight in the eye. "I want it. I want to explore it. To find out." Before he could object again, she hurried on.

"Listen. I have two weeks of vacation coming to me. I haven't had time to use it since I got there. But we've pretty much wrapped up the interview process for Gary's replacement, and he's joining the firm two weeks from this coming Friday. We're between any big pitches right now. In fact, this would be a perfect time for me to take my vacation. So what do you think? Is two weeks enough for me to know? Do you think you could stand to have me around for two solid weeks, 24/7?"

"I think I could handle it." He laughed, his eyes dancing. Sobering, he added, "Why don't we sleep on it? Check with your office, give the idea some time to percolate in your head. I have to go out of town for a few days on business. If by Saturday morning you still want this, then come to me. No briefcase, no cell phone, no agenda other than a sincere desire to submit. If you change your mind, or it's not the right time, we're the same as before, and I'm fine with that."

Elizabeth nodded. Though she didn't fully understand what she was committing to, she somehow knew with unerring certainty that nothing was ever going to be the same. She was excited, even exhilarated, about her decision, and she knew she wouldn't change her mind, no matter how many nights she slept on it. Still, she didn't press the issue. She'd finished out her work week, get Art's okay for a break, which he'd been encouraging to her to take anyway, and arrive at Cole's doorstep, ready to take that next thrilling step in this amazing sensual adventure.

Cole refilled their glasses. Elizabeth raised hers and, in a belated response to his earlier toast, echoed, "To us."

CHAPTER SIXTEEN

It had been easy to get the two weeks off, and though she had some qualms about being out of contact for so long with her team, she also knew it would be a good exercise for them to handle things without running to her for every little thing. And since they had no big projects on the table, it would mostly be business as usual, managing and maintaining their existing accounts.

While Cole was away she lay in her own bed each night, tossing and fitful as usual, she found herself reviewing the charred, pitted landscape of her failed relationships. Cole wasn't the first man she thought she was in love with. There had been several over the years, each one successful, confident, handsome and good in bed. So what had gone wrong? What was it that consigned each of Elizabeth's romantic connections to failure, sooner or later?

When she had engaged in this kind of introspection in the past, which wasn't often, she invariably blamed the guy, whether directly or indirectly. From the moment she met a man, she placed a metaphorical set of scales on his shoulders. One side was reserved for his good points, or, as she thought of them, his assets. The other would tally his weaknesses and failures.

Naturally the scales at first tipped heavily toward his assets, piled like little gold bars on the positive side. Invariably he would misstep, resulting in a shift in the balance toward the lumps of lead that weighed heavier than the gold of his merits. It could be something as significant as standing her up for a date or being a selfish lover, to revealing himself through a careless comment to be a bigot or a sexist, down something as innocuous as telling a tasteless joke that fell flat. Though it wasn't something she did consciously, she was merciless in dropping the little lead weights of his perceived failures onto the scale, until eventually, inevitably, it would tip into the negative, taking him down in the process.

Now, as she lay in bed alone, contemplating this new man in her life, and the step she was about to take in their exploration of D/s as a possible alternative lifestyle, she wondered how long it would be until the scales tipped against Cole.

And then something occurred to her, or rather, it hit her with a sudden, epiphany-like realization that had the force of a sucker punch to the gut. The reason her past relationships had all failed sooner or later wasn't because her men fucked up one time too many, but because she'd consigned them to failure from the outset, by definition.

From their inception, each relationship was doomed, because instead of falling in love with a man, with the whole fallible, imperfect man, she had fallen in love with a set of characteristics and expectations. Thus it was only a matter of time before the man shouldering her heavy scales would falter and, in her eyes, fail.

"It wasn't them. It was *me*."

She said this aloud, sitting up suddenly in her bed, the knowledge at once depressing and exciting her. Depressing because she was forced, for the first time, really, to admit she was the problem. She was the reason she had spent so many years feeling lonely and disconnected from others. Excited because she knew this time was different.

Cole Pearson was different.

Or was it that she was different?

Yes, he was certainly the most compelling, exciting man she had ever met. She was intrigued by everything about him. She found herself responding on the deepest level to the allure of what he offered, though she didn't yet fully understand the dynamics of a D/s relationship or how she would handle it when it was no longer a game.

As exciting as it was to contemplate the two-week experiment she was committing herself to, she recognized this wasn't just about exploring the intensity of experience he promised, or the thrill of something new.

It was also a new chance. A chance to redefine herself and the way she looked at men and relationships in general. She didn't have to keep a mental tally and pull the man down, even if only metaphorically, with the weights of her unspoken demands. She wanted to still herself, to let their love flow over her without grabbing it and twisting it into a death grip until she choked the life out of it.

Maybe, she thought to herself with a wry grin, *I'm growing up.*

In his absence, she hadn't been able to resist putting in a ridiculous number of extra hours in anticipation of her vacation, making sure everything was ready for her two-week hiatus from the job. Jane and Hank had finally barred her from their offices with a laugh. "Come on, Elizabeth. Give us a chance to do it on our own. We promise we won't destroy the place while you're gone. Have fun, relax, forget all about us."

She had told them she was going on a two-week cruise. Cole had suggested this, reminding her he wanted no interruptions from her office during their exploration, as he called it.

In the past week she'd begun to post comments on Slave Anna's blog, which had led to an email connection with the young woman. The more she got to know Anna personally, the more impressed she was with Anna's utter serenity. Hers seemed to be the mirror opposite of Elizabeth's frenetic, hectic-paced approach to life. Beyond that, she'd never seen anyone more in love. Elizabeth had no idea if Cole and she could achieve the sort of intense, deeply connected relationship Anna seemed to share with her Master, but she found herself willing, even eager, to try.

Now the time had come. She'd left away messages on her phone and email, closed up her apartment, packed only the clothing and sundries she'd need, and presented herself at Cole's door bright and early that Saturday morning, a suitcase in her hand and butterflies in her stomach.

They hadn't seen each other for five days. Elizabeth drank in the sight of him, tall and dark, red lips breaking into that lopsided smile over white teeth, his eyes like liquid onyx, raking over her with raw desire.

"Elizabeth." She could hear the longing contained in that one word, a longing that mirrored her own. He pulled her into his arms and kissed her, a long, lingering kiss that left her hungry for more. When he pulled away, she moved forward, her lips still parted, aching for the press of his.

"Greedy girl. There's time." He held her by the shoulders and again swept her body with his eyes. She was wearing a long, flowing black skirt with large white flowers painted in broad brushstrokes over the silky fabric. Her sheer white blouse was hidden beneath a lightweight black jacket.

He dropped her shoulders and stepped back. "Take off the jacket." She obeyed, the butterflies now doing loop-de-loops in her belly. The blouse was sheer and, per his instructions, she wore no bra beneath it. She was aware of the press of her nipples against the fabric, which stiffened further beneath his intense gaze.

"Are you wearing panties?"

She shook her head. He'd told her what to pack, and panties were not to be among the items, nor was she to wear any that morning. "Show me."

Heat rising in her cheeks, Elizabeth obeyed, feeling more like twelve than thirty at that moment. She lifted the hem of the long skirt, bunching it at her waist. Again per his instruction, she'd shaved her pubic area early that morning until she was smooth as a baby. She could feel the cool air stir against her naked sex, which served to emphasize her nudity.

He'd explained that, as his submissive-in-training for the coming two weeks, he would require complete access to every part of her body. While an aesthetic choice he found pleasing, shaving her pubic hair was also a symbolic gesture of her willingness to bare herself more completely for him.

She found herself so aroused during the grooming process in the shower, she'd had to masturbate immediately after, lying down on her bath rug, her body still damp, her mind filled with images from Slave Anna's photo gallery, and Cole's handsome face.

"Good. I'll inspect you later. For now, come over to the sofa." She let her skirt drop, his words reverberating in her head...*I'll inspect you later.* He led her by the hand and they sat together, side by side.

He turned to her. "I know we've talked about it a lot, but I want to ask you one more time if you're sure. Are you ready to submit to me? To agree to obey my rules for the next two weeks, to allow yourself to be led and used, trained and, if necessary, punished when you fail in your duties as a sub? Are you sure you're ready to explore a 24/7 D/s lifestyle? Because I want to reiterate, I'm happy with you now, just as things are. Yes, I'd like to go further, but only if you're one hundred percent sure it's what *you* want. I absolutely do not want you doing this for me. In fact, I wouldn't permit that. It's a sure recipe for failure."

Elizabeth didn't need to think it over. She'd made her decision. She wanted this, she realized, more than anything she'd ever wanted in her life. She knew it might not work. She knew she might be too willful and headstrong to make a good sub. Anna had advised her how difficult submission could sometimes be.

It's not just about the sex, Elizabeth, Anna had written to her in an email she'd read many times over. *Make sure you're clear on that. If he's a real Dom, and from what you've told me, I think he is, he's going to test you in ways that are going to push not only your sensual envelope, but all aspects of who you think you are and what you want and what you're willing to do to prove it. To submit is to give of yourself, one hundred percent. It's to bare not only your body, but your soul.*

But I can tell you this. If you can find the courage to do it, to really give of yourself on every level to the man you love, you will find such peace, such a heightened sense of self and self-worth, that you'll never want to go back to vanilla. You won't be able to. You will become something other than you are now. Or rather, something more. Your submission will become a part of you, and you will become a part of your Master.

I know that sounds very metaphysical and poetic, but, if this is right for you, you'll understand what I mean. You'll have to find out for yourself. Just remember, be honest with him. And with yourself. This lifestyle is definitely not for everyone. You'll know if it's for you.

Good luck on your journey! Love, Anna

Now Elizabeth turned to Cole and smiled. "Yes. I want it. I want to try—for me."

Cole reached for her, gathering her into his arms. "I love you," he whispered.

~*~

He let her go, ignoring for the moment his insistent erection. She hadn't answered in kind, at least not with words, but he was okay with that. She was here. That was enough.

He could hardly believe this was actually happening. He reminded himself not to project or hang on to unrealistic expectations. This whole thing might end up being a big mistake. Instead of taking her deeper into a true D/s relationship, he might alienate her to the point he'd lose her altogether.

It was a risk he had to take. Not only for her, but for himself. He'd tried twice before to train a woman as a submissive, and each time had ended, if not precisely in failure, in falling far short of the mark. He knew it was because he'd wanted the connection more than he'd wanted the woman he'd chosen.

In that regard he'd been unfair, though at the time he'd thought he could make it work. His desire had overrun his better judgment. He understood now love was an essential ingredient, at least for him, in any meaningful D/s connection. He hadn't loved either of those other women, though he'd tried to and nearly convinced himself of it each time.

He hadn't planned to say those words to her.

I love you.

He understood the love was new, tentative, not yet cemented by time and experience. Nonetheless, like a sapling that would one day be a huge oak, he felt the sturdy roots of that love burrowing into his heart.

He recognized these two weeks she'd given him were a gift—a gift of time he planned to exploit to the fullest. By the end of it she would either belong to him completely, or they would go their separate ways. He already knew there was no going back. He wondered if she knew and for a moment he was frightened. The thought of losing her was intolerable.

He pulled himself together, reminding himself of the code he lived by in all other areas of his life. A code that had stood him well—*failure is not an option*. Thus fortified, he turned to Elizabeth, aware after this moment, nothing between them would ever be the same.

"Stand up."

Elizabeth obeyed without hesitation, which pleased him. He was aware of her correspondence with the submissive online and approved of it. The more Elizabeth understood about the lifestyle, the better their chances of success.

He leaned back against the sofa, admiring the shadow of her nipples jutting against silk, and the rounded curve of her cheeks, flushed a faint pink. She was twisting her hands agitatedly in front of her body. He could feel her tension and nervous anticipation.

"Hands at your sides. For now I just want you to listen." He waited while she obeyed. "Close your eyes and take several deep, slow breaths. I want you to calm yourself. It's a skill you're going to need as we move forward. An ability to calm down when you're over-excited or frightened. I'll be here every step of the way, but I want you to empower yourself as well. Okay?"

She nodded and closed her eyes. He waited several seconds while she breathed slowly and deeply. When she opened her eyes, he continued. "There are certain basic ground rules I expect you to follow during this training period. You need to let go of the idea of us as lovers and accept your place as my submissive-in-training. What that means if you're voluntarily giving up control over just about every aspect of your life. A voluntary exchange of power.

"At first we'll just work on the basics, things like positions, commands, expected behavior when you're with me and when you're alone. I'm sure this is familiar to you, given your research and interaction online."

Elizabeth nodded. Cole continued. "The most important part of being a submissive is adopting a submissive mindset. It's a breaking down of ego—a giving up of self. There are certain rules and rituals that will not only enhance our experience, but will help you get there.

"First of all is trust. You need to trust both me and yourself. You need to be aware of your reactions and your feelings, and you need to be willing to share them with me. This is a process and nothing's written in stone. We'll be exploring together. I don't want a mindless robotic fuck slut. Ultimately I want a lover, a submissive lover who helps me create the perfect circle of our love—the yin and yang as I once mentioned to you."

He gave a small laugh. "I'm lecturing. Forgive me. You ready to get started?"

"Yes." She caught her lip nervously in her lower teeth.

"Excellent. First off, take of your clothes. You'll be naked for most of the next two weeks. Then kneel, ass resting on your heels, thighs spread apart, hands palms up on your thighs. When I tell you to kneel and present, I expect you to assume this position immediately."

He waited while she slipped out of her clothing, his mouth watering and cock straining as her lovely body was bared to him. Her face, pink before, was now red with embarrassment. She parted her legs, but barely, and her back was hunched.

She was still modest, excessively so. He would need to desensitize her. "Straighten your back, chin up, eyes on the floor. A sub is proud and your bearing should reflect that at all times." She made an effort to comply.

"Spread your legs wide. As wide as you can. Arch your back and thrust out your pelvis. I want to see that cunt."

She looked up sharply. "Hey," she blurted. "I don't like that."

"You don't like what?"

"That word. It's demeaning."

"No. It's not. It's been demeaned by its use and the connotations associated with it, but cunt in and of itself is nothing more than a word. A good, earthy word for the most beautiful, sensual part of your body. There's power in the word. Sometimes you will be reduced to nothing more than a cunt. That is, you'll become sheer lust—controlled and defined by your sex and your appetites. You'll be my sub, my cunt, my perfect whore, my possession, the object of my adoration."

He waited, wondering if she understood what he was saying, if she could someday believe it too. She said nothing. Adding steel to his voice, though he didn't raise it, Cole ordered, "Elizabeth, show me your cunt. Now." She stared at him, her eyes flashing. He stared back, willing her to bend. It was her first test, and had come sooner than he'd expected.

"Eyes on the floor," he reminded her. "Spread your legs. Then use your hands. Arch your back and spread your cunt for me. It's a gesture of submission. You say you want what I offer. If you can't obey this simple dictate, it tells me you don't really want this. In which case, we might as well forget this whole thing and go back to vanilla with the occasional spice."

Could he do that? He was convinced—she was the one— the one he'd been looking for, dreaming of, longing for. Was he going to lose her before they even started? The thought was nearly unbearable. Silently he cursed himself. Yet there was no going back. If he relented now, she would never respect him as a Dom, nor should she.

She held his gaze for several heart-stopping moments, her cheeks flaming with color, her hands clenched into fists on her thighs. Then she obeyed, dropping her head, reaching with trembling fingers to spread herself for him.

He let out his breath, which he hadn't realized he'd been holding. It was a small victory, but an essential one. He kept his face impassive and turned his attention to her spread pussy. She was lovely, the spread folds of her labia peeking between her fingers. It was all he could do to stop himself from lifting her off the floor and fucking her then and there.

Instead he said, "Good. Very good. I know this is hard for you. You have a strong will and some modesty issues. We'll work on that. Modesty has no place between a Dom and his sub. I'm sure you understand that, but you have a lifetime of ingrained behavior to break down and reshape. You can let go of your cunt now, but keep your legs spread."

He slid from the couch and knelt beside her, unable to keep from touching her. "Stay in position," he whispered, "hands on your thighs, head down, eyes on the floor." He kissed her cheek, which was warm from her lingering blush. Wrapping his arm around her, he reached for her smooth cunt and stroked the outer labia. She shivered and leaned against him.

"Stay still," he admonished. "Back straight." She obeyed. She was breathing rapidly. He reached for her pussy, this time pressing a finger inside her. She was wet, not just moist, but slick and slippery with desire. However much she protested or blushed, this was turning her on.

He drew his finger out and up, adding another as he slid in sensuous circles over her vulva. She shuddered and twitched beneath his fingers. "That's my cunt now," he whispered close to her ear. "That means it's my orgasm. You will never, ever come without my permission and without me being there. Understand?"

She nodded, her hips thrusting forward. He pulled his hand away and shook his head. *"My* orgasm. I'll give it to you when you earn it. Not a second before. It might be hours or even days before you earn that privilege."

Elizabeth's eyes were closed, her chest heaving. Unable to resist, he slipped his hand once more into her sticky sweetness and rubbed until she was moaning and trying to impale herself on him. Though always responsive, she'd never displayed such wanton abandon.

A small blinding rush of hope burst inside him like a flame—she wanted this. Not just to please him. Her reactions now, so early in their training, said more than any words could have. She began a steady, convulsive shudder, her labia swollen and hot beneath his fingers. Coming to himself, he pulled his hand away and moved from her.

She opened her eyes, their expression pleading. "Don't stop," she begged. "I'm so close."

He hoisted himself back onto the sofa and shook his head. "I told you. You have to earn it. Now compose yourself." He watched as a storm of emotions hurtled over her face. Elizabeth was not used to being denied, that much was clear. Yet it was also evident she wanted to obey and was taking this seriously. He waited to see which side in her won—the greedy slut girl or the fledgling sub.

She closed her eyes and began to breathe in a deep, regular pattern. The high flush receded on her cheeks and her shoulders eased, her back straightening. When she opened her eyes, her expression was calm.

Though impressed, Cole didn't comment directly on her level of control. "Are you ready now to hear the rules?"

"Yes."

"There aren't too many, but I do expect you to follow these to the letter, or accept that you'll be punished." Her eyes widened, the pupils dilating and again she bit her lower bit, but remained silent.

"The first rule is to demonstrate respect at all times. I don't personally care to be called Master. You may address me as Cole or as Sir, as it suits you. So, just now, when I asked you a question, your answer should have been, 'Yes, Cole', or 'Yes, Sir.' Got it?"

"Yes, Sir."

He nodded, pleased she'd chosen the more formal title. "Rule number two—you are never, ever to touch yourself sexually without my express permission. I catch you doing that and you'll be soundly punished." She thrust her chin forward in a gesture he was coming to recognize as defiance, but she made no overt protest. He let it pass.

"Rule number three—you don't orgasm without asking my permission first. That's to remind you your body belongs to me—I will control the level of pleasure and pain." Her eyes widened again but she said nothing.

He continued. "The most important rule of all, as far as I'm concerned, is open communication. Any time you feel uncomfortable or scared or confused, talk to me. You don't have to wait to speak until spoken to or any of that crap. I'm taking you at your word that you really want to explore the full potential of a D/s relationship, and that means I'm going to be taking you to places you aren't comfortable with.

"So I expect you to speak up if you're having a hard time, okay? That doesn't necessarily mean I'll stop whatever I'm doing, but I want to know where your head is at all times. And when I ask you to process the experience with me after a session, I want open, honest answers. Not what you think I want to hear, but what's really going on inside your head."

She looked so serious, staring solemnly at him. Should he have left things as they were—casual spanking games and light bondage? Had he let his own selfish desire to own her convince him she wanted this as much as he did?

"Hey," he said gently, trying inwardly to calm his own fears. "Come here." He reached out for her and she rose gracefully and moved toward him. He pulled her down onto his lap.

She nuzzled against his neck. "It's going to be intense, but I also want it to be fun. I want you to enjoy the experience, okay? Is it what you're expecting so far? I am going too fast for you?"

She pulled back to look at him. "I want this, Cole. I had a lot of time to think while you were gone. I've been..." she seemed to be searching for the word and then she found it, "...disconnected. Not just from the men in my life, but from myself. I don't know how to describe it, but since I've been with you, since we've begun to experiment with D/s and erotic submission, I've come alive. I feel vital and excited. I want to go further. I want to find out more. Yes, I know I'm going to fuck up probably, but you have to trust me too, okay? I'm not doing this to please you. I'm doing it because I want it. I want what you offer."

She paused and he waited, certain she was going to say she loved him, aching to hear it. "I trust you." After a beat she grinned, adding, "Sir."

CHAPTER SEVENTEEN

Elizabeth stared around the room, her eyes darting from here to there like a hummingbird. He hadn't taken her back to see it since the one and only time he'd showed it to her. This time she noticed the recessed lighting along the ceiling, casting a warm, soothing glow over the room. The floor was covered in thick, soft carpet, its weave dense and fine. She noticed the leather cuffs dangling from chains hanging from the cement beam were lined with white, soft-looking wool. The restraint table and spanking horse were padded with cushioned leather. The dichotomy of making sure the subject was comfortable while being sexually tortured was not lost on her.

"Safeword." Cole pulled her from her introspection. "You're familiar with the term?"

"Yes. Slave Anna's is pickle." Elizabeth grinned, though she was nervous at the thought of needing such an escape route. Would things get so intense with Cole she'd be forced to cry out for him to stop?

Cole read her mind, as he so often seemed to. "I hope you'll never need to use it with me, and if you do come, in time, to truly belong to me, you won't. But for now, while we're still learning each other's rhythms and tolerance, your safeword is red light. I like keeping things simple. You're only to use it if you absolutely can't handle what's happening. It's a panic button, and as such, I trust you won't use it lightly. If you do, the action will stop at once, and we'll regroup and figure out what went wrong.

"You can say 'yellow light' if you feel you're nearing the edge of what you can tolerate, and just need me to ease back a little. But remember, safewords are a last resort. You can always just talk to me—communicate. Tell me you're having a hard time or need me to back off. I'll be listening to you. And not just your words, but your body language, too. Okay?"

"Yes," Elizabeth said, belatedly adding, "Sir." Cole smiled faintly but said nothing. He advanced into the room and she followed. It was strange to be naked while he was fully clothed. She felt vulnerable and not a little nervous, but also aroused. Her pussy still throbbed from his touch. Being told to stay still in that subservient position while he manhandled her sex had created a deep, pulling ache of desire inside her. It had taken every ounce of control not to finish the job when he took his hand away. Intellectually, she understood the lessons—self-control and obedience—but that hadn't made it any easier.

"You'll become intimately acquainted with every device in this room by the end of these two weeks." Cole walked toward the large cross shaped like a big X, Elizabeth following a pace behind. As they came closer she saw it was covered in soft black leather. "This is called a St. Andrew's Cross. Its double frame construction allows the arm, leg, waist and chest straps to be adjusted in height to suit any size person." He pointed to the wide leather straps hanging at intervals along the cross. Elizabeth wrapped her arms around herself protectively.

To her relief, he moved past the cross. "This is a spanking horse. You can either lie across or along its length, depending on what I want to do to you. You'll notice those D rings," he pointed to large metal rings attached midway on the legs. "Those are for the wrist and ankle cuffs when I want to secure you."

"What's *that*?" Elizabeth breathed, staring at what looked like a medical inversion table, only decidedly more diabolical. She hadn't noticed this particular piece of furniture on her first visit.

"Ah." Cole's eyes lit up and he flashed an evil smile. "That's my newest toy. I can't wait to try it out. It's called an inversion rack. The leg frames are adjustable and the whole frame can be tilted to 180 degrees."

Imagining herself strapped onto the rack, tilted upside down, her legs forced wide apart, sent a cold finger of fear down her spine. "Oh, Cole. I couldn't…you wouldn't…" Her mouth was dry and she found herself backing away, toward the door.

In a moment he was beside her, taking her into his arms. "You could and you would. You will. But not yet." He kissed the top of her head and held her close. She relaxed in his arms. "Not until you're ready. We'll both know when that is, I promise."

He let her go and stepped back. "For now, we're going to start with something you're more used to. The spanking horse. The only difference is, instead of being draped over my lap, you'll be bound to the horse. I'm going to cuff your ankles and wrists to give you a taste of bondage. It also helps to keep you still and accessible for me."

Elizabeth's ass actually tingled with anticipation. She was nervous at the thought of being bound by her wrists and ankles, but at the same time she was excited. He positioned her across the horse and moved around to face her. "Grab hold of the legs." Something in his voice was different, less tender than a moment before.

Her heart speeding, she did as he said, hoisting herself forward so she was balanced on the horse at her midriff, her breasts hanging over the rounded edge, her hair falling into her face. Cole slipped leather cuffs over her wrists and ankles and clipped them to the D rings along the metal legs, locking her in place.

He moved behind her. Elizabeth's legs were spread wide. Her heart was pounding, her breath ragged, though he'd yet to touch her. She tugged experimentally at her bonds—she was well and truly helpless.

She jumped when his hand caressed her ass. "Shh," he whispered. "You're perfect. You're beautiful. Relax and give yourself to me. This isn't just about teaching you the pleasure of pain. It's about service. It pleases me to bind and expose you like this. It turns me on. I love the feel of your soft skin against my palm, the way your flesh moves, the sounds you make." As he spoke, he dropped his hand between her legs, caressing and cupping her splayed pussy.

"You're soaking wet," he observed with a small, pleased laugh. She shuddered as his fingers slipped into her passage, drawing a moan from her lips. Unable to control herself, she pressed back against his hand, as much as she was able in her bound position.

He stroked her, moving with butterfly softness over her clit while she whimpered with need. "You ready? I'm just going to use my hand, to start."

"To start?" she said faintly.

"That's right. Where we finish is up to you."

At first his touch was light. It stung, but not too much. Her pussy still throbbed at the memory of his fingers, though his hard palm distracted her. She felt the sharp sting of his hand along her inner thighs. Perversely, her pussy ached so much she thought even a smack on the tender folds would be better than no attention at all. She arched back, sticking out her bottom, further exposing her bared sex.

Obligingly he smacked it. Elizabeth squealed. He refocused on her ass, striking her harder. The sting at her sex seemed to melt into pure desire. She arched back again but was ignored, as Cole focused on her ass and inner thighs.

"Ow, it *hurts*."

He didn't respond, except by hitting her harder. She began to jerk in her bonds, but her own position, bent over the spanking horse as she was, kept her stable. "Please, please, oh, oh, oh…"

"Please what?"

"Please…" she didn't say what she really wanted, too shy, too confused to even admit it to herself. He continued to smack her ass, the sting shifting to fire, nearly too much to tolerate. At the same time, her sex was on fire of a different kind. She thrust it back at him, too hot to care what a lewd picture she must present.

"Please what? Say what you want, Elizabeth. Tell me. Say what you *need*."

She gasped as his fingers grazed her spread sex, teasing her, driving her wild. "Please, yes…" she whispered, unable to finish the sentence. How could she admit what she wanted? She could barely believe herself that she did want it, yet the ache in her pussy was nearly intolerable. She had to have it.

"I want," she said raggedly, trying to catch her breath. He smacked her ass, the force of his palm thrusting her body hard against the padded horse.

"Say it. Say the words."

"I want…for you to…smack my pussy." Jesus. Had she really just asked for that? Was she out of her mind? Yet she did want it. She wanted to feel the sting again, to experience the rapid metamorphosis to heat, to lust, to raw desire.

"Good girl. Always ask me for what you want. And remember, I'll always give you what you need." He smacked her sex, much harder than the first time. She gasped, a sudden sharp intake of breath. He smacked it again, though this time he let his fingers glide, catching and stroking her hooded clit. Waves of pleasure and pain whirled and eddied together, creating a combined sensation that was like nothing she had ever experienced.

Again he smacked her pussy, a rapid succession of hard slaps, the sound echoing wetly in the room. While she panted and whimpered, he drew his fingers along her inner thigh, still stinging from his earlier attentions. His fingers were wet, wet with her lust.

He returned his focus to her ass, methodically covering every square inch of her flesh with his hard, cupped palm until she was nearly in tears, her eyes squeezed tight, her fingers clenched around the metal legs of the horse. Just when she was about to cry out, *yellow light*, he began to caress and stroke her pussy, two fingers slipping into her wetness. She groaned, thrusting back against him

"Please," she murmured, only realizing after she'd said it that she'd spoken aloud.

"Please, what?" He drew his fingers up over her clit, rubbing in lazy, tantalizing circles around it.

"Fuck me. Please." He didn't respond. She thrust herself back against his hand, desperate for him. "Cock. I want your cock. I *need* it. Please." His hand fell away. She squirmed, whimpering with frustration and lust. She heard him behind her, the zipper of his fly, the shuffling sound of his jeans being kicked off, the tear of a plastic condom wrapper. She waited to feel his hands at her ankles, releasing her legs, and then her wrists. She expected him to take her into his arms and lower her to the soft carpet so they could make love. She was so aroused she couldn't help but squirm with anticipation.

But he didn't release her. She felt him behind her, crouching, his cock nudging between her cheeks, the tip touching her asshole, then sliding lower, pressing into her, filling her before she even realized what was happening.

She grunted, her body struggling to accommodate the sudden fullness. He gripped her hips and thrust hard against her. His movements caused her swollen clit to rub against the soft leather of the horse. Almost at once she began to climax, mewling her ecstasy with each perfect thrust.

"Oh God, oh, oh, oh..." The orgasm that overtook her was so violent she would have collapsed, had she not been held bound and bent by her position. She came to herself in time to be aware of Cole's shuddering climax, his fingers digging sharply into her shoulders as he slammed ruthlessly into her.

He leaned heavily against her. Their bodies were slick with sweat, his chest slippery against her bare back. He wrapped his arms around her and found and cupped her breasts in his hands. She could feel his heart thumping against her. She hung limp, completely spent.

She must have dozed a second or a minute, she didn't know for sure. She was cold, the sweat drying on her back making her shiver. Cole had stepped away from her. He stroked her calves, his hands running down her legs until they arrived at the leather cuffs. He released her ankles and a moment later her wrists.

He moved again behind her and helped her to stand, turning her as he did so she was facing him. She reached to hug him but her arms were weak and she let them drop to her sides. He wrapped his arms around her and lowered them both to the ground, cradling her on his lap.

Elizabeth was overwhelmed with emotions she couldn't yet sort through, confused, thrilled, elated, embarrassed, grateful. Grateful? She leaned her head back against the crook of Cole's strong arm and looked into his face. He was regarding her with a warm smile, though his black liquid eyes seemed lit from behind with a smoldering fire.

"Talk to me. Tell me what you're feeling."

Elizabeth was not used to telling men what she was feeling. She would gladly tell them what she was thinking, and had a strong opinion on everything. But feeling…deep inside, those feelings that were at once frightening, erotic and deeply compelling. How did she describe them? And what would he think of her if she did?

He was watching her, willing her to speak. She could feel his command, his control, emanating from him with a radiance that warmed her. She had the sudden odd desire to slip from his lap and kneel in front of him, dropping her forehead to the ground in homage—recognition of his mastery over her. The feeling was alien and not altogether comfortable.

Elizabeth was used to men kneeling at *her* feet, figuratively speaking. She bestowed the gift of her body and her sexual favors upon them. She had certainly never felt *grateful* after sex with other men. Cole had bound her in a humiliating position, exposing her pussy and asshole, leaving her vulnerable, squealing and jerking in her cuffs while he smacked her ass and pussy until she nearly cried.

Totally uncharacteristically, she'd pleaded with him fuck her, desperate for him, begging for cock like some kind of slut until he slammed into her, taking his pleasure with almost ferocious force. A lifetime of conditioning told her She knew she should be humiliated, angered to have been treated this way. But she wasn't. Not if she were honest. No. She was deeply, profoundly grateful. And she just didn't get it.

Cole was regarding her with a raised eyebrow. She tried to think how to put her feelings into words. A part of her resisted—to admit how strongly he had affected her was to give in, to give him power over her she wasn't sure she was ready to surrender. It was one thing to give her body—quite another to share her secrets.

"You're holding back. I don't want that." Cole shifted, pushing her gently from his lap "If you really want to experience erotic submission as you claim, you have to let go of your reserve. I understand it's still new, but I when I said I wanted to claim you, I mean all of you. I want to possess you. For that exchange of power to truly take place, you have to bare your heart and your soul to me, not just your body. Otherwise, it's just a game."

"I'm sorry," she finally ventured. "I can't. I mean, not yet. I'm not ready to talk about it."

She saw the disappointment in his eyes and felt ashamed, but still she couldn't seem to give words to her feelings. Cole's voice was gentle, perhaps a little sad, though he smiled at her. "Okay. We've got time."

He stood, magnificent in his nudity, his form long and shapely, the muscles sharply defined beneath the soft mat of dark curling hair on his chest and legs. Again the strange urge to kneel before him assailed her. He held out his hand and she took it, allowing him to hoist her up. She reached for him, expecting him to fold her into his arms. Instead he stepped back, shaking his head. "You were very naughty, you know."

"What do you mean?"

"Rule number three. You broke it. And you know what happens to sub girls who break the rules, right?"

"Rule number three?" Elizabeth thought back frantically to the rules he'd laid out before bringing her into the playroom. *Respect, no masturbation…permission to come…shit…*

That was hardly fair. It had snuck up on her, tearing through her before she even knew what was happening, much less had time to ask Cole for permission for something she couldn't have prevented if she'd tried. She opened her mouth to protest but he stopped her.

"No, I don't want to hear any excuses. Rule number three—no orgasm without permission. It's really very simple." His smile was cruel though his eyes were dancing. "You were a bad girl, now you'll be punished."

Reflexively she glanced toward the puppy cage and quickly away. "Cole…"

He had followed her glance. "No, not that. You'd have to willfully break the rules to deserve the cage. This infraction was due to lack of training. You simply forgot, am I right?"

Elizabeth nodded, glad he understood this. "Nevertheless," he continued, as he moved to pull on his jeans, "you will suffer the consequences of your behavior." He stroked his chin as he eyed her. "I just need to think of the appropriate correction. From your response on the horse, a spanking is clearly *not* a punishment, not even on your cunt." Elizabeth began to blush, though she couldn't deny what he said was true.

"I know what we'll do. We'll combine correction with a lesson in the surrendering of your modesty. You have a gorgeous body but you aren't yet comfortable with displaying it for me on command. We'll work on that. For your punishment and my pleasure, you'll masturbate for me."

She'd been with guys before who wanted to see her play with herself and she'd always refused—end of discussion. Cole was right—as odd as it seemed in light of what had just taken place between them, with her bound and spread, she was, at her core, deeply modest. No way in hell would she bare her newly denuded pussy for his scrutiny while she made herself come. She wasn't even sure she could come that way in front of someone else. The very thought made her anxious.

"No." The word burst from her lips before she realized she was speaking.

"No?" Cole's eyebrows raised and then knit over his eyes. He glowered at her. "Have you forgotten yourself so soon? I wasn't asking you, sub girl. I was telling you." He put his hands on his hips and regarded her steadily until she looked away.

"Here's the deal. You've got five minutes. I'm going to go into my study and give you some time to think this over. When the five minutes are up, I expect to find you in my bed, naked, your legs spread, your hand on your cunt. If I don't find you in that position, it will be because you've reconsidered what you really want. In which case, we'll stop the training immediately and figure out where we go from here. That's not a threat. But if you can't obey my direction, and you can't talk to me and tell me what you're feeling, we might as well accept this isn't going to work."

Without giving her a chance to respond, Cole turned on his heel and was gone.

CHAPTER EIGHTEEN

Elizabeth lay in the center of Cole's bed, arguing with herself. What was it about him that made her so desperate to please him? If it had been anyone else, would she be there now, naked and nervous, though undeniably aroused by her predicament?

Was it just because he had managed to tap into this secret well of submissive, masochistic longing within her? Was she only using him in a way, to seek that intensity of experience?

No.

It was him, or more accurately it was them. Them together. Somehow, when she was with him, she felt safe. Calm. She was able to slow down, to still her normally racing thoughts. And beyond that, she felt as if she knew him. As if she could feel his feelings, sense his moods, experience his elation and disappointment. It wasn't just that he understood her. On some indefinable level, she understood him just as completely.

Was this what he meant by the yin and the yang? A dovetailing of two people, winging around one another in a symbolic circle so complete they didn't need anyone else? Was this the stuff of fairytales and romance novels? Could it be real? Could it be sustained?

He'd whispered he loved her. She hadn't responded in kind, not because she didn't, but because he'd taken her by surprise. Those three words, words they hadn't yet said to one another in all the weeks they'd been together, had slipped past her brain, lodging in her bones, her blood, her skin, her heart.

He loved her. And, for these two weeks at least, she'd consigned herself to him—her body, her will, her separateness as a person. The session with the spanking horse had been amazing. Beyond amazing—it had stunned her. Not the spanking itself, though she had to admit that had been incredibly sexy and hot, but even more so her reaction to it.

To be bound and at his mercy, forced to yield to him, unable to stop him. Rather than just suffering through it as an act of submission, she had burst through it, burst through the pain into something she hadn't expected. She had entered an altered state—yes, that was it. Pain and pleasure were no longer clearly defined or separated. Sensation was heightened to an exquisite degree. But there was even more going on. She couldn't yet articulate it, but she knew she felt—liberated. Yes. That was it. But why?

She found herself ready to talk now, even eager. She wanted to explore these strange new feelings with the man who had brought them about. He would understand. He wouldn't think she was sick or crazy. He would help her explore what was happening inside her head.

But Cole didn't want her to talk. She was going to be punished—no, *corrected*. He wanted her to make herself come for him. Though she knew performing such an intimate act while he watched was going to embarrass the crap out of her, she couldn't deny the throb in her sex.

I can do this, she assured herself. *I want to do this—for him.*

As if on cue, Cole entered the bedroom. He was still barechested, his jeans slung low over his narrow hips. Quickly Elizabeth spread her legs as he had told her she must, covering her bare pussy with her hand.

He stood still just inside the door. She saw the flash of relief washing over his face and realized he'd come in possibly expecting her to have remained defiant. Would he have stopped the training then, as he'd claimed he would? Could they really go back to what they'd had before? She wasn't sure they could, but had no intention of finding out. She would submit to her correction and continue with the training. The thought of anything less was, she realized, out of the question, at least for her. She wanted this—bad.

He was watching her with eyes as black as the bottom of a lake. "Put your hands behind your head and bend your knees, feet flat on the bed. Spread your thighs as far apart as you can so I can see your cunt and your ass. It's time for that inspection I promised you. I'm going to make sure you're properly groomed."

To her extreme dismay, she now saw he was holding a large magnifying glass. Surely he didn't intend to use it on her? Though she was reasonably comfortable with being naked, she'd never permitted a man to examine her pussy and certainly not her asshole, in such a clinical fashion. She was nearly faint with apprehension. "But you said…"

"Don't worry about what I said. You do as you're told. I'm pleased I found you in the position I told you to be in. That was good. Now I've given you a new direction. The proper response is, 'Yes, Sir,' and then you do as you're told. You don't question me or remind me I said something else. You obey. Got it?"

She'd already defied him twice in the few hours since she'd arrived. Somehow she sensed that three times would mean she was out. Closing her eyes, trying to ignore the heat surging over her cheeks and along her throat, she assumed the position.

~*~

Cole watched from the doorway, trying not to smile. She looked so pitiful, her expression pleading, that he very nearly relented, but he knew to do so would do her a disservice. She had said repeatedly she really wanted this training and he was damned if he'd do any less than his very best to give it to her.

Not to mention it was fun and, yes, even thrilling. He'd nearly come just from looking at her bound against the spanking horse, her shapely ass thrust out at him, her legs spread wide, that hot little cunt peeking between her legs, beckoning him like a dripping honeycomb to a bee.

Each shiver, startled cry and moan was like a direct caress to his rigid cock. He'd given her a thorough spanking, watching her soft, fair skin turn from white to pink to heated red. And though she wriggled and yelped when he smacked her pussy, at the same time she was sopping wet and moans of passion were intermingled with her cries.

She'd orgasmed within minutes of his entering her slick passage, which gripped and held him like a satin-lined glove. Though of course he'd had to call her to task for coming without permission, in fact her raw, intense climax had driven him over the edge himself. Each of her responses so far had been heartfelt and genuine. He was convinced she had the potential to be a true sub, just waiting like a budding flower to come into her own.

He had been disappointed when she outright refused to talk about her experience, especially because it was clear to him she needed to process what she was feeling. But he would be patient. After all, it was only the first day.

Now he advanced into the room, noting her reddening cheeks and her eyes squeezed tightly shut as if she were expecting a blow or a slap in the face. He sat beside her and stroked one soft breast. "Hey. Take it easy. This is a just a lesson. A lesson to help desensitize you from this modesty about your body. Remember, if you're to become mine, truly mine, then your body must also belong to me. No reservations. No hesitation when I ask you to present or display yourself.

"The position you're in now is called the present position. It's one of four present positions you'll learn to assume when I ask you to. These positions give me the best access to inspect your body and satisfy myself you're properly groomed and cared for. When you're fully trained, I'll expect you to assume the requested position immediately, no matter what else you might be doing at the time."

Her eyes remained shut but at least she wasn't squeezing them tight any more. He stroked her cheek, moving a tendril of shiny, thick hair and tucking it behind her ear. He dropped his hand to her chest. He could feel her heart beating rapidly. To her credit, she'd kept her legs bent and spread wide during his mini-lecture. "Calm yourself. Deep, slow breaths. Yes. Another. Easy and slow. You want to do this for me—I know you do. You want to give yourself in a way you've never been able to with another man."

For nearly a minute he stroked her cheek, her neck, her round, soft breasts, urging her to slow her breathing and calm herself. When he was satisfied, he said, "Open your eyes. Look at me." She obeyed and even managed a small smile. He smiled back and kissed her cheek.

"Good girl. Now keep your legs spread. I'm going to examine your cunt and your ass. Don't move, no matter what I do." She swallowed hard and squeezed her eyes shut again. He let it pass, secretly finding her shyness adorable.

Crouching between her legs, he lifted the powerful magnifying glass and focused on the delicate petals of her sex. The inner labia folded over at the top, like iris blossoms. They were dark pink, tinged with purple. He moved the glass and inhaled the sensuous, alluring aroma, resisting a desire to lick along the folds.

Forcing himself to focus on the task at hand, he repositioned the magnifying glass and scrutinized her pudendum for any errant hair or stubble. To her credit, she'd done an excellent job of grooming. Her skin was soft and smooth. He ran his fingers lightly over her mons and outer labia. She shivered sensuously at his touch, a soft moan issuing from her lips.

Glancing at her face, noting her eyes were still closed, he permitted himself a smile. However embarrassed she was, she was also aroused. Just another indication of her submissive state of mind—where erotic humiliation at once embarrassed and aroused. Using the tip of one finger, he circled her entrance and gently dipped into it. Tight, wet muscle gripped his finger and again she moaned.

He withdrew the finger, licked it and touched the tiny puckered entrance between her ass cheeks. She flinched, though she kept her position. He circled the tight asterisk with his wet finger and then carefully pushed it inside. Elizabeth jerked and gave a small gasp.

"Have you been fucked in the ass before, Elizabeth?"

"Yes. I didn't like it. It hurt."

"You'll learn to like it. In fact, you'll learn to love it. Not only the submissive aspect of it, which is essential as part of your training—you will withhold nothing of yourself from me, not even this most intimate orifice." To make his point, he pushed his finger in deeper. Elizabeth shifted but didn't resist. "But from a purely pleasurable standpoint, you'll learn to relax sufficiently so not only will it not hurt, but you'll come to crave it as much as when I fuck your cunt."

She shook her head, her eyes still closed. He let her silent doubt remain unchallenged. Withdrawing his finger, he moved back, sitting cross-legged in front of her.

"Now I want to see you touch yourself. Show me how you masturbate when you're alone. And open your eyes. I want you to look directly at me while you do it. And remember—don't you dare come without permission."

Elizabeth's eyes flipped open, the color rising in her cheeks. "Oh, Cole...Really, I—"

"Elizabeth." He cut her off. "Do you want to learn and explore with me? If you do, if you're really sincere about this, you have to stop this disobedience. I know you're embarrassed. That's the point of this particular exercise. You're being corrected for coming without permission. But beyond that, you need to learn to give yourself to me in every respect. You say you want it, but when I ask you to do anything that's the slightest bit uncomfortable for you, you balk. That isn't submission. Now you decide, once and for all, that you're in this for real, or you close those lovely legs, get dressed and we'll accept this isn't for you. I'm not kidding around. Make your choice."

She didn't respond. If she refused to obey, he was going to end it then and there. Not the relationship—he couldn't bear to do that. He wanted this lovely, special woman in his life on whatever terms she would have him. But he would stop the training. He wasn't going to bully her into something she wasn't ready for. Though he was certain she had the potential and desire to submit, if she couldn't find the courage to move through things that were difficult, he had no intention of cajoling and begging her each step of the way. It wouldn't be fair to either of them.

He waited a beat, then another. Finally she answered in a low, sultry voice that went straight to his cock. "Yes, Sir."

He nodded, keeping his face impassive, though relief flooded through him like a river overflowing its banks. Only then did he allow himself to admit how desperately he wanted this D/s relationship.

Her eyes wide but focused squarely on his, she licked her fingers, her pink tongue running seductively over them. She dropped her wet fingers to her pussy and moved them in a slow swirling motion over her spread labia.

It wasn't long before she began to breathe harder, her eyelids fluttering as she rubbed herself faster. His eyes flickered from her face to her sex, watching with aroused fascination when she slipped two fingers into herself and let her head fall back, her eyes closing, lips parting. Her hand was moving rapidly, alternating between finger-fucking herself and rubbing her clit. She was breathing rapidly, a telltale flush spreading over her chest and neck.

"Please," she said throatily, "may I come?"

Now for the real test of her willingness to submit.

"No."

It took a second to register. Then the fevered rush of her fingers stilled and she opened her eyes. "Please, I need to come," she begged.

"I heard you the first time. And I said no. Drop your hand, stretch your legs out flat on the bed and put your hands back behind your head."

Defiance flickered in her eyes. One, two, three seconds passed. She took her hand from her pussy and assumed the position, if reluctantly. He moved so he was sitting next to her on the bed. He put his fingers lightly around her throat, savoring the feeling of power as she closed her eyes and shuddered involuntarily.

"My body, my orgasm, remember? You'll come when I say, never before. And if I say no, that's the end of it. You need to work on obeying my commands the second they are given. You don't wait and think it over. You obey. Period. That will come with time. Why didn't I let you come? Because this was a correction, not a chance to get yourself off." He tightened his grip for emphasis, pleased she maintained her position. He let go of her throat and leaned over to kiss her cheek.

"You did good, Elizabeth. I'm proud of you. Let's take a little break. How about some lunch? Then after, if you're a good girl, maybe I'll let you come again. Or maybe not. Just remember, it's up to me."

~*~

Elizabeth's pussy was still gently throbbing, but she managed to regain her control over lunch. He permitted her to wear a light sundress during the meal, though he'd had her lift the hem so her bare bottom touched the seat, which served to keep her achingly aware of her sex. She was annoyed at having been denied her orgasm, but at the same time curiously aroused by his refusal.

Yes, she was the one who agreed to obey—it was a voluntary relinquishing of her right to touch and use her own body as she wished—but that didn't make his control any less real or powerful. If anything, it made it that much more complete—the knowledge that she was giving herself freely to him.

She knew she'd come a hair's breadth of blowing it. She didn't mean to continually thwart him—it was reflexive more than anything. She tried to explain this as they ate sandwiches and strawberries in his large kitchen.

"I understand that," he replied. "Submission isn't easy. It's hard to push past your inhibitions and a lifetime of learned behaviors. It takes time and conscious effort to break out of old patterns. You're a strong, independent woman, used to defining yourself in those terms and no others. You're used to being in control in all aspects of your life, without considering the heavy toll it can sometimes take."

"It's true. That's what I don't get right now. Why does this stuff turn me on so much? I felt, I know this sounds really weird, but when I was bound to the spanking horse, even though the spanking hurt and I felt helpless and even a little frightened, I also felt, I don't know—liberated is the word that keeps coming into my head. Especially afterwards. It was like something that's always kept tightly wound inside me somehow loosened. Does this even make any sense?"

"Absolutely. And, while I know the experience was a very intense one for you, it's not unique. Bondage is a form of losing control. Normally, people seek control. They want power, they want to know what's going to happen to them, they want freedom, they want to have choices and options, and so forth. People want to make up their own minds and run their own lives. The quest for control is one of the most universal psychological principles. A big part of the self is devoted to gaining and keeping control.

"But when you submit in an erotic sense, you give up, in time even erase, this aspect of the self. You submit to being tied up and blindfolded, for example. You're told what to do and what not to do. You're forced to be passive, and that blots out a major part of the self. It might seem like a contradiction, but this very giving up of self can be incredibly freeing. For the first time in your life, you can really, totally let go."

"*Yes*," Elizabeth cried. "That's *it*. You just gave words to exactly what I was feeling in the playroom. I was so focused on what was happening, everything else fell away. That never happens to me. A part of my mind is always going overtime—thinking about deadlines and bills or who owes me what on a campaign. I can never shut myself down. In fact, more than one boyfriend has complained of exactly that. That I'm never really *there* all the way. I withhold a part of myself. I can't help it."

"Ah, but you did help it, didn't you? Already on your first day of training you were able to let go to that degree, to be completely focused in the moment."

"Yes, and it was incredible." She took a bite of her sandwich and pondered while she chewed, trying to organize her thoughts. "Then there was the pain," she said aloud. "How can someone like pain? I mean, the sensation itself is unpleasant—it hurts. So why did I get off on it? I still don't really get that."

"Pain is a subjective thing, really. I prefer to think of it as heightened sensation. Pleasure and pain aren't really at opposite ends of some kind of linear spectrum. I think of them more as a circle—sensations that fuse and blend when you're in the right headspace. That heightened sensation has powerful effects on the mind. It focuses attention here and now. You forget about being a home-owner, a decision-maker, a high-powered business executive. During a whipping, for example, you become just a body. You lose all the ego and get a unique chance to redefine yourself as you work through it.

"What could be more liberating than that? You're literally freed from your own identity. I think the exhilaration you experience is produced partly by this removal of who you are. All your normal roles, ways of acting, your ideas of who you are, the games you normally play with people—all these abruptly stop. All you are is your body."

Elizabeth shook her head with admiration. "You should write a paper or something on the subject. I'm curious, though. You seem to get it, to be so in tune with the mindset of a sub. How can you have such an intuitive understanding when you're the one doing it, rather than being done to?"

"I listen. I pay attention. And as I've mentioned, I'm the other side of the coin. My mindset is different, but the experience is no less intense for me. Where you crave liberation, I get my thrill from the control—the power you give to me over your body and your reactions. When you react to something I do to you, it's like we're connected. I feel your excitement, your pleasure, your letting go. It's like you're a kite caught in a strong wind and I'm the one holding the strings, keeping you in check, controlling your flight, keeping you tethered to me. It's a powerful experience. You throw sex in there and it can just about blow your mind. You add love," his voice dipped and he reached for her hand, "and it's like nothing on this earth."

Elizabeth's heart surged, though those three simple words still didn't manage to slip past her lips. Cole only smiled. "Enough time on the soapbox." He laughed. "Time for your next lesson."

CHAPTER NINETEEN

Elizabeth dipped her toe into the hot, frothing water, wondering what sort of lesson could take place in a hot tub. She settled herself in the steamy water, Cole beside her. She leaned back with a sigh of pleasure as the water jets sprayed hard against her shoulders and lower back.

Cole put his arm loosely around her shoulders. "Ready for your next lesson?"

"In here?"

"Yep. Another lesson in self-control. Ever made yourself come with a stream of water?"

"Oh..."

"Answer the question."

"Yes." This man had a knack for asking her the most embarrassing things.

"When? When did you first do it, and how? Were you alone?"

"Yeah. I was thirteen. I'd only recently discovered masturbation. I was adding more hot water to a long soak and for some reason I scooted up and let the water fall between my legs. It felt good, so I stayed in position. It was just a kind of bubbly tickle at first, but after a while my body started trembling and then all at once it welled up into an orgasm."

"I bet you were really clean that year." Cole laughed.

"Yeah. I was constantly in the bathtub." Elizabeth grinned. Then she realized what the lesson was going to be. "You don't want...I mean, not in front of you..."

"But of course. My body, remember? Lift your ass so the water stream is on your cunt. Go on. Don't make me ask twice."

Elizabeth didn't dare disobey. At least the pink in her cheeks could be attributed to the steamy water. She lifted her body until the hot, steady spray was concentrated at her sex. She couldn't deny it—it felt good. Very good.

She closed her eyes and wriggled her hips a little to get a better angle. She was aware of Cole watching her. At least the roiling water obscured exactly what was going on beneath it. She let her eyes close as the jet pummeled her sex, the stimulation almost too direct to be pleasurable. She shifted again to ease the pressure and let out a long breath as the water hit her just the right way.

"That's it," Cole urged. "Let go. Feel it." She let her head fall forward and concentrated on the sensations. The water force was so powerful it not only stimulated her clit, but forced its way inside her as well, a liquid dildo.

"Oh," she moaned, as her climax began to mount with inexorable relentlessness beneath the steady pulse of water. Remembering in time, she managed, "Please, Sir. May I come?"

"No."

What the fuck? She sat down abruptly, her pussy still tingling from the frenzied water. Maybe she'd misheard him over the tumult of the spray. "What?"

"I said no. Not yet. You obviously heard me because you sat down. Are you questioning me again?" His dark eyes held hers. Slowly she shook her head, feeling at once submissive and defiant, not sure how to reconcile the conflicting feelings.

"Good." He climbed out of the tub and began to dry himself. "Next lesson will be about service. Part of your duties as my submissive is to make sure my needs are met at all times, sexually speaking. If I wake you up at three a.m. and tell you to suck my cock, you do it. Right now my cock could use some attention and you could use some practice in pleasing me the way I like it."

He set the towel aside and pointed imperiously to the ground. "On your knees. Hands behind your back, mouth open." Elizabeth stepped out of the tub, reaching for a large towel from the rack. "I didn't say to dry yourself. It's plenty warm in here. Kneel down just as you are, wet and dripping at my feet."

Elizabeth knelt, water from the tips of her hair dripping in rivulets down her wet body. Her pussy was on fire and she ached for his cock. She admired his thick, erect member, bobbing so close the crown brushed her parted lips. Putting her hands behind her back, she grabbed one wrist with the other and leaned forward to receive him.

Cole reached for the back of her head, grabbing a thick handful of hair and pulling it into a bunch in his strong hand. He jerked her back by the hair, forcing her to look up at him. "Who do you belong to?"

Without thinking, she answered, "You, Sir."

He nodded, his eyes blazing beneath hooded lids. He let go his tight grip on her hair, though his fingers remained entwined in it. Moving his hips forward, he guided himself into her mouth.

She licked around the head and shaft as best she could, sucking along the length, her hands itching to help out. He let her service him for a few minutes, murmuring his appreciation of her skills. When he pulled back, instinctively she moved forward, wanting to keep his hard, silky shaft under her control.

"Stay still," he ordered. "Keep your mouth open and don't move. I'm going to come down your throat. Make sure you swallow it all."

Elizabeth tensed, anxious she might choke if she wasn't allowed to move. *Trust him.* The words slipped into her mind and she slowly relaxed. Yes. This was Cole. Cole, who loved her, who wanted to help her reach that place inside where she could finally and truly let go of her chokehold on life.

"That's it. Take it. Good." He slid deeper until his cock was lodged at the back of her throat. She hadn't gagged and now couldn't even if she'd wanted to. She couldn't breathe and began to pull back. His hand on the back of her head held her firmly in place. "You're fine," he told her. "Stay still. Trust me."

Yes. She would trust him. She did trust him. The seconds passed. Pressure was building up in her head and knew if he didn't release her soon, she'd be forced to struggle away to get her breath. But she didn't want to. She wanted to obey him, to prove she could do this, to prove she trusted him, even with her very life's breath.

A curious peace began to descend over her and all thoughts ebbed from her mind. She was on her knees, just where she should be, serving the man she loved. She would tell him. Yes, as soon as she could speak, she would tell him....

Elizabeth blinked, trying to focus. "What happened?"

"You started to pass out. I'm sorry. I held you in position too long. It won't happen again."

Elizabeth was lying on the bathroom floor, her head resting on a towel in Cole's lap. "You surprised but pleased me, Elizabeth. You didn't struggle at all. I wasn't expecting that. I was expecting more of a cue from you, since you're still untrained in the art of breath control. I'm impressed and touched by the level of trust you exhibited by staying still like that."

A happy warmth suffused her. She was delighted to have pleased him. She smiled broadly. "I'm glad I pleased you, Sir." The sir just came out—not planned or rehearsed.

He nodded. "You did. I think you need a little rest. Why don't you take a nap? I've got some work I have to attend to. It'll only take an hour or two at the most." He shifted, helping her to a sitting position. Tenderly he wrapped a towel around her and took her hand, leading her out of the bathroom.

He helped her up onto the big bed as if she were made of china. "Hey, I'm okay," she asserted. "Really, I'm fine." He pressed her gently back against a mound of pillows and drew the soft sheets up around her. All at once she was assailed with a sense of nearly overwhelming fatigue. Maybe a little nap would be a good thing....

Cole kissed her lips. "I'll see you later, sweetest girl. Sleep well."

Elizabeth awoke slowly, luxuriating in the comfortable, huge bed. Before she even remembered where she was, she became aware of a delicious smell permeating the air. Something with tomato sauce and melted cheese and plenty of garlic. Her stomach rumbled and she sat up, shaking back her tousled hair.

The room was nearly dark—how long had she slept? She climbed out of the bed and moved toward a window. The sun was setting, the sky a rich, pale purple, the skyscrapers tinged with luminous gold. She went into the bathroom, used the toilet, washed her face and looked at herself in the mirror.

The woman who smiled back at her looked—happy. She grinned, pleased with herself, eager to find Cole, ready for more training. She returned to the bedroom and found the sundress he'd permitted her to wear at the last meal, and left the room, following her nose.

~*~

Cole looked up as Elizabeth entered the kitchen. "Hey there. I was wondering when you'd return to the land of the living. You went out like a light. I checked in on you about an hour ago and you hadn't moved."

Elizabeth stretched like a cat, her voluptuous breasts rising and falling beneath the skimpy dress as she moved. "I feel great," she announced, her smile tugging directly at his heart.

"Hungry? My housekeeper makes great lasagna. She freezes it for me. It's just about ready. I made garlic bread too and I have a nice Australian Shiraz that should go well. Would you like a glass while you wait? I'll get it for you."

"Sure. Sounds great. I'm starving. I can't remember being this hungry in ages." Elizabeth moved toward the table to sit, as he had expected she would.

"Uh unh," Cole stepped between her and the table. "Tonight you won't be using the furniture. I put a cushion on the floor, there by my seat. That's for you."

"Excuse me?"

"You'll be sitting on the floor at my feet during dinner. Do you have a problem with that, sub girl?"

He watched her, almost hearing the internal argument as she talked herself into obeying. It wasn't yet natural for her, but that would come in time, if she gave it the chance he hoped she would.

"No, Sir," she whispered, sinking gracefully onto the cushion. He retrieved the wine bottle from the counter and poured her a glass. She took it and sipped. He scrutinized her until she looked up at him.

"What have you done wrong?"

"Me?" She looked flustered. "Um, nothing, I don't think..."

He could see she didn't know. "Lift your dress. Ass directly on the cushion, same as in a chair.

"Oh." She blushed becomingly while she shifted and pulled at her dress.

Cole turned away to hide his grin. He'd already set the table—one plate and set of silverware. He took the lasagna and garlic bread from the oven and put them on the waiting trivets. He brought his own glass and the bottle of wine to the table. Lastly he retrieved a set of metal handcuffs from a drawer.

"Drink up and give me your glass," he instructed her. Elizabeth drained the remainder of her wine and held out the empty glass, her eyes trained on the cuffs. "Kneel up and put your hands behind your back. I'm going to cuff you. This is just to help you remember not to use your hands. I don't like to use metal cuffs during a session but they're good as a reminder."

He waited while she knelt into position. He'd considered making her remove the sundress but decided, since she'd opted to put it on, he'd let her keep it a while longer. As he cuffed her, he felt the slight tremble in her arms.

He kissed her head and stroked her cheek. "Relax. Close your eyes and calm yourself. Use your breathing. Nothing's going to happen to you. I'm just going to feed you some dinner and then maybe we'll snuggle up and watch a movie. You've done great so far for your first day. I'm incredibly proud of you."

Elizabeth smiled, her shoulders easing. "That's better." Cole smiled back. He helped himself to a large serving of the lasagna. He cut a small piece, blew on it and held it close to Elizabeth's mouth. Flushing, she accepted the offered bite.

"That's delicious."

"Martha's a good cook," Cole agreed, cutting and eating the second bite himself. He tore off some of the hot, buttery bread and offered it to her. She accepted it as eagerly as a baby bird.

He fed her slowly, his cock hardening each time she accepted the food from his fork—his perfect slave girl, kneeling and docile, her nipples jutting provocatively beneath her dress, her hands secured behind her back. In between bites, he held the wine glass to her lips, letting her drink.

Elizabeth turned her face away. "I'm stuffed." Cole wiped a bit of garlic butter from her cheek with his napkin.

"Me too. I'm glad you enjoyed it. I like having you kneel at my feet like you belonged there. I like keeping you bound and helpless while I feed you. Sometime in the future, when you're properly trained, we might use food deprivation as a punishment. Not that you'll need much punishment by then, am I right?"

She looked decidedly alarmed. "Food deprivation?"

"It can be a very effective tool. A night without dinner spent in the puppy cage, cunt and ass stuffed with dildos, taped in to keep them there. Very effective indeed for a naughty slave girl."

"Cole! You wouldn't...?"

He slipped from his chair and knelt in front of her, taking her face in his hands. "Of course I would, darling. If it's what you needed. Don't you see that? I'll do whatever you need. Yes, it's about pleasing me, but in the end, it's about you and what you need. That's always the way between a Dom and a sub. That's why it's called an exchange of power, rather than merely an abdication on your part.

"In a healthy D/s relationship, the submissive ultimately holds the real power. She stops the scene with a word. She sets the limits with what she can tolerate, and with what it takes to satisfy and control her. It's a circle, a fluid exchange of power between us, even if on the surface I'm the one in charge. Does that make sense to you?"

"Yes, Sir. It does." She bowed her head. Cole reached beneath the hem of her dress, gently forcing her thighs apart with one hand. He sought and found what he was looking for—she was wet, so wet she'd stained her thighs with the sweet juice.

Jesus, he had to have her—now.

Hurriedly he released the cuffs. He grabbed a cushion from one of the other chairs and placed it on the empty side of the large oak kitchen table. "Get up. Lie on your back on the table. I need to fuck you."

He reached into the back pocket of his jeans and fished out a condom, wishing he didn't have to use it, aware she wasn't on birth control. If she stayed with him, they would need to address that, but for now he simply had to have her.

"On the table?"

"Stop repeating every order I give you," he snapped, though he really wasn't angry. She would learn soon enough. "It's your fault. You're so damn sexy I can't even wait to get you to the bedroom. Take off that dress, lie on your back and scoot your ass to edge of the table. I'm going to fuck you. Oh, and don't you dare come. Don't even think about it."

~*~

Elizabeth tried and failed to pay attention to the movie. She was too aware of Cole beside her, too aware of her own nudity and his, her unsatisfied lust, her aching desire for him. They were lying in his bed, she cradled in his arm. She hadn't realized there was a large flat screen TV hidden behind the doors of the large armoire that faced his bed.

Again she tried to focus on the action thriller, barely following the plot line, and finally giving up entirely, surrendering herself to her daydreams. She still wasn't sure how she felt about being fed like an infant. On the other hand, she hadn't felt like an infant, with her hands cuffed behind her, her bare pussy resting against her heels and her nipples perking toward her captor at stiff attention.

She hadn't been able to help the occasional surreptitious grinding of her cunt against her heels. Cunt…Somehow the word no longer offended. Because *he* used it and he liked it. It was earthy, he'd said. Honest. He was right. Pussy was a euphemism, like saying you're going to go powder your nose, when you actually intend to pee. One more thing stripped away, she thought, in this strange quest for freedom and self-discovery.

He'd fucked her hard on the table, thrusting into her, his hands pressing her shoulders down against the hard wood. She'd felt objectified—used. But instead of outrage, she couldn't deny the thrill. He had simple taken what he wanted without preamble or regard for her, like a prehistoric caveman staking his claim on a woman he'd captured and dominated.

Because he'd told her not to come, her perverse body was instantly sensitized, teetering dangerously on the edge of orgasm the entire time he was inside her. She'd very nearly succumbed to her own desperate need for release. After all, he'd purposely kept her on edge all day, forcing her twice to bring herself nearly to orgasm, only to cruelly withhold the ultimate pleasure.

She snuggled against him, rubbing her bare body suggestively against his beneath the sheets. "Hmm." His eyes were still on the screen. Absently he stroked her back, seemingly impervious to the press of her breasts against his side. After a few minutes of being basically ignored, she raised the stakes, partially straddling his strong thigh with hers, rubbing her cunt against it while brazenly reaching for his cock.

That got his attention. He turned toward her, shaking his head. "Pay attention to the movie. Am I going to have to chain you to the bed?"

"Come on, Cole. I haven't come all day."

"You came after your spanking in the playroom," he reminded her.

"That was hours ago." She knew she sounded petulant but it was his fault for keeping her on edge like this. Being denied for so long had made her irritable. She couldn't relax or focus with her cunt constantly throbbing. "I've been trying to be really good and obedient. You've been teasing me for too long. Come on. Let me come. Please? You don't even have to be involved. You can keep watching that stupid movie."

He moved suddenly, pinning her wrists over her head, pressing her into the mattress with his body. His mouth was close to her ear, his warm breath tickling her as he spoke. His voice was low and steely and for the first time, she felt afraid of him.

"You don't run the show, Elizabeth. I do. I decide when you come, how you come, if you come. Got it? Whiny little brats don't get orgasms just because they want them. You'd been doing very well this evening, and it had been my intention to reward you. Too bad you fucked it up."

He lifted himself off her and turned his attention back to the screen. Elizabeth found herself both mortified and furious. She fumed in silence for a while, staring at the ceiling, wondering for the first time that day if she really wanted to submit to this man. Yes, it was thrilling, but did she really want to give of herself to such a degree? Was she even capable of such submission?

She glanced toward Cole and found he was watching her, instead of the movie, his expression inscrutable.

"What." She knew she sounded defensive.

"You don't have to stay." His voice was soft, even sad.

She hadn't expected that response. "What do you mean?"

"Maybe this isn't right for you." He echoed her own thoughts of a moment before. "Maybe you're really not cut out for submission. The BDSM games are fun, sure. Maybe that's all you really want. All you're truly looking for, if you're looking for anything at all."

She stared at him, still angry and now afraid—afraid he was sending her away, firing her from the job of sub girl she had signed up for.

She felt tears well up in her eyes and spill over her cheeks. All at once a flood gate inside her opened. She began to cry in noisy, gasping sobs. He reached for her and took her into his arms. "It's okay, baby. It's okay. It's okay to cry. It's okay." He held her tenderly. She continued to sob, not even sure why. She couldn't remember the last time she'd cried, not just silent tears, but this raspy, undignified snot-nosed sobbing. Cole continued to hold her, stroking her hair, letting her cry against his warm, fuzzy chest.

Eventually the sobs subsided and she lay limp and still, not wanting to move. It felt good and safe to be held in his strong arms. She didn't want to ever leave these arms. Maybe she would just lie here in them forever and let the world drift by.

Finally she lifted her head to see his face. He smiled tenderly at her and reached for a tissue. He wiped her running nose, as gently as if she were a child, nothing but concern in his expression. He reached for another tissue and gently dabbed at her wet cheeks. Impulsively she turned toward his hand and kissed it.

"Feeling better?"

"Yeah, I guess." Surprisingly, she was. All the irritation and petulance had melted away. She was still horny though, she thought with an inward rueful grin.

Cole leaned up on his elbow and faced her. "You've been through a rollercoaster of a day today. The first day is always the toughest, in terms of mindset. Listen to me. I love you. I want you in my life. You convinced me before you really wanted to give this a serious try—a 24/7 effort to find out if you have what it takes to truly submit, and if it's the right thing for you.

"There's no crime in failing. Unless you try something, you can't know if it's right for you or not. Maybe you've reached that point. Maybe you'd like to go back to your place and think things through. I'll still be here. I'm not going anywhere. I promise."

"I want to stay." Her voice was firm. "I honestly don't know the answer yet—if I'm really submissive or not. I guess just saying I want to submit isn't the same as actually doing it, or following through."

She fell back against the pillows beside him. "It's your fault," she asserted. "I've never been this turned on before. This...sexualized. It's like my every waking moment since I got here this morning has been focused on my...cunt." She said the word softly, shyly, feeling odd as she said it, but also correct.

"That's a good thing. I want you sexualized and sensitive. I want you always quivering on the edge of desire. What you don't yet get is the experience can be that much more intense if you give up your control over it all. Let me guide you. Accept I know what you need, and I'll always give it to you. Always. And right now what you need is to learn some self-control. You have none." He laughed. "Not when it comes to your orgasm. You want what you want when you want it. Well, that ain't gonna fly. Not if you're to belong to me. I'm serious when I say that's *my* body. My property. You get permission to use it sexually, and then only if it pleases me.

"That's the lot of a submissive, and paradoxically it's also her exaltation. I know you don't get that yet, but you will, I promise. If you really want to stay, that is. If you really want to keep trying."

"I do." Elizabeth clamped her legs together resolutely, willing her randy sex to go to sleep. "I do, Sir."

CHAPTER TWENTY

When Elizabeth awoke the next morning she was alone. Cole had told her he would be getting up early for a phone conference with some investors from Amsterdam, but would probably be done before she even woke up.

To her disappointment, they hadn't made love before going to sleep. Though she wouldn't admit it, she had thought her tears would have brought a reprieve, and he would let her come. Instead he had placed leather cuffs around her wrists and loosely shackled them with chain. "Just a reminder to keep your hands away from that little cunt of yours."

It had taken her a long time to fall asleep. She started out in his arms, her head resting on his broad, strong chest, her hands pressed together beneath her chin as if in prayers, the chain resting between them. After a while Cole's breathing deepened and slowed and she knew he was asleep.

Slowly, carefully, she shifted off him and lay on her back, sliding her hands down to her pussy, which still throbbed with dull, aching need. She cupped it with her right hand and glanced over at him. He hadn't moved. Did she dare? With him right beside her, did she dare steal her pleasure?

He turned toward her, startling her so she pulled her hands away, the chain clinking between her wrists. In his sleep, he brought a heavy arm over her stomach, capturing her arms in the process. With a sigh, she closed her eyes and, eventually, fell asleep.

Now she glanced at the clock. It was seven-twenty. Was he still on his conference call? Quietly she climbed out of bed and went into the bathroom. She used the toilet, which was awkward with her wrists shackled, but she didn't dare remove the cuffs on her own.

Returning to the bedroom, she went out into the hall and walked toward his study. The door was ajar and she could hear him murmuring inside. He must still be on the phone. She wouldn't disturb him.

She returned to the bedroom, thinking perhaps she would shower and groom herself. She looked at her shackled wrists, wondering if she was expected to leave them on while showering. Surely not? On the other hand, maybe she should just wait until he was done with his call. Maybe he would want to shower with her.

That thought turned her mind to his strong, sexy body. She never tired of looking at his long, lean physique, of feeling his firm, well-rounded muscles and burrowing her face in his masculine chest. Her nipples perked and her pussy began to throb. Day two of training. What did he have planned for her today? Would she be able to stand it if he didn't let her come?

The mere thought made her loins ache. Maybe if she stole a quickie. To take the edge off. Nothing big, just a quick rub, a mini-gasm. No harm done and it would make her a better sub because she wouldn't be so agitated. Yes. That's what she would do. He would be none the wiser.

She climbed back into bed and lay on her back, bringing her shackled hands to her sex. Glancing toward the door, she dared to dip her fingers into the wet, tight passage. Ah, it felt so good. The cuffs and chain hindered her somewhat, but she managed to work around them.

It was her body, not his, no matter what sexy fiction they maintained. She could do as she liked when he wasn't around. A part of her knew this violation of their pact was a mistake—it would dilute the intent of her submission, but she was, frankly, just too damn horny to care. She would just have one tiny orgasm and then she would be good, she promised herself.

She rubbed her clit, letting her legs fall wide as she took her pleasure. Oh, it felt so good. She needed this. He was wrong to tease and deny her for so long. Yes, yes, that was it. Perfect. She began to pant, her eyes squeezed shut, a climax rising up through her like sap returning to a dying tree. One little cry escaped her lips and then she fell limp, her hands falling away from her sticky sex, her head lolling to the side.

She heard a sound and her eyes flew open. Cole was standing just inside the doorway, his eyes narrowed, his lips pressed into a thin angry line. Oh God, what had he seen? How long had he been watching her?

Without a word he advanced into the room. "Cole, I—I didn't, I mean, it was only…." Her words died as he towered over her and hauled her by her shackled wrists from the bed. Jerking the chain, he pulled her along behind him out of the room and down the hall.

She stumbled as she struggled to keep up. Her heart was smashing in her chest and she could barely catch her breath. "Please! I'm sorry. I just needed it so bad. Come on, I said I'm sorry. Damn it, it's my body." Her voice was rising, along with the panic in her gut. He still hadn't said a word. Where was the kind, patient Dom of the day before?

He pushed open the door and dragged her up the steps and into the playroom. Still without speaking, he unclasped the cuffs and spun her around so her back was to him. "Hands behind your back," he barked.

Trembling, she obeyed. At least he had said *something*. He cuffed her wrists again and began marching her toward the corner of the room where the puppy cage waited, covered in its black sheet. When she realized where they were going, she pushed back hard against him. "No. I can't do that. I can't go in there. It's too small. Please, I can't—"

"You should have thought of that while you were stealing that orgasm, slut." He pushed her to her knees and pulled the sheet from the steel bars. The padlock was open and he removed it from the small door and pulled it open. "Get in."

"No, really. I can't. Please. I'll be good, I swear. I don't want to get in."

Cole's voice was deadly. "You get in, now."

Elizabeth swallowed and stared up beseechingly at him. His face was impassive, except for the fiery black eyes, which flashed with anger. Her heart thumping, her breath catching, she crawled into the small enclosure.

She sat in a half-crouch, gripping the bars as he shut the door with a clank and snapped the heavy padlock into place. "Cole, don't *leave* me. Please. I can't do this. Please. Punish me some other way." She wailed his name as he left the dungeon, shutting the door with a resounding click.

~*~

Cole moved quickly down the hall to his study. His heart was beating far too fast He needed to calm down. Anger had no place in a Dom's repertoire. He sat behind his desk and closed his eyes a moment, taking several slow, deep breaths. Then he flipped on the screen of the small closed-circuit TV that was connected to the small video camera mounted discreetly on the wall facing the puppy cage.

Elizabeth came into view. He adjusted the sound. She was clenching the bars and shaking them, calling his name, begging him to come back. His heart wrenched and he half-stood but forced himself to sit back down. He turned down the volume though he couldn't tear his eyes away from the screen.

Clearly she didn't like being in that cage. But why had she done what she'd done? Was this whole thing just a game to her? He didn't want to think so. She'd been so sincere, or so he'd thought last night, assuring him in that low, sultry voice of hers that she wanted to do better, she wanted to keep trying. He had believed her. What a shock, what a disappointment, to find her with her hand buried in her cunt, the telltale rosy flush of orgasm mottled on her chest and neck.

This was not a mistake or something to be forgiven or overlooked because of her lack of training. This was a willful breaking of the rules—a conscious decision on her part to dismiss the promises between them. He shook his head as he watched her on the monitor. How he wanted her—but not like this. Not a willful, sneaky brat who only played at submission when it suited her.

She lay on her side, curling herself into a fetal ball, her back now to the camera. He was being too hard on her. He'd teased her unmercifully the day before, bringing her twice nearly to orgasm, then stopping her. He knew how aroused she was as they lay in bed and again he'd withheld her pleasure, forgoing his own desire to fuck her because he wanted her that much more needy and eager for him today.

He'd entered the bedroom with the intention of licking her to orgasm, letting her come as long and hard as she wished before beginning the day's training. But she'd ruined it.

Stop it. She didn't ruin anything. She fucked up, that's all. She's human. She's being punished and then you forgive her and move on.

Don't make more of this than it is. She's just undisciplined. Don't be such a hard ass.

He leaned toward the monitor and turned up the volume. It took him a moment to interpret the muffled, snuffling sound coming from the cage. He saw her shoulders were shaking. Ah, Jesus, she was crying. His baby was crying.

Leaping from his chair, he ran down the hall and hurtled up the steps. He burst into the playroom, fumbling with the padlock key, his hands trembling as he turned it in the lock. In a second he had the door open. He reached for her.

"Elizabeth. Hey, it's okay. Turn around. Come out of there. It's okay. *Please.*" She turned slowly toward him, her face streaked with tears. Cole's heart lurched with pain. "Oh God, baby. I'm sorry. I didn't mean to make you cry. I just wanted to teach you a lesson. I didn't know how else to reach you."

She rolled toward him and crawled out of the cage, into his waiting arms.

~*~

She'd very nearly fought Cole, ready to ruin everything, to give it all up, just to avoid being forced into that dreadful cage. She had never liked confined spaces. Crowded elevators always left her with a vague if undefined sense of unease. She didn't like to feel hemmed in.

It was a sheer act of will to make herself go in there, an act of courage. But when he'd walked out, closing the door behind him, she'd felt herself losing it. Panic had rolled over her like a mudslide, destroying the fragile self-control left to her.

When he didn't return, despite her entreaties, she gave in to her panic, curling as tight as she could and letting her sobs overtake her. When she realized he was back, calling her name, holding out his arms to her, she continued to cry, but they were tears of relief.

Now Cole took off the cuffs, dropping them to the floor. Scooting back with her on his lap, he leaned against the wall, holding her tight. He let her cry, holding her and rocking her in his arms. Eventually she calmed down, the tears drying, the panic ebbing away, replaced by an exhausted but peaceful calm.

Cole wiped away her tears with his fingertips and pulled her close so her damp cheek rested against his chest. It felt wonderful to be wrapped in his strong, warm embrace. She wanted to stay there forever. Her eyelids felt heavy after her cry and she let them close, breathing in his masculine essence, curling like a cat in his arms.

She was nearly asleep when his words pierced her consciousness. "You forgive me?"

Elizabeth was confused. She twisted in his arms to see his face. "Me forgive you? Aren't I the one who disobeyed?"

"Well, yes." Cole smiled. "But what happened just now was my fault. I should have listened better. Paid better attention to your cues. I didn't take the time to understand your limits. I didn't realize the depths of your fear of confined spaces. I shouldn't have left you alone in the cage, not even for one minute."

He gave a small, sad laugh. "It's ironic, with me on my soapbox lecturing about the importance of communication in a D/s relationship, more paramount even than in a vanilla love affair." He shook his head. "I want to test your limits, yes. But not to push so far past them you become terrified. That was never my intention. I'm sorry, sweetheart. So very sorry."

Elizabeth stared at the puppy cage, wondering now what had frightened her so. She felt almost sheepish at how strongly she'd reacted. She wanted to take the sadness out of Cole's voice. "It's okay, Cole. Really. I just panicked for a minute. I'm fine now. Better than fine. I feel like a whole new world is opening up to me. I don't want to stop because of one little setback. I want to keep going. You haven't given up on me, have you?"

Cole's expression was one of such incredulous surprise Elizabeth had to laugh. "Given up you?" he demanded. "God, no! I would never do that. It's me who needs another chance here."

"Then you've got it."

"Okay then. Clean slate." He got to his feet, still holding Elizabeth in his arms. "How about a nice hot shower?" Elizabeth nodded, still feeling a little sheepish. He was treating her as if she had just recovered from a long, lingering illness or a car accident or something. Still, she let him carry her all the way to the bathroom, loving the feeling of being held and protected in his strong, safe embrace.

The shower was huge, with jets spraying not only from overhead, but from two sides. There was a marble bench set at the back of the stall. They held one another for a long moment in the hot spray. Elizabeth felt Cole's erection rising against her stomach. She wanted to drop to her knees and take him into her mouth, but given her earlier willful disobedience, she didn't quite dare.

After they'd soaped their bodies and washed their hair, Cole pointed to the marble bench. "I'm going to groom you today."

Elizabeth sat, watching as he took a fresh razor from the shower rack. He squirted a dollop of emollient soft soap onto his fingers and turned to her. "Raise your arms and stay very still. I don't want to nick you."

She did as he asked. It felt strange to have someone else shaving her underarms. He was very gentle and he made a cute face while he was working—the tip of his tongue appearing between his lips as he concentrated.

Next he knelt in front of her and did her legs, moving with long, sure strokes over the skin. He ran his fingers over them when he was done and nodded with a smile. "Smooth as silk. Now for that lovely cunt. Scoot forward and spread your legs."

A wave of apprehension washed over Elizabeth at the thought of a sharp razor in someone else's hands being used on her delicate parts. Yet he'd been very gentle with her underarms and legs. And she couldn't deny the slow pulse of desire that had rekindled as he'd touched her body.

She moved forward until she was perched on the edge of the bench and dutifully spread her legs wide. Cole used a mixture of baby oil and the emollient soap, rubbing it gently over her mons and outer labia. She closed her eyes as the razor slid over her skin, followed by his fingers. His touch sent spasms of pleasure surging through her. She held herself still to keep from shuddering.

When he was done he had her stand and rinse herself. She thought they'd get out of the shower but he wasn't done. "Sit back down and spread your legs." She obeyed, wondering if perhaps he'd missed a spot. But this time when he knelt, he held no razor. Putting a hand on either thigh, he leaned down and licked the smooth folds of her shorn sex.

"Ah," she moaned. His tongue was like liquid fire, drawing a criss-crossed path of shivery pleasure over her sex. He licked and suckled her swelling clit and moved lower, pressing his tongue into her tunnel, making her long for his hard, thick cock. As he drew her rapidly toward climax, she let her head fall back, losing herself in the delicious sensations.

Her body began to shudder and she opened her mouth, trying to speak, to ask for what she had silently vowed to herself she would never take again without her Dom's express permission.

He pulled away from just long enough to say, "Come for me. Now."

She did.

~*~

She looked like an angel, her arms pulled taut overhead like wings, her long, shapely legs spread, her proud, bare body displayed before him. She was suspended from chains secured to the eyehooks in the cement beam, her wrists bound securely in the attached cuffs.

She'd been subdued over breakfast, quietly apologizing for masturbating without permission. He'd accepted her apology and gently questioned her about her honest feelings with regard to continuing the training. Her heartfelt response convinced him to keep going. Though he didn't mention it to her, he doubted he would ever use the cage again. He had wanted to punish, not terrify her.

It had been a mistake to force her into the cage without first taking the time to understand her reservations. The experience had only highlighted for him the importance of communication. He would make sure going forward he had a better understanding of her limits and her fears. Together they would break them down, one by one.

Now he drew the tresses of the heavy flogger over her back, admiring the contrast of black soft leather and pale soft skin. He stood close behind her and reached around her body to cup her breast. He wore no shirt, only jeans. His feet were bare. He pressed his erection against her ass and squeezed her breast.

"Are you ready for your first whipping? Are you sure?"

"Yes. I want it...Sir." He could feel her heart beating like a caged bird. She was afraid, he knew, but he believed her. She wanted this. She wouldn't still be here, after all she'd been through over the past twenty-four hours, if she didn't want what he offered.

He wanted it too, more than he'd wanted anything in his life. He'd found the girl of his dreams. He would do anything, he realized, to keep her. The fact she wanted to submit to him, to belong to him, reached something deep inside him. He knew these next few days were pivotal in establishing their relationship going forward. He would need to draw on all his discipline, knowledge and self-control to keep from pushing her too hard, but at the same time giving her what she needed.

He stepped back and stood just behind and to the side of the naked, bound girl. He glanced at the mirrored wall facing them and saw she was watching him, her eyes glittering, her lips parted, her nipples stiff and red.

He struck her gently with the flogger, more of a caress than a blow. Her eyes widened but she didn't flinch. Slowly he increased the intensity until she did flinch, gasping and jerking away, though she couldn't move far, suspended as she was.

He took careful aim, watching as the black leather landed against supple flesh. He began to whip her in a steady, stinging rhythm, not enough to mark her, not yet. He wanted her to get used to the sensation, to process the sting without its overwhelming her.

She began to moan, soft cries that could have signaled pleasure or pain, or both. Her skin was reddening nicely. He was delighted at how well she was doing. He decided to up the ante. He struck her hard, watching as the tips of the flogger curled cruelly around one hip. This time there was no mistaking her cry. He'd hurt her.

He lowered the whip a moment and leaned in, smoothing the heated flesh he'd marked a moment before. Her breath was ragged, her eyes squeezed shut. He put his arms around her and kissed her neck. "Shh," he whispered. "You're doing beautifully. You're so hot right now. You need this, don't you, baby? You need to suffer for me."

He watched her in the mirror. Slowly she opened her eyes, though her chest still heaved. She saw him looking at her and she nodded, her eyes shining. Cole stepped back and lifted the whip again. He struck her just as hard. She swayed and gasped, but her eyes remained opened, staring at him in the mirror.

He focused on her ass, making sure every inch was reddened by the stinging rain of leather. Elizabeth began to dance on her toes, gasping and whimpering. She was clutching the chains above her cuffs. He didn't stop, certain she wanted him to continue, *needed* him to continue.

Finally he put the whip down and moved in front of her. Perspiration gleamed on her upper lip and along her sides. She was breathing rapidly, her eyes closed, her body still twitching and swaying. He took her into his arms and kissed her face.

"I want to take you deeper. I think you're ready to go. I want to use a different whip to help you get there. It's braided and not as soft. It's a level up in terms of intensity. Do you want that?"

"Yes, Sir."

~*~

You can do it, you can do it. Fuck. This hurts. This hurts, hurts, hurts, hurts...oh. Oh, I should have said no. The flogger felt good. I liked the sting. It turned to heat, to pleasure, to desire. My cunt is dripping. I'm so hot for him. Ow. Fuck. This is too much. I can't do it. No.

"It hurts, oh, Cole, it hurts. It's too much. I can't do it." Elizabeth danced on her toes, twisting in a frantic, futile effort to escape the stinging lash.

"You can. You are. I can sense you're almost there. Breathe. Go with it. Stop fighting the pain. Become the pain. Become the whip. You're strong. You're brave. You're almost there."

*Almost where? Where am I going? Ah...*Elizabeth let her head fall back. She didn't have the strength to lift it again. The sting was still there, but somehow more bearable. Her skin, a moment ago on fire, began to cool. Her head still hung back, eyes closed. Her lips parted and she drew a slow, shuddery breath.

Something shifted. He continued to whip her, if anything harder than before. She felt the sting but no longer defined it as pain, no longer processed it as suffering. Her fingers, which she hadn't realized had been clutching the chains, relaxed. Her hands went limp and she sagged against the thick cuffs at her wrists.

She was aware of Cole behind her, aware the whip was still biting into her flesh but she no longer felt it. She no longer heard the whistling warning of its trajectory. Her mind emptied, her breathing slowed...

Silence.

Serenity.

Euphoric peace.

Elizabeth opened her eyes, blinking against the bright light. On one level she'd been aware of Cole dropping the whip, Cole releasing her from the cuffs and lowering her to the ground, taking her head into his lap. But she had been too deeply nestled in the cocoon of a trance to respond or speak.

She had no idea how long she'd been lying there. She hadn't been sleeping—it was more like drifting, or flying. Flying over a vast expanse of clear sky, weightless. She looked now into Cole's handsome face. He was smiling at her.

"You did it."

"What did I do?"

"You got there. You got to that place of utter peace, didn't you? I could *feel* it happening. It was the most incredible thing to watch."

"It was like flying," she offered, trying to find the right words. "Like soaring. I could still feel the whip but I didn't feel the pain, if that makes sense."

"Perfect sense. You gave of yourself, Elizabeth. You worked past the pain, you trusted me, you trusted yourself."

"I did, huh? Wow." Elizabeth found herself grinning so hard it made her cheeks hurt. She sat up, sudden joy coursing like fire through her veins. Impulsively she reached for Cole, wrapping her arms tightly around him.

Nuzzling against his neck she whispered the words she'd rarely said before and had never meant in the all-encompassing, fiercely tender way she did now.

"I love you."

CHAPTER TWENTY-ONE

Elizabeth was into her sixth day of training before she realized she hadn't thought about work once. Cole had continued to transact business now and again from his study, but she hadn't even looked at her cell phone to see if there were any messages.

She decided not to check. They were obviously managing without her. The world had not stopped when she'd decided to step out of it. She stared at herself in the mirror. She was kneeling naked in the playroom, practicing the positions Cole had been teaching her. She still looked like herself, but the pinched, anxious expression around her eyes had eased and she had a small secret smile on her face. She had an appetite for the first time in ages and she was sleeping deeply, waking refreshed and rested. She liked who she saw staring back at her. She looked happy and, yes, serene.

How did one reconcile chains with freedom, pain with serenity? But as Cole had promised she would come to understand, she now knew in her bones how freeing it was to completely give herself to another. For the first time in her life, she was in the moment, completely focused on the now, with no thought to past or future.

"You gave this to me," she had marveled, when talking about this new sense of serenity with Cole."

"No, you found it in yourself. I just helped you realize it was there."

She glanced at the list, written with fine ink in a strong, angular hand. *Attention.* She stood, squaring her shoulders, chin up, breasts out, feet and ankles together, arms at her sides.

Present-back. She lowered herself to the ground, drew her legs up, feet flat on the ground and let her knees fall open, displaying her pussy and ass. She crossed her wrists crossed over her head.

Present-facedown. She rolled over, lifted her ass high and touched her forehead to the floor, stretching her arms out on either side of her head.

Present-Stand. She stood, feet shoulder width apart, fingers laced behind her neck with elbows back, head up and eyes lowered.

Present-Kneel. As she had during her first day of training, she knelt back on her heels, her palms resting face up on her thighs, her legs spread wide. She closed her eyes and concentrated on emptying her mind while she waited for Cole.

When she heard him enter the playroom a few minutes later, she didn't move, though her nipples stiffened to attention and her pussy tingled. Square-toed boots of soft, black leather appeared in her line of vision. She lowered herself until her lips met the leather, which she kissed. He stepped back and she remained as she was, her forehead touching the carpet. She brought her hands to the small of her back and grasped her wrists.

Cole moved behind her, running his hand over her ass, dropping it lower to fondle her sex. She shivered with pleasure but otherwise didn't move. He stroked and teased her until she was trembling. Then he pulled his hand away and touched her head, the signal for her to stand.

She rose as gracefully as she could and stood in the at-ease position she was to assume when not given specific instruction, her legs comfortably apart, arms loosely at her sides. As promised, he'd been working his way through the various pieces of torture equipment in the playroom. He'd tethered her to the St. Andrew's Cross for an extended whipping session, during which she'd again entered that euphoric, soaring trance.

Feet tied into the stirrups of the bondage table, she'd been forced to suck a thick black rubber dildo, which Cole then eased into her spread pussy, fucking her with it until she came. He tied her ankles and wrists high on the arms of the leather bondage swing and impaled her on his cock, standing still while he pulled and pushed the swing to penetrate her.

The only toy he hadn't yet used was the inversion rack. Today, he had informed her calmly over breakfast, was the day. He led her to it and she leaned against the leather-covered frame, her heart tapping nervously as he strapped her into the device. It was the thought of being upside down that had her uncomfortable. Though her fear was nowhere near the level of being forced into the cage, she was anxious nonetheless. Cole had talked her through her fears, promising her he would pay attention to her reactions and keep her safe.

Along with the fear she was, as usual, highly aroused at the prospect of being once again at the mercy of her sexy, masterful Dom. She had come to understand manageable fear, as Cole termed it, added to the experience, making it more intense, not in spite of but because of her ability to work through it and triumph.

All of this went through her head as Cole bound her at the thigh, below the knee and at the ankle with padded leather straps. An X-shaped harness fit securely over her torso to hold her in place. He secured her wrists loosely behind the leather frame.

"How're you doing?" He bent down and kissed her lips.

"Okay." Her voice sounded small in her own ears.

"Good. You ready?"

She blew out a breath, as ready, she supposed, as she'd ever be. "Yes, Sir."

Slowly he tipped her back until she was perpendicular to the floor. He pushed apart the frames that held her legs, exposing her ass and cunt. He ran his fingers lightly over her sex and then slipped his thumb inside her. "Wet, as always," he chuckled.

He moved to her side and slowly tipped the rack until she was completely upside down. She felt disoriented and vulnerable, but she didn't feel panicky. She could handle this. Cole walked away a moment and then returned.

"Stay relaxed," he advised her. "I'm going to prepare you for anal play." Elizabeth stiffened. Cole had brought up anal sex several times over the past few days, and she knew it was just a matter of time before he used her in that way. Unlike the few times she'd done it in the past—reluctantly with a man she didn't really want to be with—she knew this would be different. He promised her she would like it, if not at first, after a while. The submissive aspect of it did arouse her, she couldn't deny that.

She felt a cold wetness at her nether hole as he smeared lubricant onto it and pressed his finger inside her. "Relax," he urged. "Deep breaths. I'm going to put this anal plug in, slow and easy.

The hard rubber tip of the plug pressed against her entrance and despite her efforts to relax, she began to tense. He pressed slowly, inserting just the tip, giving her time to adjust. Slowly she relaxed, her muscles easing. He pressed farther and a jolt of pain shot through her. She yelped.

"Relax," he ordered again. She tried, but it was difficult with her head where her feet should be and her legs spread wide. He twisted the plug as he pressed it gently but inexorably into her. It didn't hurt anymore. He pulled it out and then plunged it back in again and she gasped. He did this several times until her muscles had relaxed to the point she could easily handle the plug.

This time he pressed it in deep and warned her, "Just a bit of pain now, as the flared base is pushed home. Here we go." Before she had time to tense and work herself up, he'd already popped it in. She gave a small squeal but already the pain was fading.

With the anal plug in place, he produced a small pussy whip, which he held out to show her. "Ready to suffer, sub girl?"

"Yes, Sir," she whispered, both terrified and thrilled. She wouldn't be able to get away. She wouldn't even be able to close her legs. The first strokes against her sex were light, even sensual, but quickly he stepped up the pace and intensity until she was writhing and crying out.

He alternated between her cunt and her inner thighs. Upside down as she was, she never knew when or where he would strike next. It stung like angry bees, but as usual, the pain had a curious way of transmuting into pleasure, or something greater than pleasure. Just when she thought she'd either faint from the pain or orgasm from the pleasure, he dropped the whip and pulled her up so she was again perpendicular to the floor. She couldn't see what he was doing, but in a few moments she the fat head of his cock pressed against the stinging wetness of her sex.

"Come for me. Now."

She exploded in a powerful orgasm almost as soon as he entered her. He fucked her hard and fast at first, and then slowed to a sensual rhythm, making her come twice more before he climaxed inside her.

He pulled himself from her and, after tossing the spent condom in the small trashcan near the door, returned to release her. He held her tight as the blood rushed away from her head, leaving her dizzy and disoriented.

"Not so bad, huh? You survived."

"Yeah." She touched the base of the plug still lodged deep inside her. "But can I take this thing out, please?"

"Sure. Right after lunch."

It was hard to believe the two weeks were nearing their end. Elizabeth hadn't left Cole's apartment once during that time. She'd been content to stay in the sensual, encompassing world Cole had created for her. She knew she would have to return to work, return to the real world of bills and schedules and obligations.

In a way she wanted to get back, but she didn't want to lose the incredibly close connection they'd established. She didn't want to revert back to the tense, driven, stressed-out woman she had been.

As they lay snuggled together in the bed Cole soothed her fears. "You don't have to go back to that. Sure, you can return to work and your life, but the cool thing about D/s is you can take it with you. It becomes a part of you. You won't lose that serenity you've found—you'll be able to harness it in all aspects of your life. And it's not like you're leaving me, right?" He chucked her playfully under the chin but she saw the flash of anxiety in his eyes.

"No, no," she hastened to reassure him. "Never. I love you, Cole. You're the first man I can say that to with no reservations, no hesitation, no qualms. I don't have one foot out the door like I realize now I always did with my past relationships. I want to be where you are for as long as you'll have me."

Cole swept her tightly into his arms. "That's forever." He kissed her. She could feel his cock hard against her. "I want you," he whispered.

"I'm yours," she answered. He lowered himself over her, pinning her body with his while his lips sought her mouth.

She wrapped her legs and arms around him, pulling him into her, wishing she could take him deeper, into her very soul. He felt perfect inside her as they moved together. It wasn't about his pleasure or her pleasure, like some kind of transaction or tally, as lovemaking with other men had always been. The joy rising inside her was wordless and complete. She was where she needed to be at last. She was home.

EPILOGUE

Gary Dobbins leaned back contentedly in his first class seat. He was flying to San Francisco and an offer that had seemed almost too good to be true.

After a miserable six weeks holed up in his apartment, drinking way too much whiskey and working himself back up to a pack a day, things were finally turning around. He'd been surprised but pleased to receive the phone call out of the blue from Mistress Storm of Storm Dungeons. Despite the smear campaign conducted by his enemies at Wallace & Pratt in Manhattan, his reputation as a top-notch marketing strategist was still intact, at least on the West Coast.

He still seethed at having been outsmarted by that bitch. He'd spent hundreds of hours plotting and planning how he'd get back at Elizabeth, at Wallace, at them all. He looked into ways of hacking into the company's computer system, destroying their records, planting false rumors about a troubled financial situation or leaking false reports of impropriety among the top brass. He even considered stalking and kidnapping the bitch, holding her hostage in a farmhouse in upstate New York, making her his personal sex slave, though these fantasies only achieved full flower when the whiskey bottle was nearly empty.

In the end, he'd done nothing, telling himself he was biding his time, waiting for the right moment to strike. Revenge, he would remind himself, while nursing a very large glass of booze, was a meal best served cold.

And now things were, for the first time, looking decidedly up. If things went well with this job, maybe he'd just leave New York altogether—make a fresh start on a new coast. He'd been recommended, Mistress Storm told him, by an old friend, though he hadn't recognized the man's name. No matter, a job was a job and, at this point, beggars shouldn't be choosers, he reminded himself bitterly. True, it was just one job, but she was willing to fly him out, all expenses paid, to assess the marketing and advertising needs for her string of high-end BDSM dungeons.

How ironic, yet how wonderfully appropriate to be tapped for such a venture. He hadn't admitted his personal penchant for the scene, remaining strictly professional during the phone call. Time enough for that later. If she were hot, he might even engage in a scene with her, once the business was completed between them.

"Another drink, Sir?"

"That'd be great." He watched the flight attendant walk away, her hips swaying beneath the tight skirt of her uniform. He undressed her in his mind as he watched her, wondering how she'd respond to a good whipping.

When she returned a moment later, she leaned in close as she placed the drink on his tray. Her perfume wafted pleasantly toward him, her breast brushing his shoulder in what he felt sure was a deliberate gesture.

She was in her late thirties, he guessed, young enough to still be attractive, old enough to appreciate the attentions of a handsome, well-dressed man like himself. After he had sized up Mistress Storm, both professionally and otherwise, he thought with a smirk, he might toss this girl a bone.

Yes, things were definitely looking up.

~*~

The phone by the bed rang. "Cole Pearson."

"Hey, Cole. It's Storm. I baited the hook and he bit down—hard. Now I'm reeling him in. The guy has an ego the size of Montana. He totally bought the story you laid out for me. He thinks he's on his way out here to create a new image for my dungeons. From what you've told me about the little creep, I can't wait to give him a taste of his own medicine."

"So everything's arranged? The GHB for his drink? The video camera?"

"Yep. He'll walk into my office, but he'll wake up in my dungeon, naked and shackled to a whipping post, a ball gag in his mouth, a pony tail shoved up his ass, a video camera recording the whole scene. I'll make sure he's way too humiliated to even think of pressing any kind of charges. If he does, it's his word against mine, and I've got some powerful friends in this town, as you know."

"I do know. I knew you'd be perfect for the job." Cole laughed. "Keep me posted." He hung up, reaching for Elizabeth. "What was that you said, that day at the deli?"

Elizabeth's eyes twinkled. "Don't get mad—get even."

CPSIA information can be obtained at www.ICGtesting.com
Printed in the USA
LVOW11s0045260915

455846LV00001B/29/P